# WRITTEN

A DJINN WARS NOVEL

CHRISTINE POPE

DARK VALENTINE PRESS

WRITTEN



ISBN: 978-1-946435-74-3

Published by Dark Valentine Press

Cover design by Indie Author Services

Ebook formatting by Indie Author Services

# Chapter 1

Rowan Aames crested the hill behind Montezuma Castle and performed the usual check of her surroundings, gaze scanning the heavily forested landscape and the two-lane road that led onto the sprawling property.

As usual, there was nothing to see.

Still, she couldn't help being relieved that not a single thing seemed to have changed about her surroundings...and that she hadn't caught sight of any hostile djinn descending on the place that had been her sanctuary for the past four years.

A pair of dead rabbits dangled from one hand; her snares had done their job the night before. Once upon a time, she would have recoiled at the thought of killing such innocent creatures, let alone having to skin them and dress them so she'd have a filling meal. But the Rowan she'd been when she first came to work at United World College—a fancy boarding school that used the former luxury hotel called Montezuma Castle as its campus—was so different from the person she'd become since the Dying changed the world, she doubted anyone would have believed they were the same person.

Internally at least. Outwardly, she knew she had the same red hair and brown eyes, the same short little nose and friendly mouth, even if she'd gotten leaner and tougher over the past few years. Every once in a while, she allowed herself to wonder why she kept working so hard to keep herself alive when there didn't seem to be much point anymore, but it appeared her survival instinct was far too strong to allow herself to simply lie down and die.

Even though she'd had times when it felt far easier to give up than continue to struggle through yet another lonely day.

A brisk wind pulled a few strands loose from her ponytail, and her eyes narrowed as she once again surveyed the horizon. Clouds were building to the north, but they didn't look organized enough to be a harbinger of a storm.

At least, she hoped not. According to the big calendar she'd created out of butcher paper at the beginning of the year and taped to the wall in the kitchen—a calendar that was based on the one she'd used up the year before, the last of the "real" ones that had existed on campus—it was now a few days into November. In general, it didn't snow this early in the year, but if there was anything Rowan knew about living in northern New Mexico, it was that the weather here could be notoriously unpredictable.

Especially the past couple of years. She hadn't been an expert on climate change or anything close to it, but even she could tell that the winters had gotten colder and wetter since the Dying, the monsoon storms of summer more intense. All the moisture was good for the trees and plants, and yet she couldn't help thinking it had made her life that much more difficult.

As she headed down the hill, though, she told herself it could be worse. There was no denying that her isolated location had probably kept her safe from the djinn, since even they didn't seem much interested in scouring such a remote spot simply to kill a single human.

One part of her brain still didn't want to admit that creatures who should have been mythical had turned out to be real. However, she couldn't deny what had happened after the Heat killed almost every man, woman, and child on the planet. Or rather, although she'd never seen the murderous elementals for herself, she'd witnessed the aftermath of their attacks when she went foraging in Las Vegas, the closest town to United World

College. The djinn were too thorough to leave any bodies behind, but they hadn't seemed much interested in cleaning up the blood spatter.

And the only reason she knew they were djinn at all...and maybe not illusions conjured by a mind gone mad from isolation...was because of the radio transmissions from Los Alamos. A man named Miles Odekirk had broadcast on several bands, warning anyone out there who might be listening about the otherworldly creatures...and also claiming he'd invented a device that seemed to keep them at bay. His transmissions had included detailed instructions for constructing the devices, but because Rowan had been a communications major in college and had come to the United World campus as their new P.R. person...and therefore didn't have any kind of technical background...she didn't have the foggiest idea how to build one of the little boxes on her own. Sure, she'd dutifully assembled the bits and pieces—screens scavenged from iPads that had once belonged to students at the school, wires and circuit boards from the science classrooms.

Unfortunately, all she'd ended up with was a jumbled mess.

However, she hadn't allowed that failure to deter her and had instead recovered a ham radio and antenna from a house in Las Vegas, thinking she could at least reach out to the people in Los

Alamos to let them know she was alive, since the unit she'd discovered in the school president's office wouldn't allow her to broadcast. But by the time she had the radio set up and working, a few months after the world had ended, there no longer seemed to be anyone sending, no one to answer her pleading calls.

For all she knew, she'd done something wrong yet again, and that was why she'd never gotten a single response.

Or, worse, Miles Odekirk's devices had failed them after all, and everyone in Los Alamos was dead.

Not knowing what had happened to all those people might have driven her crazy, except she made sure to keep so busy that she wouldn't allow herself to brood on might-have-beens. She read books in the library on making snares and caught rabbits and the occasional squirrel, and she scrounged a fishing pole to catch trout from Gallina Creek, which flowed nearby and had been part of the reason why people had first decided the location would be a good spot for a hotel.

Well, that and the hot springs, which she had to admit were a godsend. It wasn't really possible to use them in the depths of winter, but the rest of the time, they were the reason she was able to keep clean and at least somewhat presentable, mostly because she refused to allow herself to descend into a complete disheveled mess. When it was too cold, she used water from the well and took cold baths while surrounded by space heaters, gritting her teeth the whole time and wishing for the return of summer.

Rowan entered the kitchen and glanced around. Almost at once, the cattle dog mix she'd rescued during one of her trips to Las Vegas got to his feet and trotted over to her, black feathered tail wagging. He'd been wearing a collar with a tag when she found him, and that's why she knew his name was Darby.

"Hey, boy," she said as he nosed the pair of rabbits she still held in one hand. Most of the time, she took him with her when she went to inspect her snares and see if they were going to eat well that night, but today he'd been sleepy and hadn't seemed too inclined to go on any adventures.

Which was fine—her little expedition had been utterly without incident, and if Darby wanted to sleep in the relative warmth of the kitchen rather than face that biting north wind, Rowan couldn't really blame him.

His tail wagged a little harder, and she couldn't help smiling. Early on, he'd made his preference for rabbit over trout well known, although he'd eat bits of fish if there wasn't anything else available.

"Roasted or stewed?" she asked the dog, and he tilted his head to one side. He had a black patch over his right eye that gave him a roguish look, although he was probably one of the sweetest dogs she'd ever met. And thank God she'd found him, because otherwise, she wondered if she might have gone crazy during all these long, empty years.

"Roasted it is," she said with a grin, a comment that made Darby's tail start going all over again. She had to admit she wasn't too fond of stewed rabbit, although it was all right when she threw in some of the carrots and potatoes she grew in the garden out back. Her first winter here, she'd had to subsist on whatever she could scrounge from empty Las Vegas and had eaten way too much processed food, making her vow to grow as much as she could the following summer, even if her kitchen garden attracted djinn attention.

But it hadn't. She could only guess as to the reason why they hadn't detected her presence here, although it still seemed most likely that they'd made one sweep of the area, had done away with the few survivors they'd found, and had moved on. There wasn't much point in lingering in this quiet corner of northern New Mexico, not when they probably would have found much better hunting in Albuquerque or Las Cruces or even Santa Fe.

And although the big ovens in the campus kitchen had run on gas and were therefore useless to her, she'd found a decent-sized convection toaster oven during one of her foraging expeditions in Las Vegas, just big enough to fit a rabbit if you cut it up first. The people who'd founded the college had been heavily into sustainability, which meant there was plenty of solar power most of the time, enough to run the little oven and the induction cooking plate she'd found, not to mention all the space heaters she could scrounge. It was nowhere near enough to heat the entire building, not when it encompassed nearly 90,000 square feet, and running the big industrial hot water heaters, designed to accommodate the needs of hundreds of people, had also been out of the question.

No, Rowan had closed off all the unused rooms and heated only the kitchen, her bedroom, and the nearest bathroom. Whenever she needed to use the library, which was located in an entirely different building, she simply bundled up during the cold months and tried not to spend too much time there. Maybe it wasn't the most comfortable existence in the world, but it worked...most of the time. If a storm got bad enough, then the amount of solar power to run the space heaters was reduced considerably, and she usually tried to stay in her room with Darby, hoping that one heater would be enough to get her through until the clouds broke and the sun shone again.

With any luck, though, the real winter weather would hold off for another month. She'd already harvested everything she could from the garden, drying and canning and freezing, making sure she and Darby would have enough to get them through the cold season when supplemented with fresh fish and rabbit. Elk and deer roamed these woods, but although she had "liberated" a bow and a bunch of arrows from a store in Las Vegas, she doubted she'd be able to hit much of anything with them, even though she'd been practicing her archery for the past few months.

No, she'd survive this coming winter just like she had the preceding three. The diet got monotonous, but it was nourishing enough, and she'd scrounged plenty of dog food for Darby in Las Vegas, although she knew the supply would have to run out one day.

Well, she'd deal with that eventuality when the time came.

What else could she do?

---

Jamal al-Qadir came to a stop on Highway 518 at a place called Storrie Lake State Park. He still wasn't entirely sure why he'd gone this way, except, after he'd taken his leave of his older brother Aamir at the other djinn's house in Telluride a few days earlier, he'd decided to wander for a while, reluctant to return to his own home in Jackson Hole. The place was beautiful enough, he supposed...just like all the homes assigned to the djinn by the elders, the nominal rulers of their people...and yet he'd felt curiously restless, unwilling to go back to his quiet life when such a fundamental change had been wrought within his family.

Aamir had fallen in love with a human woman and made her his Chosen.

Some might have argued this was not such a rare occurrence, not when a thousand of his people had done the very same thing, saving those humans from the purge that occurred after the djinn-created plague commonly referred to as the Heat killed off most of humanity. But Aamir and Omar —the youngest of the family—and Jamal had been among those who participated in the purge, making sure that those immune who were not Chosen would not live to see another day.

For a reaver djinn such as Aamir to put aside his disgust for the human race and make a mortal woman his partner for eternity...well, that was not what anyone could call a regular occurrence.

However, Jamal hadn't tried to argue with his brother or tell him he was a traitor to his people, mainly because he could tell for himself how happy Aamir was, and he did not see what use it would be to try to dissuade him from his current course of action. No, he had only wished Aamir well and left, even while deciding it would be best to keep this latest development to himself for as long as possible.

Somehow, he doubted his hot-headed youngest brother would take the news with equal equanimity.

No, it was better to wander thus and learn more about the countryside in this part of the world. Jamal couldn't help thinking of something he'd heard in a movie once—over the years he'd realized that he enjoyed consuming human media and culture, enjoyed using it to learn more about mortals...a weakness he'd done his best to hide from his brothers. Yes, there had been a comment one of the characters had made to his partner in crime after everything in their world had, in human parlance, gone completely sideways.

*I'm gonna walk the earth.*

A curious phrase, and yet one that had resonated with Jamal nonetheless. Not that he planned to cover the entire surface of the planet, but he thought he could make his way through this particular corner of it, taking in the wild beauty of the landscape, from the ponderosa forests to the high plains rippling with yellowed grass. An earth elemental, he could not fly from place to place, so it seemed somehow right to increase his connection to the world that was now his home, feeling its power right through the soles of his boots.

Now, though, he paused as he took in a sign he hadn't been expecting.

*United World Campus: 5-1/2 miles*

A college of some sort, out in the wilderness like this? He hadn't been expecting to encounter anything like that, here in what felt like the middle of nowhere, and yet he knew New Mexico was the sort of place that could conceal all sorts of unexpected treasures in its untamed landscape.

Time to investigate.

Walking briskly, he followed the signs and turned off Highway 518 at the appropriate place, heading toward a spot called Montezuma. The back roads here were narrower but still paved, although he noted how the pavement had begun to crack and buckle following years of neglect. It was like this all over the world, he supposed, as the artifacts humankind had left behind gradually fell into disrepair with no one to maintain them. The process would take years, but eventually, this world would return to its green, pristine state, for the djinn had no wish to bend its beauties to their will the way men once had.

He passed several ranches, abandoned to return to the earth like all the other works of humanity. Whatever horses or cattle or sheep had once lived here were now long gone, although he guessed that they—or their descendants—thrived elsewhere, since the djinn had made sure that all the animals would be provided with food and shelter, even as they wandered from place to place as they wished.

The narrow road Jamal currently followed began to slope upward, but he barely noticed. It would take much more than a slight grade such as this one for him to even begin to exert himself.

When he reached the peak of the hill, however, he found himself catching his breath, for the sight in front of him was one he certainly hadn't expected.

A huge building constructed of warm-hued stone sprawled across the landscape, dominated by a large turret to one side and a graceful covered porch that curved to match the shape of the turret. Several smaller structures surrounded it, with more he could barely glimpse through the pine trees and other growth that dotted the landscape.

Who would have thought a castle would be hidden here in the wilds of northern New Mexico?

All right, it wasn't precisely a castle, but something he guessed had once been a hotel of some sort. No sign of life, of course, but he wouldn't have expected anything else. He had not been among those who swept through this part of the world immediately following the Heat, for at the time, he had labored with his brothers in Colorado, performing the important work of removing any survivors who remained in that state's larger cities. Still, what the fever hadn't quite accomplished, any reaver djinn in New Mexico would have finished.

A glint of copper caught his eyes, and he blinked in astonishment.

So much for the apparently lifeless landscape he'd observed only a moment before.

Someone had just emerged from the rear of the large stone building, someone with bright red hair.

A woman.

Even from this distance—for djinn eyes were keener than those of a human—he could tell she was young, perhaps in her middle twenties, and tall. Slender, he thought, although the true outline of her form was hidden by the bulky jacket she wore. At her side bounded a medium-sized dog, black and white, whose tail wagged ferociously as he followed her over to what appeared to be a well of some sort, since she lowered a bucket into it and then pulled it back out a moment later, heavier than it had been when she began.

Task accomplished, she went back inside the building, the dog still a faithful shadow at her side.

Was it truly possible that this human had managed to survive out here for all these years?

Jamal supposed it must be, since he couldn't ignore the evidence of his own eyes. And although he was numbered among those who had worked to eradicate humanity, even he had been forced to admit to himself that there was always a chance a stray mortal might have survived here and there, tucked away in hidden spaces that his people hadn't bothered to revisit...or had never reached at all.

The question was, now he had found her, what did he intend to do about the situation?

Some reavers would have charged in and taken care of what they considered unfinished business, but Jamal and his brothers had long ago agreed amongst themselves that they would not spill the blood of women and children. Even if they had not made that decision, he was not sure he would have had the stomach for such a brutal act, not when faced by someone who had managed to survive all these years despite such incredibly long odds.

He wanted to know how she had accomplished such a thing, what it was about her that had allowed her to persist even after losing everything and everyone she'd ever loved.

It would not be possible to simply walk into the astonishing structure she had taken as her home and ask her outright, of course. He was a djinn and she was a human, and she would have no reason to trust him or believe he was not there to take her life.

Well, then, he would not be a djinn. It was not that difficult for those of his kind to represent themselves as mortals, since the two races resembled one another a great deal. A few scars here and there, some stubble, and an overall picture of being weary and footsore should do the trick. And he also had to believe that his ongoing fascination with human media and literature would give him an advantage most djinn did not possess. From watching those movies and TV shows, he understood how humans spoke, how they reacted to things.

He would not be Jamal al-Qadir. No, he needed a name that would make more sense to her, one that would still match his appearance.

James...James Aguilar. It was close enough to the name his parents had given him that he didn't believe he would hesitate if the woman addressed him by it. Of course, he would need to hand her a plausible story to explain his presence here, but he thought he could come up with something easily enough, especially considering he knew much more of what had been happening in the outside world during the years she'd been cloistered here.

First, though...first, he needed to meet her.

# Chapter 2

Potatoes simmered in the pot on the induction burner, and one of the rabbits—much more skillfully butchered than it would have been a few years ago—was roasting in its pan in the toaster oven. Rowan knew she should have been able to sit and relax while she waited for the food to be ready, but for some reason, she was jumpy, almost nervous. She couldn't say why she was feeling that way, since absolutely nothing had happened today to make her think this day was any different from the hundreds of ones that had preceded it.

She got up from the chair where she'd been sitting and peered out the window, but of course she saw nothing, only the bulk of the mountain to the west of her, where the sun had already disappeared as long shadows began to creep toward Montezuma Castle. Over the past couple of years, she'd begun thinking of it that way rather than its official title of United World College, simply because with only her remaining and all the students and faculty and staff dead, it didn't feel much like a college anymore.

Why she had survived, and not any of those bright, hopeful kids who'd come here from all over the world to study and learn how to be involved, educated citizens, Rowan had no idea. It was clear that a few people in Las Vegas had been immune to the Heat...but they hadn't been immune to the violence visited on them by the djinn in the days following the plague. And because she'd cowered here in Montezuma Castle for almost a month before hunger drove her out in search of food, she had no real idea exactly how many survivors there had been.

Well, she might as well let Darby out one more time this evening...and she could stand to clean her hands in some of the hot water from the springs before dinner was ready. It wouldn't be fully dark for at least an hour, which meant she had plenty of time.

"Hey, Darbs," she said, and the dog immediately got to his feet, expression hopeful. "Let's go down to the springs, okay?"

His tail wagged in agreement, and Rowan went over to the back door and opened it, then shrugged on the puffer coat she kept hanging from a hook there during the colder months. Strictly speaking, the door was on the side of the building and not the back, but since the house she'd grown up in had a kitchen door that allowed access to the backyard, she had begun to think of it that way.

Darby went running out, just like he always did, while she followed at a more leisurely pace. In the beginning, she'd worried he might run into a pack of coyotes or a bobcat or even a bear, but although she'd seen physical evidence of those predators nearby—paw prints, some scat—none of the animals ever seemed to come close to the castle and were never visible when she and the dog went out to fish or visit the hot springs.

Because she only wanted to wash her hands and not actually bathe, Rowan decided it would be easiest if she went to the spring known as "the Cube," which was smaller than some of the others and set into level ground. She headed in that direction, Darby a little ways behind her since he'd paused to sniff a tree stump and anoint it with pee.

He caught up with her soon enough and then surged ahead, tail wagging. In fact, he gave a quick, sharp bark and all but ran toward the spring, while she followed, frowning a little. That wasn't Darby's warning bark—it was the one she'd heard often enough when she'd left him behind at the Castle for whatever reason and he'd greeted her at the back door.

As she approached the Cube, though, her entire body froze in shock.

Someone was in the spring. His back was to her, so all she could see was longish dark brown hair pulled back into a ponytail, but that was enough.

At once, she pushed her puffer coat out of the way, hand going to the knife she always wore on her belt. Early on, she'd gone everywhere with at least a pistol—her firefighter father had taught Rowan and her two older brothers to shoot while they were in grade school—but after a while, the precaution hadn't seemed necessary, so she'd started to leave the gun at the Castle when she went out.

Now she was really, really regretting not strapping it on her waist...or maybe bringing her bow and arrow with her, even though she knew she wasn't as good at archery as she was at shooting.

Since Darby had continued loping toward the spring, looking way too happy about their intruder, it wasn't as if Rowan could turn around and bolt for home. No, she'd have to run into this head-on, just like the dog.

She stopped a few paces away from the spring and said, in the toughest voice she could muster, "Who the hell are you?"

The stranger turned around, expression startled. He looked like he might be a few years older than she was, maybe as old as thirty, with dark eyes that matched his deep brown hair and warm olive skin.

And he was...gorgeous. Even, chiseled features, a trace of stubble that couldn't hide the sensual shape of his mouth or the strong set of his jawline.

Cold shock moved through her.

Was he a djinn? She'd heard they were supernaturally good-looking.

He raised his hands, even as he stood up, revealing a body just as jaw-dropping as his face. However, the fading light showed some half-healed scrapes along his arms and hands, making her falter a little.

Hadn't Miles Odekirk said in one of his radio messages that djinn couldn't be wounded?

"Sorry," the stranger said, and his voice sounded completely normal. A nice warm baritone, true, but.... "I didn't mean to startle you. I didn't know anyone was here."

Well, of course he didn't, because he'd probably thought this forgotten corner of New Mexico was just as dead and empty as the rest of the state.

Before she could respond, he went on, "I'm James Aguilar. I'm from Los Alamos."

Rowan blinked. "So, you're not all dead?"

His brows lifted, seeming to tell her he hadn't been expecting that question. "No," he said, his tone even. "We're all fine. But do you mind if I get out of this spring? I'm starting to feel a little cooked."

He would have been feeling even more that way if he'd chosen one of the hotter springs, like the Lobster Pot or either of the Toasters, but she didn't argue. "Sure," she said, although she made sure to keep wearing what she hoped was her best *High Plains Drifter* steely-eyed expression. "Just don't try anything funny."

"Not planning on it," the stranger—James—said with a grin.

A push on the concrete edge of the spring, and then he was out, showing all six-foot-plus of dripping male perfection. Rowan did her best not to goggle, although she wasn't sure how successful she was.

It had been a long time since she'd seen another human being, and even longer since she'd gotten an eyeful of anyone even close to James Aguilar in looks.

But he dried off quickly enough after plucking a towel from the big rucksack that waited at the edge of the spring, then pulled on some jeans and a long-sleeved T-shirt. A brief pause while he put on socks and hiking boots, and then he bent down to pat Darby on the head. The dog had waited patiently through all of this as if he somehow knew he needed to stand by until their visitor was socially acceptable again.

Or maybe Rowan was reading way too much into all of this.

"That's a great dog," James remarked. "Australian cattle dog, right?"

"Right," Rowan said, knowing she sounded slightly less frosty. "He wasn't mine...before. We just kind of adopted each other."

James acknowledged this piece of information with a small nod, his pleasant expression growing more serious. "I'm sure it helped to have him with you."

"It did," she said. Then she pulled in a breath and added, "Do you want to tell me what you're doing here?"

In another time and another place, she would never have asked such a rude question. Now, though....

If James was offended, he didn't show it. No, he just inclined his head again and said, "I saw the sign for the hot springs and figured I could try to get in a dip before the sun went all the way down."

All right, she could almost understand that. If he'd been walking for a long time, the prospect of bathing in warm water would have been pretty enticing. But that didn't explain the rest of it.

"No," she said, realizing an edge had entered her voice. "I meant, what are you doing out and away from Los Alamos at all? It's a long way from here. It's not safe."

He smiled again. "Oh, it's pretty safe. It's been safe for a while." A pause, and his dark gaze seemed to probe her expression. "You don't know, do you?"

"Know what?" she demanded.

Rather than reply directly, James glanced up at the sky, as if to gauge the coming dusk, the way the world was getting dimmer and dimmer. "We should probably go inside. It's going to be dark soon."

She already knew that, but if he thought she was just going to let him walk into her sanctuary, no questions asked, then he wasn't very good at reading the room.

"How am I supposed to trust you?"

A lot of guys she'd known would have attempted some kind of facile reply to such a question. This James Aguilar, on the other hand, only stood there in silence for a moment, appearing to carefully consider her words.

"Either you do or you don't," he said, and his gaze strayed down toward Darby, whose tail gave a quick, friendly thump before going still yet again. "I guess it depends on whether you think your dog is a good judge of character. He does seem to like me."

Well, there was no denying that. Not that Rowan had a lot of basis for comparison, since

James was the first human being either she or the dog had seen in the past four years.

But Darby had been a faithful companion that whole time, and even though most of the local predators had stayed away from the Castle and its environs, there had been a couple of times when he'd gone into a fit of barking and taken a defensive stance, even though she hadn't been able to see exactly what had set him off. Because of that, she had to believe he wouldn't have been nearly as friendly toward James if he'd thought the stranger posed any kind of a threat.

"All right," she said at last, even as she hoped she wasn't making a colossal mistake. "I'm Rowan Aames. Follow me."

---

So far, so good. Jamaal hadn't been sure what he would do if the woman denied him entry to the place where she'd been living, but—thanks largely to the welcome he'd gotten from her dog, who seemed happy to see him—he hadn't been forced to face that particular problem.

No, he'd picked up the large rucksack he'd adopted as part of his disguise, hefted it onto his shoulders, and then trailed after Rowan as she led him away from the hot springs and up to the large building of rosy stone he'd spied from the hilltop only an hour or so earlier. It was something of a climb to get where they were going, since the place sat on a rise that allowed it to look down toward the road and the little complex of springs with their concrete enclosures and sheltering trees, but eventually, they reached a door at the side of the structure.

Inside, it was warmer than he'd expected, thanks to a couple of space heaters chugging away and doing their best to keep the early November chill at bay. A welcoming, toothsome scent filled the air, and he couldn't keep himself from giving an appreciative sniff.

Something that was almost a smile pulled at Rowan's pretty mouth. "I hope you like rabbit. That's what's on the menu tonight."

"Rabbit sounds great," he replied, preventing himself at the last minute from saying "wonderful." He had to remember to sound casual, like a human male in his late twenties and not a djinn who'd been alive for centuries. Then he added, "We eat a lot of it in Los Alamos, too."

"Hopefully not as much as I do," she said, her lips still quirking a bit. "That's basically been it for the past four years...rabbit and trout."

"There aren't deer around here?" Jamal asked as he pulled off his heavy rucksack and leaned it up against the nearest wall.

"Oh, there are plenty," Rowan said. "But I still

haven't worked myself up to trying to bag one. That's a much bigger butchering job than a rabbit or two."

He supposed she had a point there. Also, even though she'd said nothing about who she was or where she'd come from, he had to believe she hadn't been raised learning how to dress a carcass and had been forced to fend for herself as best she could.

Which obviously had been fairly well, since she was still alive, and appeared strong and healthy enough. Very slim, he realized as she pulled off her puffer coat and hung it from a hook near the door, but not thin to the point of malnutrition or anything close to it.

"Water?" she asked, heading toward one of the two large stainless-steel refrigerators that occupied one wall. Jamal realized this kitchen was quite big, and must have been constructed to serve the needs of the hundreds of people who had once occupied the space.

He didn't bother to ask if she had electricity; the single light shining down from overhead already proved that point. However, he realized she must have removed the bulbs from the other fixtures or disabled them in some way, probably to make sure any illumination inside was dim and not something that could be easily seen by any hostile eyes.

Instead, he said, "Yes, please," and watched as she reached inside the refrigerator and pulled out an aluminum pitcher, then poured some water into a glass she'd fetched from a nearby cupboard.

After she gave it to him, she fixed him with a steady gaze. In contrast to her bright red hair, her eyes were a warm brown, almost amber. It was an unusual combination, one he wasn't sure he'd ever seen before.

"You said something before about it being 'safe' to be out in the world," she told him. "Want to explain that?"

He sipped some of the water. It was cold and sweet, reminding him of the way he'd spied Rowan earlier filling her bucket from a well behind the building. His gaze strayed to the small oven that sat on the countertop, where the savory smell had originated, then past it to the little induction burner that held a pot of water simmering away.

Correctly interpreting his gaze, she said, "The food's got at least another fifteen minutes before it's ready. So that should be plenty of time to tell me what's going on."

There wasn't any reason to withhold the information, especially if telling her the truth might make her soften her stance a bit. So far, she seemed wary as a doe ready to take flight at the slightest crunch of a twig or hasty movement, and he wanted her to relax enough to explain to him how she'd managed to survive here for so long. It seemed she'd had to work with what she was given...he suspected that the large ovens on the other side of the room had run on natural gas and therefore were useless in a world that no longer had the infrastructure to support them...but still, he thought it might be better if they had this discussion sitting down.

"Fifteen minutes," he echoed, adding, "But how about we take a seat over there?"

He inclined his head toward the small bistro-style table and two chairs that had been set under a window near the door. Because they seemed out of place there, Jamal guessed Rowan must have put them in that spot so she could stay near the food while it was cooking but still keep an eye on whatever might be happening outside.

Or possibly not, since he noted that the blinds were shut tight. It seemed to him she valued safety far more than expediency.

"All right," she said after a grudging silence.

Without waiting for him to reply, she headed over to the table, pulled out one of the chairs, and sat down. He would have thought she might have let her guest seat himself first, but then realized she'd been alone here for so long that she might not even guess her actions seemed a little rude.

He shrugged it off and sat as well, bringing his glass of water with him. Once he'd taken another sip, he said, "I made that comment about the roads being safe because they are. A couple of years ago, the djinn elders made an agreement with the reavers that it was time to move on and not worry about what few survivors might remain out there in the world."

Rowan's russet brows drew together in confusion. "'Elders'?" she repeated. "'Reavers'?"

At another time, he might have smiled at her ignorance. Now, he only reminded himself that she had been cut off from the world for a very long time.

"The djinn are ruled...if you even want to call it that...by three people, two men and a woman," he said. "They're the elders. I guess they have the final say on anything djinn-related. I don't know all the particulars, but it sounds as if they got the reavers —the djinn who were hunting down any immune survivors—to lay down their swords, so to speak. Ever since then, it's been pretty safe to move around outside Los Alamos."

"Where you have those devices protecting you," she said, and Jamal felt his eyes widen in surprise.

"How do you know about those?" he asked, knowing that the shock in his voice was genuine.

A shrug. Even though she'd abandoned the puffer coat, she still wore a thick fleece zip-up, probably because it wasn't overly warm in here despite the space heaters doing their best to combat the frigid air outside. "I heard Miles Odekirk's broadcasts back when all this was new," she replied. "There was a radio here. I found a ham radio in town, but I could never get it to work and wasn't able to reply. Then eventually, the broadcasts just... stopped." A pause, and she gave Jamal a weak little smile. "I guess that's why I thought you must all be dead."

"No, the community in Los Alamos is thriving," he said, which was only the truth. "I guess we stopped broadcasting because we thought there wasn't anyone else out there to hear us, and we all had a lot to do."

There, that sounded like a reasonable enough explanation. Or at least, it did to him. Whether Rowan would believe a word of it was an entirely different proposition.

But she nodded, as though she thought his story made sense. "I get it. I probably wouldn't have kept wasting time on trying to get the word out when it was clear no one was listening. It still helped, though." She stopped there, fingers drumming an unconscious little rhythm on the tabletop as she seemed to think things over. "Are there any other communities like Los Alamos out there?"

"No," he said at once. Again, only the truth. For a moment, he wondered if he should mention the community of djinn and Chosen in Santa Fe, then decided against it. That felt as though it would be throwing far too much information at her all at once, especially since she had no reason to believe djinn were anything except the deadliest of foes and the reason for the destruction of mankind. "No one else had the devices, even though Miles also broadcast instructions for making them."

To Jamal's surprise, Rowan almost grinned at that comment. "I know," she said. "I listened to his directions and tried to follow along. All I got for my efforts was a bunch of busted iPads."

Her expression was so rueful, he couldn't help smiling as well, even as he reflected it was a good thing she hadn't been successful in replicating Miles Odekirk's terrible devices.

Otherwise, this encounter would have turned out very differently.

The countertop oven made a little binging noise, and at once she got up from her seat, saying, "Sounds like dinner is about ready. Can you get us some plates from that cupboard over there?"

She pointed to the same one where she'd fetched their glasses, and he obediently rose from his chair to get the dishes. They were plain white, utilitarian, and he guessed they'd been used to feed whoever had once lived here.

As he set the plates down on the table...even while reflecting that he wished they had a cloth or at least some mats to cover the wooden surface...he said, "What was this place, anyway? A hotel?"

Rowan had been in the middle of extracting the rabbit from the oven, so she waited until she was done before replying, "It was a hotel a long time ago. But for the past thirty years or so, it's been a kind of high school."

He frowned. "I thought I saw a sign on the road that said 'United World College.'"

To his surprise, she didn't frown at his ignorance. Instead, she went and fetched the pot from its little induction burner and, as she poured out the water, said, "They were all called that. There was a network of these schools all over the world, training kids to be independent thinkers and maybe future diplomats or policy people. But everyone here was between fifteen and nineteen, except the faculty and staff."

"And you were a student?" Jamal asked. She seemed a little older than that, but not old enough to have actually worked at the institution.

Another of those smiles that warmed her amber-brown eyes and helped erase some of the shadows of strain in her face. He realized then that she would have been strikingly beautiful if she hadn't seemed so tense.

"Thanks for the vote of confidence," she said, pulling a masher out of a drawer and getting to work on the potatoes in the pot. "But no, I worked here. It was my first job out of college, and I thought I'd really lucked out. I only started working here in July, and then...."

And then a few months later the Heat had arrived, along with the end of the world. What must it have been like to be trapped out here, forced to watch all those young souls perish of that terrible fever?

Jamal found he didn't want to think about that. True, he and his brothers had been among the reavers, and once upon a time, he had truly believed they were doing this world a service by removing those who had polluted and almost destroyed it, but...

...but after seeing Aamir fall in love with a mortal woman and realizing that perhaps there were far more sides to the issue than they'd previously considered, he wasn't quite sure where he stood. Before his brother had taken Isla for his Chosen, Jamal had thought those of the djinn who'd selected human partners must be suffering from their own particular madness.

Aamir was not mad, though. Jamal knew that much. And perhaps part of the reason why he'd made the impulsive decision to assume the persona of James Aguilar and get a chance to interact with the red-haired survivor at the castle was to discover for himself whether there might be much more to human females than met the eye...or what he'd seen of them in films and television shows.

"And then the Dying happened," he said quietly.

Rowan got some olive oil out of the pantry and started drizzling it into the potatoes. "Sorry about the olive oil," she said. "But obviously, I don't have any butter or milk. It works...mostly."

"It's fine." Realizing that he should perhaps offer to contribute to their meal in some way, he added, "I have some jerky and other trail food in my pack, if that will help. It's nothing fancy but—"

"No, that's all right," she cut in. "I don't want to take away the food you had for the road. The rabbit and potatoes will be enough."

For a moment, he considered pressing the issue, but the firm tone in her voice had told him he probably wouldn't get very far.

"If you're sure," he said.

Her shoulders lifted, but she didn't say anything for a moment, and instead seemed to focus on the potatoes on the stove before her.

"Anyway," she went on after a pause. "I hid here for a long time. But it got to a point where I had to go into town to find out what had happened, even though I'd heard Miles Odekirk's warnings on the radio. We had solar here, so there was power, although I didn't have gas to cook or running water. The springs worked fine for a bath, so I suppose it could have been worse."

"That must have been a long walk," he said, and again she gave one of those negligent little shrugs, as if doing her best to dismiss all the privations she'd suffered.

"I didn't have to walk," she said. "A couple of the students here had e-bikes, so I charged one of them up and rode it to town. Still more conspicuous than walking, I guess, but at least it was quiet, and I did my best to use trees and buildings for cover, whatever I could think of to make it harder to track my progress. And then I found...." The words trailed off, and her mouth compressed as she reached into the cupboard to get a bowl for the potatoes. "Well, I found a whole lot of nothing. No survivors. So, I hurried over to the Walmart, got the biggest backpack I could find, and loaded it up with stuff. Ever since then, I've been going back and forth to town about once a month, trying to find whatever might help me survive out here."

She came over to the table and set down the bowl of potatoes. Something about the stiff set of her shoulders and jaw told him she didn't want any words of commiseration, so he wouldn't bother to murmur, "I'm sorry," the way a mortal usually might have in such a situation.

Instead, he asked, "Need any help with the rabbit?" and she shook her head.

"No, I'm good. Just need to grab another plate."

Which she did, and then brought their main course to the table and set it next to the potatoes. Up close, the rabbit didn't look very impressive, and Jamal guessed it would have been barely enough to feed Rowan, let alone the two of them.

However, he got the impression any offer to let her have the lion's share of their main course would be rebuffed, so he didn't say anything and only allowed her to put some on his plate, with the remainder going on her dish. The potatoes likewise seemed skimpy, but he thought that was probably because of their lack of any dairy to make them fluffy.

However, the combination of olive oil and salt and pepper tasted better than he'd thought it would, and the rabbit, while on the small side, had been roasted to perfection, its seasonings simple but effective.

"Thank you for this," he said after he'd had a few bites. "It's been a while since I've had a hot meal."

"I guess so," she responded, then sent him a searching look. "Why were you out there on the road, anyway? I mean, even if it's safe, you'd think you'd be a lot more comfortable in Los Alamos."

That observation might have been accurate...if it weren't for the djinn-repelling devices deployed all over the mountain town and everywhere else within a ten-mile radius.

"I volunteered," he said, seeing a flicker of surprise in her warm-toned eyes. "I thought it would be a good idea to get out and get the lay of the land, so to speak. We've expanded down into the Española river valley and grow most of our crops there, but none of us have gone out into the wider world. It just seemed like a good idea to do some scouting, so that's why I headed in this direction."

Something about the lift of her eyebrows told him she wasn't completely convinced. "There wasn't much out here during the best of times," she commented. "Why not head down to Albuquerque or even Las Cruces?"

Jamal knew those had been the two most populous cities in the state before the Dying, so her question made sense. However, it was easy enough to deflect.

"Las Cruces was way too far," he said, which was true. The hidden valley where they now sat was located on the opposite side of the Sangre de Cristo mountains from Los Alamos, but still, it wasn't so many miles as the crow flew. Las Cruces, on the other hand, lay at the far southern edge of the state, more than three hundred miles away. "And most of the survivors in Los Alamos came from Albuquerque. It was the kind of place where the reavers would congregate just because there were a lot more victims to be found there."

Again, the simple truth, one he knew, if not firsthand, at least from those who had made it their mission to ensure not a single soul there survived.

Rowan didn't quite wince, but he could tell she hadn't liked hearing his bald-faced assessment of the situation. "So, you headed east."

He nodded, waiting to reply so he could finish chewing the morsel of rabbit he'd just placed in his mouth. "I thought it was worth a shot, so I went through Taos and came down past Cimarron and picked up the highway on the east side of the mountains. I'd planned to spend the night in Las Vegas, but then I saw the sign for the hot springs, and—"

"And the rest is history," she finished for him.

"Yes," he said, attempting a smile to see if she might respond in kind.

Which she did...only a half smile, but enough to let him guess she was beginning to soften a little. Or at least, to allow herself to believe his story.

It was a good start.

# Chapter 3

Rowan had to admit it was a little surreal to sit there and talk to James, pausing every now and then so she could feed a morsel of rabbit to Darby. It had been so long since she'd had a conversation with an actual human being that every once in a while she wanted to stop and pinch herself just to make sure she wasn't dreaming.

She didn't, however, and hoped she sounded mostly normal as she asked questions or responded to James's comments. On the surface, his story sounded plausible enough. Yes, she was still reeling inwardly at learning there hadn't been any real djinn threats for the past two years, but did that knowledge change anything?

All right, she probably would have dispensed with the e-bike and instead used one of the electric cars left on campus for her trips back and forth from Las Vegas, but otherwise, would her life really have been any different? Would she have had the courage to leave her sanctuary here and go out into the world to look for survivors?

No real way of saying. She liked to think she would have been brave, would have armed herself, packed up her stuff and the dog, and headed out to face whatever future might present itself, sort of like Sarah Connor at the end of the first *Terminator* movie.

But she didn't know that for sure. It was entirely possible she would have hidden out here until she dropped dead of old age or made some fatal mistake that a first aid kid from Walmart and some pilfered antibiotics...now probably expired... wouldn't have been able to fix.

"And after Las Vegas?" she asked.

James put another bite of mashed potatoes into his mouth. As far as she could tell, he didn't seem to have a problem with the total lack of dairy...or maybe he was just being polite.

"I was going to follow the highway and go through Santa Fe, then loop back up to Los Alamos," he replied. "I figured that route would have given me information on a pretty big section of northern New Mexico."

Was she imagining things, or had there been the slightest flicker in his dark eyes as he spoke the name of her state's former capital?

No, it must have been a trick of the light. It was pretty dim in here, thanks to the way she'd unscrewed all but one of the can lights set into the ceiling and had unplugged the fluorescents altogether. She'd done all that partly to save energy and partly to keep as much betraying illumination as possible from leaking past the blinds, but right then, she sort of wished she could see her unexpected companion's expression a little better.

"Well, there's still a lot beyond there," she said. "You know, up by Chama and those parts."

"Not many people, though," he replied. "Even back before."

True enough. One summer when she was ten, her parents had taken her and her brothers Henry and Charlie to camp for two weeks near Chama and ride the old restored railroad that went to Raton and back through some absolutely gorgeous country. She'd had a blast, but even at ten she'd realized that, as small as her hometown of Las Vegas was, it felt like a total metropolis compared to tiny Chama.

"You're right," she said. "So...did you find anyone?"

"Just you."

Two simple words that confirmed a bitter truth she'd known for a long time. Oh, sure, James had told her Los Alamos was still there, apparently thriving, but all humanity had to show for itself was that single outpost out of all the millions of cities and billions of people who'd once existed on the globe.

The rabbit and potatoes seemed sour in her stomach. Rowan reached for her glass of water and gulped some down, wishing it was instead some of the wine she had stored in the basement. She didn't drink much, would maybe allow herself to consume a bottle over three or four days once a month, but having it there was still reassuring somehow, kind of a "break glass in case of emergency" sort of thing.

And obviously, it would be stupid to share a bottle with a man she hardly knew. She was already taking a big enough risk just by having him here, although she had to admit he seemed relatively harmless. Unbelievably good-looking, true, but that wasn't a crime.

Somehow, she made herself give a half-hearted chuckle, then said, "And now I suppose you're going to try to convince me to come back to Los Alamos with you."

"Well, it would be smarter," he said, apparently not too surprised by the turn their conversation had just taken. "I mean, you've done fine out here by yourself, but we have a lot more resources than you do."

"How many of you are there?"

He hesitated, then said, "I don't have an exact count. But well over a thousand."

A thousand people. Rowan tried to remember what it was like to be surrounded by that many individuals, but her brain didn't quite want to go there. Just having James sitting across the table from her right now felt almost overwhelming. Being in a familiar place and having Darby there watching the two of them helped a little, made her feel just grounded enough that she knew this was really happening.

But to go to Los Alamos and have to interact with people again?

Part of her wanted to laugh at herself, just because back in the day, she definitely would have said she was a people person. Or at least, she'd read something online where someone had referred to themselves as an extroverted introvert, and she'd thought that phrase described her pretty well, too. She liked being in groups and going out and socializing, and yet she was also very happy to go home and read a book or watch a movie so her batteries could recharge. Those first days and weeks and months had been awful, not just because her mind was still trying to grasp the enormity of what had happened to the human race, but also because she kept desperately needing to hear a voice that wasn't hers, to see a face that belonged to someone else.

Now, though...now, so much time had passed

that she didn't know whether she'd be able to handle much more than one person at a time.

"It's nothing I'd expect you to decide right away," James went on, and his tone had turned gentle, as if he'd somehow been able to guess at some of the thoughts that churned in her mind. "But it might be a good idea."

"Maybe," she allowed.

He seemed to understand she didn't want to discuss that particular topic any longer, because he shifted in his seat and said, "So, what did you do here? Were you a teacher?"

"No," she replied. "I worked in the administrative offices. They hired me to be their P.R. person—stuff for the website, press releases, community outreach. That kind of thing."

"Ah."

That was all he said, but she could tell he was wondering if she'd actually had enough to keep her busy. On the surface, it might have seemed like a fluff job, but the United World Colleges were serious about their mission, and the one here in New Mexico was no different. She managed the social media accounts and kept the website up to date, wrote press releases, conducted tours of the property, and so much more. True, it had been a hell of a lot more work to keep herself alive these past four years, but she still thought she'd done a good job during the limited time she'd been a staff member here.

And she'd performed one last, much grimmer duty—after the Heat had struck down every single person at the school except her, she'd carefully gathered up the dust of their remains and buried it in small, individual holes she'd dug out past the Dwan Light Sanctuary, a lovely place constructed as a spot where people could go to meditate or pray or just be alone with their thoughts. It had seemed the most suitable location for the resting place of everyone who'd perished here, and she'd made sure that each small pile of gray ash had its own place, wasn't mingled together in one large communal grave. She hadn't put up markers, partly because she hadn't yet known all the students' names...and partly because she thought even a series of small stones laid out in neat rows might attract unwanted attention if any djinn were hanging out nearby, trying to track down any survivors.

"I grew up in Las Vegas, which helped, because the college tried to hire local people whenever it could," she went on. "How about you?"

James blinked, as if a little startled by the question. Then he said, "I grew up in Moriarty. You know, just east of Albuquerque?"

Rowan nodded, more because she'd heard the name than because she'd ever visited there. Her family had always headed north for their recreation, whether to the more northern parts of New Mexico or even into Colorado, than to go south for their vacations. Both her parents were natives of Las Vegas as well and had always seemed content to stick close to home.

Well, they'd died where they lived, which she supposed was something.

Even after all this time, thinking of the family she'd lost brought on a sudden sting of tears. She blinked, hoping the light in the kitchen was dim enough that James wouldn't notice her momentary loss of control.

"But I was living in Rio Rancho when it happened," James went on. Nothing in his expression or tone had changed, which made Rowan think he was oblivious to the betraying glitter in her eyes. "And I headed north with a group of survivors after we heard Miles Odekirk on a portable radio one of us was carrying."

The scientist definitely had been a beacon for the people left behind, she supposed. Too bad she'd been too frightened to strike out on her own. If she hadn't cowered here like a scared little mouse, she might have spent the past few years surrounded by people rather than having to fend for herself.

"That must have been scary," she said, then helped herself to another bite of rabbit. She supposed it was a good thing they were talking so much, since it made the food last longer, made it seem as if there was more to eat than they actually had.

James grinned. The sudden flash of white teeth reminded her once again how absolutely good-looking he was, even as she told herself it shouldn't matter. What mattered was that he was human... and that he'd found her.

"We were running so fast, I don't think I had time to be scared."

"You went all the way to Los Alamos on foot?"

His smile faded. "We didn't have much of a choice—the sound of a vehicle attracted djinn like a shark to chum. Also, the roads were choked with abandoned cars, so it would've been almost impossible to get around anywhere that was paved."

Right. Rowan had also noticed how cars were left in the middle of the street or sometimes halfway up on a sidewalk, as if their drivers had dropped dead while they were trying to get home or to a hospital. It wasn't as bad in Las Vegas, mostly because her hometown wasn't a big city, but still, even if it wasn't already better because of the stealth it offered, the e-bike she rode to and from the college allowed her to weave in and out of all those discarded vehicles in a way that a car definitely couldn't.

"But we made it," James said. "And that's the important thing."

She gazed across the table at him, at his friendly

dark eyes...at the kind of smile she hadn't thought she'd ever see again, simply because it belonged to someone other than her.

"Yes," she said. "That is the important thing."

---

All during their meal, Jamal couldn't help being haunted by a sensation of guilt—not just because he was consuming resources he knew Rowan desperately needed, but also because of the mountain of lies he'd told her. Perhaps he'd begun this venture coldly, thinking only that he wanted to learn as much from her as he could, but now he realized this was a thinking, breathing person who sat across from him, someone who'd suffered the kind of loss and privation he couldn't begin to imagine.

However, he doubted she noticed anything odd about his comments or his responses. Not a single flicker of suspicion in her eyes, nothing to show she believed him to be anything more than what he'd said.

After they finished their meager meal, she took the plates and set them on the countertop, saying, "I can't really offer luxury accommodations, but at least there are lots of empty bedrooms here. And you can have one of the space heaters—I've got plenty."

Perhaps she did, although Jamal thought rather that she was willing to make a sacrifice for her guest, even if he was little more than a stranger. "That's all right," he told her. "Just having a bed after roughing it for the past week would be great. My sleeping bag is really warm."

Her gaze moved to his rucksack, which he'd left propped against one wall. He really did have an Arctic-rated sleeping bag rolled up on the thing, more for the sake of verisimilitude than anything else.

"It can still get pretty cold in here," she said. "I'd really feel better if you had a space heater."

Jamal could tell she wasn't about to let it go. Better to give her this one small victory.

"Okay," he replied, with what he hoped was a disarming smile. "But just one."

Her mouth twitched in response. "All right. Just one."

She'd taken him out of the kitchen after that, and up a flight of stairs to what had clearly been a dormitory level.

"I'm right here," she said, pointing at an open doorway immediately to her right, just past the staircase. "It's probably better if you take another one on this same floor, because I did what I could to block off the other levels to conserve heat. Whatever you pick might be a little dusty, but it should be livable."

She hadn't mentioned the bathroom arrangements, and he wondered if he should ask. With only electricity and no running water, he guessed they must be fairly primitive.

"There's a bucket," she added, cheeks turning a little pink. "I just emptied it this morning, so…."

The words trailed off there, but he got the point. "I can manage."

"Okay. See you in the morning."

And she inclined her head toward her room. Darby, who'd been sitting nearby during this exchange, seemed to understand that was his signal, because he trotted inside. As soon as he had passed the threshold, Rowan went in as well and closed the door behind her.

Because he hadn't been expecting anything else, Jamal wasn't put off by her sudden disappearance. Instead, he carried his borrowed space heater into the room across the hall, since that seemed easiest, then eased off his rucksack. She'd flicked on the overhead light as they'd come upstairs, so he could see the space contained two twin-size beds with a desk in between them, along with a short shelf crowded with books next to the wall that contained a small closet.

Everything looked tidy enough, although, as she'd said, the room could have used a good dusting. Just ordinary dust, however, not the fine, grayish kind left behind when a human body burned to ash after being infected with the Heat. It seemed obvious enough to him that Rowan must have gone through the place and cleaned out all evidence of the former residents' passing, and he had to be grateful for that.

Even though his people had created the disease, he did not like to be confronted by the reality of its aftermath, not in a place where the majority of the people who had died had been little more than children.

He set the space heater down on the floor next to an outlet, then eased off the rucksack and leaned it against the bed. As Rowan had warned him, the air in here was quite chilly, although the temperature was something he noted almost in passing, since djinn were not affected by such things the same way humans were.

Still, he'd been given the space heater, and it seemed churlish not to use the thing. He plugged it into the outlet and turned it on the lowest heat setting. Immediately, warm air began to push its way out, letting him know the solar power here was sufficient to get them through the overnight hours.

He unfolded the sleeping bag and spread it out on the nearer of the two beds. The material flopped over somewhat at the foot, telling him his own feet would probably do much the same thing.

Best not to think about the luxurious, oversized bed at his ranch in Jackson Hole, especially since it was by his own choice that he was here now.

But what if he blinked himself home to sleep, then returned in the morning before Rowan even realized he'd been gone?

As tempting as the idea was, he guessed it would be better if he didn't take such a risk. Not that he believed the woman who had given him this place to sleep would have any reason to check on him during the night, but if there was anything he'd learned in all his long life, it was to take nothing for granted.

No, he would sleep here and make the best of it.

With the bed made up, he opened the door and risked a peek down the hallway. Rowan's door remained firmly shut, which told him she must have planned to stay inside until she knew for sure he was settled for the night.

He went down the hall to the bathroom, which was scrupulously clean and smelled strongly of disinfectant. The aforementioned bucket stood in one corner, but he had no intention of using it. Once he'd locked the door, he took himself away to his house so he might avail himself of the facilities there. It was one thing to sleep with his feet hanging over the bed, but quite another to be forced to relieve himself in a place with no amenities.

When he returned, though, he cupped some water in his hands and dropped it in the bucket, just so Rowan would think he'd used it. Exactly what he planned to do when it came to leaving more solid waste, he wasn't sure, but he supposed he'd figure it out at some point.

After removing his jeans and socks and shirt, he climbed into bed. The fabric of the sleeping bag was cool against his bare skin for a moment, but soon warmed up to match his temperature, a modest feat of engineering accomplished by a team of people who most likely were no longer alive.

No, better not to think about that, or how Rowan had tidied up this room but hadn't touched any of the mementos its former occupants had left behind. With the lights out, he didn't have to see the laughing faces in the photographs that sat on the shelves, or view the brightly colored pillows that decorated the bed opposite his—pillows, he guessed, that hadn't been part of the official items supplied by the school. They would have been constant reminders of the people who had died here...people who should have had their entire lives to look forward to.

Instead, he thought of the woman who'd given him this place to sleep, and how she'd somehow managed to prevail despite such long odds being stacked against her. Humans had proven to be much tougher and more resourceful than one might have expected, given their complete lack of any kind of magical powers, and Rowan Aames was no exception.

But still, she was not a djinn, or she would have been living in far greater comfort these past several years. If it weren't for the lies he'd told her and the identity he'd assumed, they'd already have working bathrooms and central heat.

A slow smile spread across his lips as an idea occurred to him. He might not be able to manage the central heat...but he thought he could take care of their other problem.

Yes, Rowan would have quite a surprise waiting for her tomorrow morning.

# Chapter 4

HER MORNING ROUTINE DURING THE COLD months was always the same—sleep in fleece-lined leggings and a sweatshirt, then slide out of bed and into a pair of Uggs and her puffer coat so she could let Darby out to do his business. This particular morning was no different, except once she emerged into the hallway, Rowan remembered she and the dog weren't alone.

Or...were they?

The door to the room she'd given James stood open, and although the overhead light was turned off, she could just barely tell that his bed was already made, with his sleeping bag rolled up at one end.

No sign of James himself, though, and she frowned. She doubted he would have left the sleeping bag behind, but because the door to the bathroom was also open, she couldn't see any sign of him on this floor.

Well, maybe he'd already gone downstairs to make himself some coffee. She had bags and bags of the stuff, both ground and whole bean, although she'd been working her way through the ground variety first just because she knew it would go stale faster. Her stash also included lots of loose and bagged tea as well, since she preferred to drink that in the afternoon when she needed a pick-me-up.

And because both the kettle and the coffeemaker sat out in full view in the kitchen, it wouldn't have been too difficult for him to put together whatever morning beverage he preferred, even if she thought it seemed a little presumptuous for him to go down there and make himself at home when he'd shown up on her almost-doorstep completely uninvited.

Darby cocked his head up at her, expression a little puzzled, since they usually headed right down the stairs as soon as she had her jacket and boots on. At least she could tell that the morning outside was gray only because it was too early for the sun to have come up, and not because any clouds had moved in overnight.

"We're going, Darbs," she assured him before heading for the stairs.

However, she'd only gotten halfway down before she had to stop short, as James was walking up the steps toward her, wearing a smile she thought was a little too wide for barely six o'clock on a cold November morning.

"Did you see my surprise?" he asked, and now it was her turn to give a confused head tilt.

"What surprise?" She didn't think she'd seen anything surprising on her way to the staircase, unless you counted the way he'd made his bed. The couple of guys she'd dated in the before times hadn't been that neat, but still....

James's smile didn't slip even a fraction of an inch. "In the bathroom. Come on—I'll show you."

Increasingly mystified, Rowan followed him up the stairs and partway down the hall to the large bath the entire floor had shared. He opened the door so she could go inside, then moved past her to the closest sink. Still wearing that shit-eating grin, he reached over and turned on the tap.

Water gushed out...hot water, with steam curling up into the cold air in the space.

She stared at the water in shock. If James had suddenly produced a unicorn with a snap of his fingers, she couldn't have been more surprised.

"How...?" She swallowed, then gathered herself. "How in the world did you manage that?"

If the dancing light in his dark eyes was any indication, he was mightily pleased with himself for shocking her like this.

"It wasn't too hard," he said. "I mean, we have

pretty much solar everything in Los Alamos. Some wind, too, but it's mostly solar for the individual houses. And because we rotate duties, I've had plenty of time to get to know how the systems work. All I had to do was connect the pump system from the well to the solar that's already powering the electrical, and that gave us running water."

All right, his explanation made some sense. Not that she would have been able to manage such a feat on her own, because even though she'd dug up as many texts on solar power as she could from the college library, they were long on theory and short on actual practical knowledge.

But....

"That explains the running water," she said, hands planted on her hips. Next to her, Darby gave a very small whine, as though to remind her why they'd gotten up in the first place. She leaned down to give him a reassuring pat on the head, letting him know she hadn't forgotten, although she kept her gaze fixed on James the whole time. "But that doesn't explain how it's hot. The hot water heaters and the furnace all ran on gas."

"They did," he replied. He didn't look particularly upset by her line of questioning, as if he'd somehow guessed she wasn't going to take this miracle at face value. "But all I had to do was a little rewiring, and they're hooked up, too. I'm not sure I'd run the furnace, though—it was set up to heat the whole building, and you'd blow through your battery stores in no time running a system that big. It's better to keep using the space heaters."

Just a little rewiring. Rowan wanted to kick herself for not managing a similar feat all the time she'd spent here alone at the Castle, but she wasn't sure she could have accomplished such a thing on her own. More likely, she would have shorted out the whole place and deprived herself of even the limited stores of electricity she'd been using to survive. She didn't have a background in electrical engineering or anything close to it, and she didn't have the practical experience James had obviously gained during his tenure in Los Alamos.

Sure, her father had made sure she knew how to change a tire and the oil in her car, and had taken her and her brothers shooting. However, even though those were good skills to have, she was pretty sure her fire chief father also wouldn't have known how to rewire a solar setup so it powered more than just a structure's electrical panel.

"I think I can manage that," she said, a lopsided smile touching her lips. "And this is...amazing. Thank you. But now I really need to take Darby out."

"No worries," James replied. "I think I'll have a hot shower, if that's okay with you."

"It's fine," she said faintly. Since she knew it wouldn't be very polite to admonish him to save some hot water for her, not when he'd just given her something she never dreamed she'd have here in this post-Dying world, she didn't say anything else, only beckoned Darby to follow her down the stairs and outside so he could finally have his morning bathroom break.

All the same, she couldn't wait to take a hot shower of her own.

---

Jamal didn't linger in the shower as he normally would have, partly because he'd bathed in the hot springs the afternoon before and didn't require much cleaning up, and partly because he didn't know how long the hot water would last and wanted to make sure there was plenty left over for Rowan.

He had no doubt that his younger brother Omar would have laughed to see Jamal showing such solicitude for a human, but luckily, Omar was not here.

Thank God.

But Rowan had suffered enough over the previous four years, trapped here by her fear of the great unknown that lay beyond her doorstep. If anyone had earned a hot shower, Jamal thought she definitely had.

So he was in and out in only a few minutes,

and dried off and put on a fresh set of clothing. He conjured the sweatshirt and jeans directly on his body because his backpack had been mostly for show and didn't contain much beyond some spare socks and some bars of dried fruit and nuts. If Rowan went snooping, she might wonder why he was traveling so light, but he didn't think she was the sort of person to pry in such a personal way.

When he emerged from the bathroom, he detected the scent of coffee drifting up the stairs and gave an appreciative sniff. He'd thought perhaps Rowan would prefer to shower right away, but he guessed she'd needed her morning dose of caffeine first.

He found her in the kitchen, just as she finished pouring some steaming coffee into a mug. "That was fast," she remarked as she reached into the cupboard to pull out a second mug and fill it as well. "I thought for sure you were going to stay in the shower longer and enjoy the fruit of your labors."

"I didn't want to use up all the hot water," he replied, then took the mug from her. Wisps of fragrant steam rose to his nostrils, and he breathed in deeply. A djinn could drink coffee that hot and come to no harm, but he knew the human he was masquerading to be would have to wait a minute or two for it to safely cool down.

"Well, thanks for that," she said. "I just

figured I'd have some coffee and toast first. There's no butter, but I've got plenty of jam and honey."

"You made the bread?" he asked...before realizing that was a foolish question. It wasn't as though she could go to the local grocery store to buy some, and she certainly couldn't snap her fingers and have it appear out of thin air the way he could.

Her mouth twitched a little but stopped short of turning into an actual smile. "Yes, I made it. That little toaster oven does a decent job, although you should count yourself lucky that you weren't around to taste my first dozen or so tries. Baking wasn't exactly on my resume when I came to work here."

Jamal wasn't too surprised by this, as he had the impression that many people in the world before didn't have the time to bake or cook, and bought everything at the store or ordered takeout. However, some fresh bread sounded like a good accompaniment to his morning cup of coffee, even if there wasn't any butter to be had.

"Do you want some?" she asked next, and he nodded.

"Yes, please."

She went to the pantry, brought out a bread box, and then produced a fine-looking loaf with a nice golden crust. It was clear she'd already cut several slices from it, but there was still plenty for both of them.

Jamal took a cautious sip of coffee while she popped the bread into the toaster oven. It was probably still a little hot for a human tongue, but he guessed Rowan wouldn't notice he'd begun drinking it a little sooner than was wise. And the coffee was excellent, rich and hot. If there was no butter, then he guessed there probably wasn't any cream, either.

She turned away from the toaster oven and gave him a rueful smile. "I used to have some non-dairy creamer, but then I started to worry that even the shelf-stable stuff was beginning to go bad, so I trained myself to drink my coffee black. I hope you don't mind drinking it that way, too."

"No, it's fine," he assured her. "I very rarely use cream myself."

This response seemed to be what she'd been hoping for, because she appeared to relax slightly. "Every once in a while, I'll catch myself daydreaming about a frappuccino from Starbucks. Something over the top with whipped cream and about a gazillion calories, even though I only had those maybe once a month back before." She paused there, then asked, "I don't suppose you have anything like that in Los Alamos."

A very good question. While Jamal and his brothers had done their best to spy on the comings and goings of the people of Los Alamos, the djinn-defying devices had made it so the three of them couldn't get close enough to know much about the humans' daily lives. They knew they had work crews coming and going from Española because they witnessed them going about their business at the fringes of the territory protected by the devices, but whatever had been happening in the mountain town itself might as well have taken place at the bottom of a coal mine, for all they could see.

However, it was easy enough to guess that, even if the Los Alamos townsfolk had cobbled together some facsimile of a restaurant or coffee house, they certainly wouldn't have the resources to make fancy drinks topped with whipped cream.

"No," he said. "No frappuccinos for us, either. In fact, we have to ration coffee because we can't grow it here in New Mexico, and eventually it will run out."

That comment was a complete fabrication, and yet Jamal thought it sounded plausible enough to him. Northern New Mexico didn't have the sort of climate conducive to coffee growing, and no matter how many bags of coffee the Los Alamos crew might have liberated from the shops and houses in Española, there would have to come a time when their stores were depleted.

Unless, of course, the djinn in Santa Fe took

pity on the hapless mortals and conjured a warehouse full of coffee for them.

Rowan's expression was thoughtful. She sipped from her mug of coffee, then said, "I suppose I hadn't thought about it that way. What I've got here will probably last a lot longer, since I'm the only one who's been drinking it."

Jamal didn't bother to comment that he was drinking her coffee, too, not when he could tell she expected him to stay here for perhaps a day or so before he moved along with his supposed "scouting" expedition. To be honest, he had expected much the same thing, thinking he could gather what information he wanted from her before returning to his home in Jackson Hole, but now he was not sure. Even though he and his brothers had been the last active reavers—and even they had not been very active these past couple of years, preferring to plot and plan rather than act so as not to draw attention to themselves—it didn't seem right to leave Rowan in her solitary refuge.

Especially since his "rewiring" of the solar grid here had also been a complete lie, and the hot running water was due to his djinn powers propping up the system and nothing more. As soon as he left, she would be forced to return to bringing in buckets from the well and having to use the springs to bathe if she wanted hot water. In the summer months, that probably wasn't much of a hardship, but he doubted it was anything she enjoyed in December and January and February.

Or even March, considering how long winter lingered in this part of the world.

The toaster oven made a "bing" sound that was already becoming familiar to him, and Rowan hurried over to pull out the four slices of toast she'd cut and set them on plates.

"Jam?" she asked. "Or would you rather have honey?"

"Jam is fine," he replied. In general, djinn preferred honey, but something about standing here and drinking coffee with Rowan Aames seemed to call for jam.

She went to the refrigerator and got out two jars. "I've got strawberry and black currant open right now."

"Black currant," Jamal said at once. He enjoyed its more subtle flavor, and it wasn't anything he'd eaten for some time.

"Same here," she said with a smile, then opened a drawer so she could pull out a knife. Soon enough, she had all four pieces of bread smeared with the stuff, and she handed one of the plates over to him. "It's not exactly French toast at Charlie's, but I guess it's better than nothing."

He had no idea what this "Charlie's" was, but he guessed it must have been a restaurant in her hometown down the road. "I was never much for

French toast," he said before taking a bite of toast. Yes, it could have used some butter, but it was still more palatable than he'd expected. "I'm more of an omelet kind of guy."

Rowan nodded. "I can get on board with that. I actually thought about getting chickens a while back, but then I worried about where I would put them and whether they might attract coyotes...and other things."

Meaning djinn, he supposed, which he couldn't say was an entirely unfounded fear. A coop full of squawking chickens was the sort of thing that would definitely invite attention. It wouldn't have been worth the risk simply to have fresh eggs and perhaps the occasional chicken dinner.

"It was probably better not to have them," he said. "Although I can see why you might have wanted to."

She nodded, but because she'd just taken a bite of toast, she had to wait until she was finished chewing before she could reply. "I'm just glad that bread only needs water and flour and yeast...and salt. Once I got the hang of it, I could make some more bread any time I started to get food cravings. It helped a little."

"It's very good bread," Jamal said. That wasn't empty praise, either; the piece of toast he'd just consumed had been nicely crunchy on the outside but still moist on the inside, telling him the bread had probably been soft and fragrant when she first baked it.

However, his comment seemed to embarrass her, because she ducked her head and seemed to be far more focused on taking another bite than might have been necessary. Once again, he was struck by how long she'd lived here alone, and how difficult it must have been for her to adjust to having only a dog for company.

Speaking of whom, Darby had finished eating his bowl of kibble and had now settled at Jamal's feet, wistful dark eyes staring up at him…or, more accurately, at the piece of toast he held.

"You can give him a little bit of the crust," Rowan told him. "Just make sure there isn't any jelly on it. I don't want him to have any sugar."

That request seemed manageable enough, so Jamal broke off a corner of his toast and fed it to the dog. At once, Darby's tail started wagging and he sat up a little straighter, clearly hoping that if he looked enthusiastic enough, he might get a second piece.

Rowan chuckled. "You can give him a little more…but not too much." She ate the last bite of her own piece of toast, then set her empty plate on the counter. "Do you mind keeping an eye on him for a little while? I want to try out that new shower."

"Not at all," Jamal replied at once. His mind wanted to conjure an image of her with warm water cascading over her glorious copper-hued hair and dripping down her bare body, but he immediately shoved it away. He had no intention of that kind of dalliance during his time here. Perhaps his older brother had been seduced by a human woman's charms, but he wanted to think he was made of stronger stuff.

Or at least, he hoped he was. Perhaps that forbidden vision had popped into his head because quite some time had passed since he had been with a woman of his own kind. He and his brothers had been so focused on piercing Los Alamos's defenses that none of them had bothered to seek our female companionship, and he had told himself he could worry about that sort of thing later, once they had achieved their goal.

But that goal seemed very far away right now, most likely impossible. And while he had slipped in and out of partnerships during the course of his long life, he had never felt such a strong connection to any of those women that he wanted to settle down for a while, perhaps have a child. It had always felt better to move on to the next person or, failing that, allow himself to be alone for however long might suit his current situation.

Rowan nodded in response to his answer about the watching the dog, then bent down and ruffled

Darby's ears before heading out of the kitchen. Jamal continued to eat his piece of toast as if he had no other cares in the world, although he wasn't so sure about that.

Because if he truly had no interest in Rowan Aames, then why would his traitorous mind have conjured an image of her naked in the shower?

# Chapter 5

The hot water beating down on her felt better than anything in the world. Better than those frappuccinos she'd dreamed of, better than a bacon cheeseburger, better than a pedicure or a massage or any of the other comforts of her old life that she'd been missing these past four years. And all right, she'd only gotten a massage once, as part of a birthday spa package her mother had bought her when she turned twenty-one, but still.

Better than sex?

Good question. One of her boyfriends hadn't been that great in bed, the other a lot more skilled, and she'd definitely enjoyed herself...right up until the moment when she found out the reason he was so good in the sack was that he'd been sleeping around with three other women. She'd dumped him and decided to stay single for a while, especially since she was just about to start her new job at United World College and thought it better to focus on her career for the time being. Back then, she'd believed she had all the time in the world to find a new relationship.

There was a joke.

She rinsed out the shampoo and applied some conditioner, knowing that now she'd finally be able to get all of it out the way she never could when she washed her hair in the sink and used a bowl to pour water on it to get rid of the shampoo and conditioner. For the first time in several months, ever since the nights and mornings had gotten cold again, she felt truly warm in a way she never did when she had to rely on space heaters to remove the chill from the air.

Maybe it was because she was so comfortable right now, but she couldn't quite keep her thoughts from straying to the man who waited downstairs with Darby. James hadn't said anything about how long he intended to stick around, and yet she found herself hoping he planned to stay for at least a few days. It was nice to have someone to talk to...and she had to admit he was pretty easy on the eyes.

Okay, scratch that. He was drop-dead gorgeous. Even more important, he'd managed to figure out a way to give her hot water, running water, a luxury she hadn't thought she'd ever be able to experience again. Right then, she wished she had bagged a deer on her hunting expedition the day before, if only so she could make him a dinner tonight that would be an adequate thank-you for the enormous miracle he'd given her.

Well, maybe they couldn't have venison, but she had that second rabbit in the fridge, and she'd see if she could figure out a way to prepare it that was a little more special than simply roasting it.

And wine. Having running water again was definitely a good reason to break out the cabernet... or whatever it was that went best with rabbit. She had to admit she didn't know a lot about that kind of thing, but she supposed with the world the way it was now, people didn't care too much about satisfying some snooty wine expert's pairing specifications. At least, James didn't seem like the sort of person who had the time to be pretentious.

He'd fixed the water situation for her, even though he'd made it sound as if he thought it was better for her to go to Los Alamos in the end. Rowan still wasn't sure why he would have done such a thing, except maybe he also hadn't known how long he planned to linger here, and it just seemed smarter to enjoy a few creature comforts before he got back on the road again.

While she could see why it might be better to finally leave Montezuma Castle behind and join what remained of humanity, some part of her wasn't sure if it wanted to accept that possible future. She'd been alone here for so long. What if she simply couldn't integrate with a community after so many years? There had been a few times during her conversation with James the night before when she'd felt as though she'd stuck her foot right in her mouth, although he hadn't seemed to notice. Was he only being polite, or was she being too self-critical?

Without much context, it was hard to say.

Reluctantly, she reached over and turned off the taps. Almost at once, the room felt far colder, although she'd left a space heater going over by the sinks so the bathroom wouldn't turn into a complete meat locker the second she shut off the water.

Even so, she toweled off quickly, then put on some underwear and a long-sleeved T-shirt before she got to work using a different towel to blot as much water as possible from her hair. Although she had a blow dryer, she didn't dare use it, not when every precious drop of energy the solar panels collected was needed for more important things like the lights and the heaters and the various small appliances in the kitchen. But she'd learned that if she used the towel on her hair long enough, it would get to a state where it only needed another half hour or so to dry, which was better than walking around with dripping wet hair in the depths of winter.

After she hung up both towels, her gaze went to the drawer where she kept the few cosmetics she owned. All right, it was just mascara and tinted lip balm, and she wore the latter every day because it kept her from looking like an extra from a zombie movie and also protected her lips from the dry, rough air of northern New Mexico. She'd been wearing some when she first encountered James the day before, so it really shouldn't be a big deal if she applied a bit now, right?

*No mascara, though,* she told herself. *Because that would make it look like you're trying too hard.*

Luckily, her lashes were several shades darker than her hair, so she could live without mascara. To be honest, she couldn't even remember the last time she'd put some on. Had it been her birthday the year before? Maybe Christmas, just to make the day feel quasi-special?

It probably didn't matter all that much.

Dressed and ready to face the day—whatever it might bring—Rowan descended the stairs and headed for the kitchen. When she got there, though, she saw at once it was empty, with neither James nor Darby anywhere in sight.

Frowning, she went to the window and raised the blind, but the landscape beyond was empty, with no sign of the pair playing ball or whatever other activities they might have engaged in after venturing outside.

Well, the Castle was big, but even so, there were only a few places they could have gone. Including....

She pulled in a breath and told herself it wasn't that big a deal, even as she hastened her pace and hurried toward the big dining hall at the other end of the corridor. It probably would have made a lot more sense for it to be located closer to the kitchen, but she hadn't designed the place.

When she got there, one of the double doors stood open, and early morning light poured out into the hallway. She knew that door hadn't been open the day before, because she'd closed it the last time she was in there and that had been two days ago.

Lifting her chin, she walked in and did her best to keep herself from blinking in the sunlight that blazed in through the dining hall's multiple windows. Standing in the middle of the space was James, his expression bemused. Then he caught sight of her and asked, "What is all this?"

Rowan pressed her lips together, feeling the smoothness of the tinted balm on her mouth. If asked, she might not have been able to explain why nervousness clenched her stomach or made her hands icy cold, except that he'd stumbled onto something intensely personal for her, something she'd never expected anyone else to see.

The dining hall held approximately twenty round tables. At one time, a set of eight chairs had been grouped around each of those tables, but she'd moved the chairs out of the way and stacked them against one wall, only leaving a single chair here and there as needed for her to work. Twelve of those tables held multiple piles of notebooks eight or ten high, or—in the case of the one where she'd been working most recently—stacks of lined paper.

"It's...." She took in a breath and told herself not to be such a coward. His question wasn't all that strange, considering what he'd just stumbled across. "I didn't know what to do with myself once I knew I was alone out here. And I worried I'd start to forget things. So...I started writing."

James's dark eyes widened. "These are all novels?"

Rowan wouldn't allow herself to chuckle, not when she supposed it was a normal enough question to ask. "No. They're just...memories, I guess. I wrote down everything I could remember about my life and about the way the world was. Plots of movies and books. Names of actors and musicians and writers. Bits of song lyrics. Just...whatever I could think of. I guess I thought if it was all written down somewhere, maybe one day someone would come along and find it, and those things wouldn't be lost forever." She stopped there, a little surprised at the flood of words that had just escaped her lips. "It's probably kind of stupid."

At once, James shook his head. He didn't move toward her, as if he somehow guessed that wasn't what she wanted right now, although Darby had come over and pressed his cold nose into her hand. He must have heard the strain in her voice and decided to offer her whatever comfort he could.

"It's not stupid at all," James said. "I mean, you're right. There are so many things that will be forgotten if they're not recorded somewhere."

"You're not doing anything like this in Los Alamos?" Rowan asked. Now that her secret had been discovered, she found herself relaxing slightly. It was okay. James didn't think she was stupid or crazy, which meant all those times she'd wondered if she was expending way too much energy that could have been put to better use elsewhere had been nothing more than her trying to second-guess herself.

He hesitated for a second or two, then shrugged even as he shoved his hands into his jeans pockets. "I don't know," he said. "I mean, some of the people there may have kept a record of events or written down their memories, but I don't know of a formal effort to keep track of everything. Mostly, people just focus on surviving."

"So do I," Rowan said. She couldn't see

anything except friendly curiosity in his face, which meant she thought it was safe to keep on talking. "But I still had lots of time on my hands even after gutting fish and dragging water in from the well or whatever, so I started doing this. I mean, did you know that medieval peasants worked a lot fewer hours than modern people did?"

Another one of those lightbulb-flash smiles brightened his face. "No, I didn't. Where did you hear that?"

"In one of my history classes in college," she replied. At the time, she'd mostly been annoyed by the piles of reading the professor expected of her—did he think his students didn't have any other classes to keep up with?—but she had to admit that she'd learned a few interesting tidbits. Since James still seemed relaxed and friendly, she figured it was probably okay to ask a question of her own. "Where did you go to school?"

"I didn't," he said, and she blinked at him. Still smiling, he went on, "I was never that interested in going to college, so I worked a bunch of jobs after high school—I waited tables and did a stint at a landscape company. But when it happened, I was working at a motorcycle shop in Albuquerque."

"Like a mechanic?" Rowan asked, and he nodded.

Well, that explained a few things. Or at least, while he'd told her they rotated duties in Los

Alamos and that was why he knew how to work with the solar setup she had here at the college, she had to believe he'd already been pretty handy and was the kind of person who could pick up a variety of technical skills easily.

Whereas she could manage a DIY project here and there if she really had to, but she knew that wasn't how her brain was put together. Otherwise, she would have figured out how to reroute the wiring for the solar panels years ago.

"This is impressive, though," he said, gaze moving to the stacks of notebooks once more. "Even if they'd had this kind of time on their hands, I sort of doubt many people would have done the same thing."

Maybe he was right. As a kid, she'd always had her head stuck in a book, and she'd enjoyed writing essays and book reports when most of her friends had groaned over that kind of homework. However, the prospect of writing a novel seemed far too daunting to her, which was why she'd had to laugh when James had suggested that was what might be in the stacks of notebooks and papers around them.

His expression grew a little more serious as he went on, "I know you weren't expecting me to barge in like this...but I was kind of hoping it would be all right if I stayed another day."

Wow, he'd put it out right there. In a way,

Rowan was relieved, because that meant they wouldn't have to dance around whether or not he planned to stay a while longer or if he was going to hit the road just as soon as he'd broached the subject with her.

Funny how she should be so relieved that he didn't want to take off right away. After all, they barely knew each other.

But she knew in that moment she wanted to get to know him a lot better.

"Sure," she said, doing her best not to show him how relieved she was. "It's fine if you stay."

---

Until Rowan had given her permission, Jamal hadn't realized how much he was hoping she'd tell him he could remain at the Castle a while longer. He might have admitted to himself that he found the place itself somewhat diverting, and her various makeshifts to get around dealing with the reality of a world with no true infrastructure were interesting on their own. However, after seeing how she'd spent the past four years, how she'd done her best to chronicle a world that was now gone, he thought there was much more to Rowan Aames than he would have previously acknowledged.

Still, he did his best to show he was glad of her

invitation without letting her see how relieved he truly was.

"Great," he said. "And I should say thank you by getting us something special for dinner tonight."

Her eyebrows—a medium brown that contrasted with her bright coppery hair—lifted slightly. "Oh? Are you going to head down to the grocery store and pick up a couple of steaks?"

Jamal allowed himself a chuckle. It was true that he could snap his fingers and have a veritable feast appear before them, but doing so would only reveal to her that he was a djinn and not a simple mortal.

No, he had something a bit less ostentatious… and dangerous…in mind.

"It would be nice if I could do that," he said. "But I was thinking more of looking for some wildfowl. You must have ducks or quail or something around here, right?"

The amused tilt of her eyebrows lessened slightly. "They come and go," she replied. "I don't think it's the right time of year for them. But I suppose it might be worth looking. If you don't find anything, we still have that second rabbit I caught yesterday."

"Thanks for the vote of confidence," he said with a grin, and she couldn't help smiling back, showing a hint of a dimple on one cheek.

"Just keeping it real," she said.

He supposed that was one way of looking at the situation. A thought occurred to him, and he asked, "Do you mind if I bring Darby along? Cattle dogs are good hunting companions."

To be honest, he wasn't sure if he was correct in that, but the dog probably knew the landscape around here much better than he did, and would help guide him back home if he lost his bearings. Yes, he could always blink himself to the Castle, but doing so would run the risk of Rowan spotting the way he'd suddenly appeared out of nowhere, and he preferred to avoid such a confrontation by acting as human as he was pretending to be.

For a moment, she looked dubious, and then her shoulders lifted and she said, "Sure. He usually comes with me when we go into the forest, and he'll be able to guide you back if you get lost. Just... just keep an eye on him, okay?"

The request was made in a casual enough tone, but Jamal understood. Darby had been Rowan's only companion these past four years, and he knew she'd be devastated if anything happened to the dog.

Well, nothing was going to happen. There was no safer place to be than at the side of a djinn... unless you were a mortal, of course.

"I will," he promised. "And since the sun's up

and the day is looking decent, I figure we might as well head out."

"Okay," Rowan said. "But let me pack you a little lunch before you go, just in case you're out there for a while."

This sounded like a good idea, so he agreed, then followed her into the kitchen, Darby at his heels, tail wagging. The dog might not have understood every word of their conversation, but it seemed he'd gotten the gist of it and knew an outdoor expedition was in the offing.

Rowan wrapped up some cold rabbit and a few slices of bread in an old tea towel and handed it over, saying, "If you follow the creek, you'll be less likely to get lost. Just remember that there are bears and mountain lions out there, and they've had four years to get over being scared of humans."

She had a point. Not that the predators she'd mentioned had ever been overly intimidated by human beings, but with no one out there hunting them with guns or even trapping them and removing them to more remote parts of the forest if they encroached on mortal territory, they no doubt thought they had free rein to do whatever they liked.

But even a bear knew better than to attack a djinn, and any other wildlife in the area would stay far away...unless he gave the signal for them to come closer. He wouldn't do such a thing, simply because he had no wish to frighten Darby. Although Rowan hadn't provided a lot of details, Jamal got the impression that she hadn't ventured very far into the forest, fearing what might happen if she was attacked by a wild animal and had no one around to provide medical attention.

That had been prudent of her, of course, but he had no reason to harbor the same fears. No, he would find something good for them to eat...a turkey seemed the most realistic option, since even a human in the prime of health and strength would have a hard time bringing back a deer on their own without a vehicle to carry the carcass...and then Rowan would have even more reason to want to keep him around.

A day earlier, that thought would have sounded ludicrous to him. Now, though, he could only allow himself an inner smile...and hope she would also smile when she saw what he had brought for their supper.

# Chapter 6

James hadn't been armed except for a hunting knife he wore at his waist, almost identical to the one she carried with her at all times. She brushed aside her inner misgivings—it wasn't as if she couldn't fetch herself an identical gun if he absconded with the one she gave him—and handed over a .22 rifle and a box of bullets.

"That should be enough for wildfowl," she said as he took the gun from her. "But if you see a mountain lion, I'd suggest running."

An amused glint entered his dark eyes. "What about the bears?"

"I'm pretty sure they're already hibernating. It's been below freezing overnight for at least the past two weeks."

This reassurance...such as it was...seemed to be enough for James, because he didn't ask any other questions and only said, "I'll be back as soon as I can."

"I'll be here."

That silly comment—where else would she go?—made him smile a little, as she'd hoped. Even after being around him for less than twenty-four hours, Rowan found herself craving those smiles. They made her feel warm even on a bleak day.

Which this one wasn't, thanks to the bright sun that now rode high in the sky. Yes, the air itself was cold, probably in the low forties at best, but it was easier to ignore the chilly temperatures with the sun shining down like that. And even though the forest canopy was quite thick here, she still thought James would be able to use the sun's angle to gauge how much time had passed, and also to help guide him back to Montezuma Castle.

All the same, she told him, "Remember to follow the creek," right before he headed out the kitchen door, Darby at his side. She stood there and watched until they disappeared into the trees on the far side of the Dwan Light Sanctuary, and a little pang went through her.

They should be safe...she'd gone into those woods dozens of times, although not any farther than a quarter-mile or so...but what if they weren't?

*Don't be silly,* she told herself as she closed the door. *Darby knows the way, and James obviously knows how to take care of himself. Otherwise, I doubt he would have made it all the way here in one piece.*

Those words should have been comforting enough, but Rowan couldn't shake off an uneasy feeling nonetheless. What if a mountain lion really did attack them? Or, more plausible, what if James lost his footing somehow and sprained an ankle or broke an arm?

*Then Darby would come back and get me and take me to him,* she thought. *He's a smart dog. He'd know what to do.*

Or at least, she hoped he would.

Realizing the best thing to do was to distract herself, she tidied up the kitchen—once again marveling at how water came right out of the tap—and then headed into the dining hall. The bright sun coming through the tall windows with their edgings of stained glass in warm shades of amber and green helped to reassure her a little. After all, what could go wrong on a gorgeous day like this?

She headed over to the table where she'd last been working when James appeared the day before. Once she'd gotten through this stack of paper, she'd put it all in a notebook and add it to one of the piles on the other side of the room, then go on to the next.

More than once, she'd thought this was all an exercise in futility, that no one was ever going to read a single word she'd written, but she hadn't stopped.

What else did she have to do with her time?

She'd been in the middle of writing about a trip her family had taken to Durango when she was a child, where they'd taken the restored narrow-gauge railroad up to the historic mining town of Silverton. It had been a bright, sunny day in August, although monsoon clouds had been piling up all afternoon, and they got to experience a massive thunderstorm almost as soon as they returned to their hotel.

Reading over those recollections, Rowan wished it were monsoon season now. Yes, the Castle could sometimes get downright hot during the summer months, but those unexpected rainstorms always helped to cool things down, and she thought she'd much rather be a little warm than feel as if she was freezing all the time.

But the monsoon storms didn't start until the end of June at the earliest, which meant she had a lot more months to go before she could head outside and dance in the rain, the way she sometimes did when it was pouring but there wasn't any lightning to make that kind of activity both stupid and dangerous.

Instead, she picked up her pen and started writing, describing Durango's fun downtown and the fields of wildflowers her family had driven past on their way in. Discussing Durango made her think of Pagosa Springs, where they'd stopped for lunch at a place right on the river, and where you could watch people floating by on inner tubes they'd rented farther upstream. She and Charlie and Henry had begged their parents to let them go inner-tubing, but they couldn't stop for that long, so the outing had been put off for another day.

A day that had never come, because they'd never found the time to go back to Pagosa.

Rowan let out a breath, then set down her pen. There was a lot more she could have written about, but right then, she found she didn't have the desire to.

What was James doing right now?

*Looking for dinner,* she told herself. *It's fine.*

She got up from her seat and went over to the wall where she'd tacked up the large butcher-paper calendar. Right after the Heat, she'd found a two-year calendar in one of the administrator's offices and used that to keep track of the days passing, but after it was used up, she'd had to create one of her own, painstakingly writing out the months and the weeks with a Sharpie so everything would be easy to read. When she'd set out to create the calendar for this year, she'd goofed because she'd forgotten it was a leap year until she was done filling out all the months up to June, and had had to take it down and start all over. Still, she was glad of the work because it gave her something different to do...and also because she knew if she didn't continue to mark off the days and weeks, she'd start to forget what month it actually was, let alone the day of the week.

A box of markers sat on the floor beneath the calendar, and she pulled out a green one and made a careful slash across November fifth, since that was yesterday and she wanted to make sure she continued to keep track despite James's distracting presence here.

Four years, one month, and five days since she'd been left alone here.

*You're not alone now,* she told herself, which she supposed was partially true. James didn't seem too eager to hit the road, and she was fine with that, but she had to believe at some point he'd need to get going.

The question was, would she go with him?

There wasn't much keeping her here, after all. Yes, the Castle had done an admirable job of providing her with the sanctuary she needed, but now that she knew people were alive in Los Alamos, it seemed stupid to stay here on her own. Much smarter to go with James and see what kind of life she could have in that sole remaining outpost of humanity.

Maybe they could have some kind of future together.

No, that was ridiculous. She'd only just met the guy. She didn't know a single thing about him, except that he'd grown up in Moriarty and he'd been a motorcycle mechanic in Albuquerque when the world ended.

Well, and that he seemed kind and Darby liked him.

And he'd made the plumbing here work, something she'd never even contemplated as a possibility.

Put together, that combination of sterling qualities did seem kind of amazing. The problem was, she'd still only known him for about twenty-four hours. As starved as she'd been for human company the past four years, that didn't mean she should throw all rational thought out the window.

So she wouldn't. She'd let him stay tonight... and maybe the night after, and the night after, if he asked...but she wasn't going allow herself to get all moony over him just because he was probably the most beautiful man she'd ever seen.

And the nicest she'd ever met, and....

Oh, hell.

The room darkened, and Rowan blinked. She'd been standing there and staring at the calendar and not paying much attention to the world around her, but even she couldn't miss the way the light outside the dining hall's numerous windows had changed.

In this part of the world, that was never a good sign.

She set down the marker she held, then hurried over to the window. As she'd feared, heavy gray clouds had begun to drift across the valley where Montezuma Castle was hidden from the rest of the outside world. The light shifted again as the sun slipped between several of those clouds, but she had a feeling it wasn't going to hold on for much longer.

Better to go outside and check, though.

She took the stairs as fast as she could and went out the kitchen door so she could stare up at the sky. Yes, there were more clouds fast on the heels of the ones she'd just spotted, dark, ominous. The wind picked up, pulling at her loose hair, sending chills down her spine. She turned and gazed in the direction of the woods where James and Darby had disappeared only an hour or so earlier.

*Come back,* she thought. *Come back...before you can't.*

---

The easiest thing to do, of course, was to simply conjure a dead turkey and carry it back to the Castle, then pretend he was the great hunter who had saved the day. Or rather, the absolute easiest thing would have been to blink that turkey right into the refrigerator in the Castle's kitchen, but Jamal doubted such a maneuver would go over very well with Rowan.

However, something about having Darby at his side made Jamal think he needed to go about this the human way if at all possible. No, it wasn't as if the dog could tattle on him, but still, it just seemed better to follow the forms when he could. That wasn't to say that he wouldn't make sure any shots he fired found their way unerringly to the turkey's neck or head, but that was the sort of djinn intervention no one would be able to detect.

It was rougher going in the woods than he'd expected, and yet he supposed he shouldn't be so surprised. Many years had passed since the last park ranger had guarded these forests or someone from the forest service had thinned the trees and picked up the dead fall.

Still, he made his way steadily through the forest, always keeping the creek within eye- and earshot, with Darby ranging forward and then doubling back. The two of them were making enough noise that he thought any sensible animal within a mile radius would have headed for the hills, but he didn't have the heart to bring the dog to heel, not when he was clearly enjoying himself so much.

And then, off in the distance, he thought he could catch the odd, ululating call of a wild turkey.

Darby obviously heard it as well, because he pointed, nose positioned in the exact direction where the call had originated.

"Good boy," Jamal said in a murmur. "Let's go."

They headed deeper into the woods, away from the creek. He hadn't forgotten Rowan's admonition, but because he knew he could get himself back to the Castle no matter what, he wasn't going to worry about the way that one obvious landmark was falling farther and farther behind them.

The sound of the turkey—or turkeys, as Jamal realized he had heard more than one—grew louder. He slowed his pace, and Darby, although obviously wanting to bound forward, slowed as well, even dropping behind him so he would have a clear shot without the dog getting in the way.

Yes, there they were. Three of them, in a small clearing dotted with bare aspens. They pecked at the yellowed grass, probably looking for seeds. And even though Jamal knew that he and Darby had been anything but stealthy, it seemed the birds hadn't noticed a thing.

Then again, no one had ever accused a turkey of being overburdened with intellect.

Jamal raised the .22 and sighted on the bird nearest him. As he did so, he couldn't help thinking the djinn way was much kinder. No need to slaughter an animal, not when his powers could simply conjure the component atoms of whatever he needed and assemble them wherever was most convenient, sort of like the elemental version of the replicators he'd seen on the *Star Trek* TV shows he'd watched.

But if he wanted to keep up the pretense that he was as human as Rowan, then he would have to do this the hard way.

The sound of the rifle going off was louder than he'd expected. He winced but didn't forget himself so much that he didn't make sure the bullet struck the turkey directly in the head. Its two companions exploded up from the ground, squawking, and disappeared into the forest.

That was all right, though. He'd felled the tom, a beast that looked as though he must weigh at least eighteen or nineteen pounds, and that was the important thing. This single bird would feed him and Rowan—and Darby—for days.

The dog had run over to the turkey's carcass and was now standing by its head, his tail wagging furiously. Jamal followed at a more sedate pace and had just entered the clearing when the sky momentarily darkened.

Instead of kneeling by the turkey, he gazed upward, eyes narrowing. Heavy clouds, their undersides shadowed and gray, were moving in fast from the north. They hung so low that they'd already begun to obscure the higher peaks of the mountains upslope from the clearing where he and Darby stood.

Jamal swore, an oath that had been ancient when the conquistadors had yet to set foot in the Americas. No, he could not truly suffer from exposure the way a human would, but still, heavy snow would make it that much more difficult for him to return to the Castle.

And he had that turkey to carry.

Although he had always enjoyed being an earth elemental, finding solace in the energies of soil and rock, at times like this he wished he might have been a djinn whose element was the air. If that had been the case, then he could have simply sent his powers upward into the sky and shunted the coming storm harmlessly off to the south and west.

Now, though, he could only listen to the wind as it began to whistle in the treetops and send searching fingers of cold through the human garments he wore, and hope he'd be able to beat the weather.

Hard to say, though. It was coming in fast.

He bent and grasped the turkey by its legs and slung it over his shoulder, then straightened. Yes, it was a large bird and might been quite a burden for a human being to carry all the way back to the Castle...but he wasn't human.

"Come along, Darby," he said. "We need to head home."

The dog came to him at once, tail wagging, nose sniffing at the turkey's head, which now dangled near Jamal's waist. At the same time, though, he sent a glance upward, as though he, too, had realized that rough weather was coming in.

"That's why we need to move fast," he told the dog. Somehow, it seemed right to address the animal as he would another person, since he'd noticed that Rowan spoke to Darby the same way.

And it certainly seemed that the dog understood, because he began loping back the way they had come, ranging sometimes as much as ten or fifteen feet ahead, but always taking a moment to pause and look back, as if to make sure Jamal hadn't fallen too far behind.

They'd only gone a few hundred yards when the first flakes of snow began to fall.

Feathery at first, drifting through the trees like fine down being shaken loose from a quilt, but that stage didn't last very long. No, they grew thicker and wetter, coming down at such a rapid pace that they began to accumulate almost at once. Just a rime of ice to begin with, but Jamal could tell the snow would be a few inches deep within the quarter hour, and much deeper still within minutes after that.

How long had it taken for him and Darby to get this deep in the woods? An hour? Two?

Probably closer to two, since the noon hour

had almost arrived when he set out, and the sun had definitely slipped past its zenith and begun to slide to the west when those first clouds appeared.

How much snow would fall over the next two hours?

Quite a bit, he feared.

At least he'd been outfitted for this, wearing heavy boots and a thick puffy jacket designed for inclement weather. No headgear, though; his hair was already wet through, sticking to his skull in a most unpleasant way.

Well, he didn't have to fear catching a cold, so the best thing to do was to soldier on.

Darby appeared to love the snow, bounding through the ever-deepening drifts, his tail wagging so quickly, it seemed that sole exertion might be enough to keep him warm. The day grew darker and darker, but Jamal knew, from the same inner time sense all his people possessed, that the darkness was born of the storm...and not because he'd lost all sense of the hour and the sun had begun to set.

However, that knowledge didn't make the going any easier.

The snow was up to his ankles now. He continued, mouth set, wishing he would just say the hell with it, grab the dog, and blink himself back to the Castle. Somehow he doubted Rowan would be outside in this kind of weather, so it would have been simple enough to select a secluded spot that couldn't be easily seen from any of the main building's windows.

But....

Darby barked, and Jamal realized they'd made it back to the creek. From here, they probably had a slog of at least another half hour, but now he didn't have to worry about them wandering around in a trackless wilderness while the snow piled higher and higher.

That seemed to decide things.

The world narrowed down to the swirling white in front of his eyes, the black and white shape of the cattle dog moving steadily along a few feet in front of him, guiding him back to a place of refuge. Now the snow was up to his lower calves, past the tops of his ankle-high boots, but he did his best to ignore the cold and the wet seeping into his socks, the way those same boots became heavier and heavier as the snow caked itself onto them. The turkey on his back seemed to weigh twice what it had when he'd hefted it onto his shoulder hours ago, but there was no way he would let go.

No, he'd promised Rowan a big dinner, and he was going to make sure she got it, no matter what.

Then....

A light ahead, a rectangle of golden illumination barely visible through the swirling snow. Darby gave one sharp, happy bark and bounded across the blank white surface that an hour ago had been the yellowed grass of the lawn that surrounded the Castle. Jamal stumbled ahead, certain that he'd never been so exhausted in his life, even though djinn weren't supposed to be weary, weren't supposed to allow physical labor to affect them.

If this was even a taste of what humans went through on a regular basis, he would have to revise his opinion of their physical and emotional endurance.

And then a second light, this one much taller, as Rowan flung open the kitchen door and ran out into the snow. She took him by the hand and led him up the steps and inside, then took the turkey from his shoulder and carried it over to the kitchen counter so she could set it down.

"God, I was so worried," she said. Her face was white and strained as her amber-hued eyes met his. "Are you all right?"

Was he? Right then, his fingers and toes were numb, but he knew they would recover quickly enough.

Djinn didn't get frostbite.

"I'm fine," he said. "Something hot to drink?"

"Coming right up."

It seemed she'd been anticipating his arrival—or at least had hoped he would be back soon—because the water she poured from the kettle steamed as it went into a mug waiting on the counter. Jamal could glimpse a small string and a tag hanging over the side of the mug and guessed she was making him some tea.

A moment later, she came over with the mug and pressed it between his cold hands. The heat of it pushed its way past the numbness, waking pins and needles in his fingers.

"Thank you," he said.

She stood a foot or so away from him, hands on her hips. "Where the hell did you go? You were gone for hours and hours."

Her tone was sharp, but he thought he understood. It was only worry and fear that made her sound that way. If she hadn't cared about what happened to him, she wouldn't have been nearly so brusque.

"Deep in the woods," he said. "Darby and I heard some wild turkeys and needed to go find them. Which we did," he added, head tilting toward his prize where it sat on the counter, looking as though it might be ready to fall over the edge.

"True," she allowed. A corner of her mouth lifted as she added, "That is one big bird. I have no idea how I'm even going to cook it."

Yes, she'd been unable to use the oven because there was no natural gas. Jamal supposed he should figure out some way to make her think he'd fixed the stove as well, since that fine bird didn't deserve the ignominy of being chopped into pieces small enough to fit into the countertop oven.

"Well, we can figure that out later," he replied. "Or maybe not. What time is it?"

"A little after four."

How long did it take to cook a turkey of that size? He had absolutely no idea. While he enjoyed the game bird, he'd certainly never had to prepare one.

About all he could do was smile and say, "Well, I think we're going to be dining fashionably late tonight."

# Chapter 7

"FASHIONABLY LATE" WAS RIGHT. WHILE Rowan had helped her mother prep the Thanksgiving turkey multiple times during her childhood—with her brothers assisting with the side dishes, since Jennifer Aames had believed everyone needed to learn their way around a kitchen—she'd never in her life had to actually dress and pluck one of the oversized birds. By the time she and James were done, they had a huge pile of feathers near the table, but at least the thing was ready...she hoped.

He hadn't seemed too daunted by the task, though, had even taken the turkey out into the storm so he could perform the messy business of removing its head and feet. After that was done and the bird was sitting in a cool water bath in the sink, he said, "I just thought of something. Give me a minute."

"All right," Rowan replied. She had no idea what he was up to, but honestly, she was so relieved he and Darby had made it back from their hunting expedition unscathed that she was willing to cut him a little slack.

As long as it didn't result in their eating at eleven o'clock tonight, though. It was now past four-thirty, and she knew a bird that size was going to take at least four hours to roast even if they cheated a bit and boosted the oven temp to four hundred.

And that didn't take into account the teeny complication of not having any gas to run the oven in the first place.

However, when James reappeared a while later, hair dusted with snow once again and a propane canister in either hand, she got an idea of what he had in mind.

"Where in the world did you find those?" she asked. Although she preferred not to hang out in the Castle's basement unless she absolutely had to —the old boiler equipment down there creeped her out—she knew she hadn't seen any propane canisters stored in the cellar. Good thing, she supposed, since her father had always pressed on her the need to store the things someplace where there wasn't any chance of them blowing up the house.

He set the canisters down near the oven and shook the snow from his hair. "When Darby and I were heading out, I saw a building that looked like it was used for storing the campus's landscaping equipment. I figured it couldn't hurt to look. Now all I have to do is attach one of these canisters to the oven. We'll need to pull the stove out from the wall, though."

No arguments here, not when it meant they'd be able to cook the turkey like civilized people. "Okay."

She went over to James, and together they managed to shimmy the big industrial oven far enough out from the wall that he was able to kneel and disengage the gas line and instead attach it to the propane. The whole time, Rowan watched with a combination of wonder and annoyance—wonder that the whole procedure was so simple, and annoyance that she hadn't thought of this herself.

James didn't seem to notice her consternation, however, and only remained intent on his work. After he was done, he straightened and told her, "Go ahead and turn it on."

"Are we going to leave the stove pulled out from the wall like this?"

"It's safer," he replied. "I don't want to kink the line, and it's not like we'll be able to fit the propane tank back there anyway."

He had a point. Holding her breath—although the setup seemed secure enough, she still couldn't quite keep herself from worrying that she was about to blow them both sky-high—she pressed the button to turn on the gas and set the temperature to four hundred.

At once, a familiar clicking sound began, telling her the oven was releasing the gas. A second later, she heard it ignite, and released a breath.

"I think it's working."

James nodded. "Sure sounds like it. I guess we can get the turkey ready while it's heating up."

There was no butter, but Rowan could still coat the bird with olive oil and herbs. Luckily, the kitchen had been well-equipped, so there was a big roasting pan and matching rack that could support the turkey, and soon enough, the two of them had popped the whole setup in the oven.

"So...nine o'clock dinner," she said after glancing at the clock on the microwave. After so many years, she wasn't sure whether that clock was entirely accurate anymore, but it still worked to keep track of the time passing.

"It's fine," James replied with another of those flashes of a grin. "That'll give us plenty of time to figure out the side dishes."

About all she could do was smile in return. "I've got just the thing."

---

Once upon a time, Jamal might have considered himself enough of a purist about his food that he would have turned up his nose at the cylinder of canned cranberry sauce Rowan plopped into a bowl. Now, though, he could only be glad she'd had the presence of mind to grab it during one of her foraging expeditions. While he felt fully recovered from his ordeal in the snow, his stomach had been growling at him for the past half hour or so, letting him know it expected to be refueled after all that time spent slogging his way back to the Castle.

"It's been around for a while," she told him as she set the bowl on the table. "But I figure this stuff would probably survive a nuclear holocaust."

He allowed himself a chuckle. "Possibly. But it wouldn't have tasted like a turkey dinner without it."

She smiled. They'd both decided that the kitchen table wasn't the appropriate setting for this kind of feast, so while the turkey was roasting, they'd moved one of the tables from the dining hall into a smaller room that had been a salon when the Castle was first built but had been turned into a kind of study area. It was a smaller, much more intimate space, with the extra bonus of a fireplace.

Rowan had protested that she'd never used it, mostly because she feared the smoke drifting up from the chimney would be a sure signal the former college wasn't as unoccupied as she wanted people to believe. However, Jamal had pointed out that they didn't need to worry about anyone seeing the smoke now, mostly because it was snowing so hard that there would be no way to distinguish it from the big white flakes falling all around it. She'd relented and he'd ventured out into the storm once again, this time ostensibly to chop some wood, but really just to disappear around a corner of the building so he could conjure a stack of the stuff, enough to keep them going through tonight and quite possibly tomorrow morning as well.

A fire crackled in the hearth now, and because the cranberry sauce had been the last thing Rowan had set on the table, they were ready for their feast. Yes, the hour was nudging past nine-thirty, but that didn't matter so much. It wasn't as if they had anything in particular they needed to get up and do the next morning.

She'd even surprised him by fetching a bottle of pinot noir from the basement, saying, "I hope this is okay. My parents always served pinot with Thanksgiving dinner."

It was actually an excellent pairing. However, the man he was pretending to be probably wouldn't be too conversant on such matters, so he only shrugged and replied, "Sounds good to me. I'm not exactly an expert."

"Well, I hope you're an expert at opening wine

bottles," she returned. "Because I've never been too good at it."

"I think I can manage."

To tell the truth, he'd rarely been required to open a bottle on his own power, since he could use djinn magic for that. But he made a good show of using the waiter-style corkscrew, nudging it along with his mind so the cork came out smoothly and with a satisfying *pop.*

"It's such a fun sound, don't you think?" Rowan said as he poured a measure of the deep red wine into her glass.

"Yes," he replied. "Probably because it tells you about what's coming next."

She grinned and raised her glass. "We should toast."

An excellent idea. He lifted his glass as well and said, "What're we toasting?"

"To...." The word trailed off as she appeared to ponder the best thing to say. The firelight reflected in her eyes, warm and sultry, as she went on, "To weathering the storm."

"'To weathering the storm,'" he echoed.

They clinked their glasses together, and he took a sip. It was good, with noticeable fruit but no residual sugars. He guessed it would be an excellent complement to the turkey.

His estimate proved correct, because after he'd carved slices for the two of them, and they'd each helped themselves to cranberry sauce and pan gravy and roasted potatoes and bread, he took a bite of the turkey and washed it down with some wine. Yes, it was excellent, the turkey not dry at all despite the lack of butter during its preparation.

"This is wonderful," he said.

Was it just a trick of the lighting, or had color flared along her cheekbones? He guessed it was the latter, since she had fair skin to match her bright red hair, the kind of skin that showed a blush easily.

"Well, it was a great bird," she replied. "I've never made one that was so fresh. So I'm sure that probably had something to do with it."

"Still, a lot of people would have been out of their depth making something like this."

She shrugged, then reached for her glass of wine so she could take a sip. "My mother was very big on making sure all of us knew how to cook. She said maybe we'd all end up eating takeout once we were out of the house, but in the meantime, we were going to learn how to take care of ourselves."

A wise woman. Jamal did not doubt that Rowan might have fared much worse during all these long years alone if she hadn't been taught how to manage for herself. "Were you still living at home when you came to work here?"

She ducked her head, now looking even more embarrassed. "Yes. It made more sense to stay at home while I was in college, and my parents didn't mind, since both my brothers had moved out by then. I was sort of hunting around for a place after I graduated, thinking I'd need one after I got a job, but then this position came up with housing included as part of the compensation package, so I didn't have to worry about finding an apartment anymore." Her expression sobered, and Jamal saw how her fingers tightened on the stem of the wine glass she held. "I can't help thinking that if I'd gotten a job and an apartment in town, I probably wouldn't be alive today."

"Because of the djinn," he said, and she nodded.

"They made a clean sweep of Las Vegas and were long gone by the time I was brave enough to venture out." She set down the wine glass, but she didn't reach for her fork and instead sat there, expression brooding. Then she looked up at him, amber-brown eyes almost russet in the firelight. "How did they know?"

"How did they know what?" Jamal returned, doing his best to look puzzled.

"How did the djinn know where to find people, how to hunt them down?"

Rowan might have been ignoring her wine glass, but he knew he needed a sip before he could even attempt to reply to that question. Once again, nagging doubt assailed him, although in that moment, he wasn't sure whether it was because of all the deaths he had on his hands or the way he continued to lie to her about who he truly was.

After swallowing some pinot, Jamal said, "I'm not sure. I mean, I've kind of heard through the grapevine in town that djinn have a way of sensing when humans are nearby, but I don't know exactly how that works. But I guess after the Heat did its job, they went from town to town, hunting down any survivors."

An accurate enough description of what had happened, he supposed. While the vast majority of his people hadn't been involved in the "mopping up" operations, so to speak, there had still been enough of them to fan out across the globe, dividing the world into territories so no corner of it would be overlooked. They'd focused first on the big cities, and then, once those were empty, they'd gone on to small towns such as Las Vegas. The operation hadn't been perfect, or single survivors such as Rowan would also have been found, but it had been effective enough.

Sitting there and watching the dancing flames in the hearth awaken a different kind of fire in Rowan's coppery locks, Jamal found himself very, very glad she'd escaped notice. Not a sentiment most might have expected of a reaver, but he would allow himself the contradiction simply because he knew the world would have been a lesser place if she had not survived.

"Some kind of sixth sense," she said in musing tones, then reached for her wine again. "No wonder we didn't have a chance."

Most of them, anyway. There was that .02 percent who were immune, whose bodies contained some unique combination of the genetic factors required to fight off a disease that had been designed to be as lethal as possible. But even they had no true chance of surviving, not with reaver djinn such as he determined to finish what the Heat had begun.

He found he didn't want to think about that, didn't want to think about the blood that had stained his hands during those chaotic weeks and months. At the time, he'd thought he was doing necessary work, but now...?

*At least you never spilled a woman's blood, or a child's,* he told himself. *You only took the lives of those who might have tried to return this world to what it once was.*

Perhaps. And yet he now found himself wishing he had been like the majority of his people, those who simply went to the homes the elders had given them and begun a new life, content to let someone else carry out the dirty work of cleansing the planet.

He doubted any of them worried too much about the manner in which this world had become empty, since now it was theirs once again. It had taken countless millennia, true, but the djinn could finally claim Earth as their own, once humankind had proven they did not deserve it.

Although she remained silent, he could almost see the physical effort Rowan made to push all those dark memories aside and pick up her fork so she might take another bite of her turkey. The fire helped to keep their meal from getting cold, but the food wouldn't stay warm forever...especially since he didn't dare help it along to retain its fresh-from-the-oven heat the way he otherwise might have.

Clearly wanting to change the subject, she said, "Were you able to get a good look at the storm before it closed in? Any idea how long it's going to last?"

Even as a djinn, Jamal didn't have the answer to those questions, since he was not an elemental of the air. He shook his head. "The only thing I could tell was that it was coming from the north, probably sliding along the mountains and dropping down from the Rockies. But it came in so fast, I wasn't able to see much more than that."

Her expression was disappointed, he could tell, but she only gave a philosophical lift of her shoulders as she speared a piece of roasted potato with her fork. "Well, here's hoping it won't last too long. The batteries can keep up for about twelve to eighteen hours without being recharged, but if we don't get sun sometime tomorrow, it could be a problem. When I first came to work here, they'd just put the funding aside to upgrade the system, since it was almost twenty years old at that point and the battery tech wasn't anything close to modern. But the new equipment never got installed, obviously, so I've had to work with what was already there."

That was unfortunate. True, having to only support Rowan and Darby meant there wasn't a lot of load on the system, but the most frugal usage couldn't overcome a lack of battery storage. Jamal couldn't have the batteries run forever on djinn power without raising her suspicions, but he thought giving them a little extra help for the short time he was here shouldn't be the sort of thing that would attract much notice. Once he left, Rowan would probably believe that any reduced capacity would be the fault of the aging system and nothing more.

"Well, we can cook on the stove now that it's powered by propane," he said, hoping he sounded reassuring. "And there's plenty of firewood. We might have to sleep down here in the salon, but we'd still be able to keep warm."

The dubious look she sent him seemed to indicate she wasn't too thrilled by that prospect. However, since she'd been doing whatever she needed to survive for the past four years, he doubted she would balk at bunking down here if matters became dire.

He thought he would be all too happy to share his sleeping bag with her.

Such an invitation would probably not be very welcome, though, so he pushed aside the mental image of her snuggled against his shoulder as best he could and instead sipped some more wine. His people had a much higher tolerance for alcohol than humans did, but still, he definitely had a curious sense of well-being in this moment, of realizing that, even with the entire world at his fingertips, there was nowhere else he would rather be.

Confounding as the situation was, he thought his brother Aamir might understand.

Rather than reply to his comment right away, Rowan broke off a piece of turkey and handed it to Darby, who'd been watching them the entire time, waiting for them to notice he was there and all too ready to help them with any morsels they didn't want to eat. He gobbled it down and then sent a hopeful look in Jamal's direction.

What could he do except chuckle and hand over a bite as well, one that disappeared down the dog's gullet in the blink of an eye and was followed by a happy thunk of his tail against the floor?

"The fire does help a lot," Rowan allowed. Her expression had shifted to one of amusement, probably thanks to that exchange with Darby. "And you're right—I'm not used to having those resources, but as long as we don't open the refrigerator too much, everything should last until the storm passes. God knows after this meal we'll have enough leftovers to feed us for a week."

At least a week, considering how huge the turkey had been. It might get monotonous after a while, but they definitely wouldn't starve.

"I suppose that depends on how much Darby eats," Jamal observed, and Rowan's eyes twinkled, good humor restored.

"Oh, I'm pretty sure he'd gobble up the whole thing if we let him," she said. "But we need to make sure there's plenty for all of us. Speaking of which, can you pass the cranberry sauce?"

Jamal handed it over, and she used the edge of the spoon to cut herself another slice and deposit it on her plate. While she was busy with that task, he added a few more potatoes to his plate, and they ate in silence for a moment.

That was all right, however. Although he could see she was still a little wary of him—understandable, considering the short duration of their acquaintance—he could also tell she was beginning to relax a little. Soon enough, he thought they might be quite comfortable together.

To what end, though? He was not Aamir, to fall in love with a mortal the second he let his guard down, for his own heart was not one that was easily given. He found Rowan Aames to be an interesting case—certainly, he had never heard of a human surviving on their own for so long in the world that had followed the Heat—and nothing more than that. They would spend this time together, and he would learn something more of humans and their ways, for he knew interacting one-on-one like this was very different from observing human behavior in a film or television show. After the storm had passed, he would offer to accompany her to Los Alamos...or at least, as close as he could get without the djinn-repelling devices affecting his well-being... and then he would leave her in the care of the people who dwelled there, knowing she was safe in the company of her own kind and he was free to go on with his life.

Whether that would be in his home in Jackson Hole or continuing to wander as the mood took him, he wasn't quite sure. At some point, he supposed he would figure it out.

In the meantime, though, he was quite happy to be snowbound with Rowan.

# Chapter 8

THE COLD SEEMED TO SEEP PAST THE window frame and burrow its way through all the layers of blankets and quilts that covered Rowan's bed. She shivered and told herself she should be glad of the space heater...and of Darby's presence, since the dog was snuggled up against her and providing some much-needed warmth along the back of her legs.

*Definitely a three-dog night,* she thought, remembering the way she'd smiled when she first heard the name of that old band from the seventies and the origin of the phrase.

But she'd have to make do with just one dog tonight, which was okay. What bothered her right now was how much colder this storm felt than the ones she'd experienced during the past four winters here at the Castle, how something about it felt almost inimical, as if it possessed its own dark and malicious personality.

She knew that was a silly thing to think. This was just weather, and sooner or later, it would have to blow over.

Problem was, she worried it would be later... much later.

Well, James had pointed out that they could still cook even if the solar batteries failed them, and there was lots of wood. No fireplaces on this floor, which meant they'd have to camp out downstairs, but....

Actually, that was a very big "but." Dinner had been fine...great, really, and she knew her stomach was feeling much more satisfied than it had in years...and yet she couldn't help thinking something had shifted between the two of them tonight. They'd gone from two strangers sharing the same space to people who, if they weren't anywhere close to intimate, still had begun to develop a bond. Even the wine she'd drunk hadn't blurred her mind enough that she could have missed the admiring way he'd looked at her, the way their gazes had caught and held once or twice.

What was she supposed to do about that?

*Nothing,* she told herself. *Come on...it's the oldest story in the book—caught together in a storm with no one else around.*

Maybe that was true, but still....

But nothing. She would allow herself to think James was cute and definitely helpful to have around, and nothing more. The only thing she could do at this point was wait and see how the situation played out. It was stupid to think anything real was going on between them when all they'd done was share a couple of conversations and not much more.

For all she knew, those supposedly admiring gazes could have been the result of the half bottle of wine he'd consumed with dinner. She hadn't asked about what kind of drinking they did in Los Alamos, but she had to believe they weren't exactly downing cases of Dom Perignon or anything close to it.

The wind howled outside the window, and Rowan pulled the quilts and blankets more tightly around her, even as Darby shifted, pressing his warm body closer to her legs. She'd thought she would be fine, since she was wearing two pairs of socks in addition to her usual fleece-lined leggings and sweatshirts, but right then, she felt as if she would never be warm again.

How was James faring across the hall? He didn't have Darby to keep him warm, but he did have that Arctic-rated sleeping bag. For all she knew, he was much warmer than she, despite all the quilts and blankets piled on top of her. Maybe she should have thought about taking a sleeping bag from Walmart or one of the local outdoors shops when she was scrounging supplies in Las Vegas, and yet something about the idea hadn't seemed very appealing the couple of times she'd considered it. With all the makeshifts she'd had to struggle with during her isolation here, she already halfway felt as if she was camping most of the time. Sleeping in a bag would have only reinforced that notion.

No, she needed to stop letting her mind wander so much. The important thing to remember was that she was full and protected from the elements, and for the first time in years, she wasn't alone here at the Castle, had someone sleeping across the hall. Even if he ended up going his own way after the storm had passed, at least she hadn't been forced to suffer through it by herself.

That had to mean something.

With that thought to reassure her, she closed her eyes and finally allowed herself to drift off to sleep.

---

Jamal sat up in bed, eyes straining against the darkness. Something about it felt different, although it took him a moment to realize what that difference was.

The little space heater sat cold and silent, and

the air in the room was positively icy. True, he couldn't suffer from the cold the way a human might, but he still found it uncomfortable...and disconcerting.

Sometime during the night, the batteries must have released their last bit of power. Not terribly surprising, since they wouldn't have gotten a full charge the day before, thanks to the way the storm had rolled in before the afternoon was even halfway over, and yet he knew he now had to make a decision. If he was cold here in his Arctic sleeping bag, then he could only imagine that Rowan must be freezing. In fact, he was somewhat surprised she hadn't come to wake him.

But perhaps she had been deeply asleep and hadn't yet noticed the shift in temperature. Still, she'd notice soon enough, and that meant he had to decide whether to send a little of his power through the building's electrical system to make it seem as if the batteries had in fact lasted through the night, or whether he should let this play out as if he had very little control over the situation.

Possibly that would have been the wisest thing to do, and yet he didn't much like the prospect of having to rouse Rowan at this hour, or for the two of them to be forced to carry all their bedding downstairs so they might sleep in front of the fireplace. Doing so would be disruptive at best and uncomfortable as well.

No, better to keep the batteries limping along for now. If the storm continued, then he knew he couldn't continue to feed the system with djinn energy, for Rowan would certainly begin to suspect something odd was going on. But at least he could put off the time when they'd have to rely entirely on firewood to heat the place for a few more hours.

Barely a conscious thought, only a flicker of his will toward the battery system in the basement, filling its cells with enough extra energy to keep them running through the night. The heater flared on, its red indicator light—and a quick rush of warm air—letting him know it was back online for now.

Satisfied, Jamal laid his head against the pillow once again. He would worry about tomorrow, tomorrow.

---

The gray light seeping around the edges of the blinds had already warned Rowan as to what she would probably see outside, but she went ahead and lifted them a few inches anyway.

"Damn it," she said aloud.

Snow must have continued to fall all night, because now it looked at least eighteen inches deep, maybe more. She was honestly surprised that the batteries had continued to feed the electrical system that entire time, but they had to be running on fumes now.

Because she was already mostly dressed, she only pulled on her Uggs and wrapped a wool shawl she'd found in a downtown shop around her shoulders. Even now, she couldn't help experiencing a pang as her fingers touched the warm, nubby yarn —it was a handmade piece that was supposed to have sold for several hundred dollars, and although she knew no one had been left to care that she pilfered it from the boutique, she still felt as if she had gotten away with some sort of crime.

However, comfort trumped guilt every time in this post-djinn world.

Darby didn't seem too worried about the winter wasteland that awaited him outside, and bounded into the snow drifts as soon as she opened the back door. Surprisingly, his paw prints weren't the only ones out there—it looked as if several rabbits had left their distinctive snowshoe-like tracks behind, and there were some slightly larger ones that might have been from coyotes.

Whatever had left them, it seemed the animals were long gone; Darby was the only living thing moving out there right now. As she watched, she felt rather than heard James come up behind her.

"That's a lot of snow," he remarked.

"And more to come," she replied, since the snow had continued to fall, maybe not quite as thick as it had been the afternoon before, but enough to make it clear that none of them were going anywhere today.

"Well, then, we should have some coffee," James said. Now he stood next to her, already dressed in a thermal shirt with a plaid flannel one on top. "Do you want me to get it started?"

"Assuming we still have water," she said. "I'm kind of shocked the batteries are still going."

His shoulders lifted. Not for the first time, she noted how broadly he was built, how his thick biceps seemed to strain at the fabric of the shirts he wore. If he'd been even a little bigger, she doubted he would have been able to layer them the way he had.

"Well, if they die on us, we'll figure something out," he said, way too cheerful for such a bleak morning. "But in the meantime, I'll go fill the kettle."

Rowan reflected that he didn't seem too worried about the situation. Then again, he seemed ready and willing to chop as much wood as they needed, so at least they wouldn't freeze.

Hopefully.

He left the doorway and went back into the kitchen. A moment later, she heard the welcome sound of the water running, so it seemed as if they had enough power for now. Whether it would be sufficient for her to have a shower, she wasn't sure, but she'd worry about that when the time came.

Darby came partway up the steps and then paused, shaking himself so bits of snow went flying everywhere. Rowan couldn't help smiling at the sight—there was just something about having a dog around that helped keep her grounded, that allowed her to push her worries aside and simply enjoy the moment.

However, she was more than happy to shut the door after her canine companion was safely inside. James already had the burner on the stovetop going, adding some welcome heat to the room. It was still cold, but bearable.

"What's the plan if everything dies on us?" she asked, and he only shook his head.

"Like we talked about last night—we'll keep a fire going, and we'll sleep down in the sitting room. I'll probably have to heat water on the stove for us to wash, since the solar won't be powering the water heater, but we'll survive. It's not like this storm can last forever."

No, she supposed not, but it sure looked as if it planned to stick around for a good long while. However, brooding about it wasn't going to change anything, so she came closer to the stove, glad of the little bit of warmth it sent out, and gladder still that the batteries were hanging on gamely.

"You're right," she said, and managed a smile. God only knows what she must have looked like right then, with her hair mussed from sleep and not a speck of makeup on her face, but she realized James had never seen her at her best, so what difference did it make? "I'll grind the coffee."

She got out the beans and the little grinder, and got to work. Just as she was finishing up, the kettle began to whistle, and her unlikely companion turned off the propane. A minute later, hot water was trickling through the coffeemaker, and the welcome scent of mocha java began to fill the air.

James had also fetched a pair of mugs for them, so once the coffee was done, he poured a decent measure into each mug and then handed one to Rowan. "Coffee makes everything better, don't you think?"

"Absolutely," she agreed. Although she wouldn't say the words out loud—they would have sounded way too self-pitying—she couldn't help thinking that she didn't know if she would have survived the past four years without that pick-me-up to get her going in the morning. Tea was great, especially on a cold winter afternoon, but it didn't have the same jolt as coffee.

They drank in companionable silence for a moment, the quiet only broken by Darby's contented crunching of the kibble she'd put in his bowl when they first entered the kitchen this morning. With someone else, it might have felt awkward to stand there and sip coffee and say nothing at all, but something about James's presence felt comforting in a way Rowan couldn't quite explain. It was almost as if she realized there wasn't a lot he couldn't handle, and with him around, worst-case scenarios weren't quite the stuff of nightmares they once might have been.

Once she was done with her coffee, though, she set her mug down on the countertop and said, "Do you mind if we put off breakfast for a bit? I just figured it would be safer if I showered now before the power craps out on us."

"Go ahead," he said at once. "I already took a quick one, so I'm set."

That must have been a fast shower, because she didn't think he was even awake when she came downstairs with Darby. But then, if James had only done a quick spritz and hadn't worried about washing his hair or shaving, she supposed he could have been in and out in less than five minutes.

"Back down in a minute," she told him, then hurried upstairs.

Ever since she'd gone into hiding here at the Castle, she'd limited her hair washing to once a week. Luckily, her hair had always been on the dry side, so it didn't get oily too fast. And since she'd washed it recently, she had a while before she needed to worry about it again.

Maybe by that point, this damn storm would have finally let up.

But that was why she was also in and out of the shower in record time, and back downstairs within ten minutes. James was sitting at the table by the window, expression contemplative as he watched the snow continue to fall outside.

"No sign of clearing?" she asked as she approached, and he shook his head.

"Not so far. But it descended kind of fast, so I guess I'm hoping it'll disappear just as quickly."

Nice notion, but Rowan wasn't sure the weather worked that way. But since she also knew there was nothing wrong with trying to maintain a positive attitude, she didn't bother to argue with him.

"How about some oatmeal?" she asked. "It's nothing fancy, but like my mother used to say, it'll stick to your ribs."

"Oatmeal would be great."

And really, once it was done and they'd swirled it with cinnamon and a little maple syrup, it tasted pretty darn good. Maybe not the Denver omelet with bacon and hash browns she'd been dreaming about for the past couple of years, but definitely more decadent than they had any right to expect, considering the situation.

Just as James turned on the water to start washing the dishes, the heaters shut off, and the flow of water from the tap slowed to a trickle and then stopped altogether.

"There go the batteries," he said, not sounding overly concerned about the situation.

However, Rowan wasn't ready to be quite that cavalier about the loss of power. "Great," she returned. "Would have been nice if they'd at least held on until we got these bowls cleaned out. Oatmeal turns into glue if you don't wash it off right away."

"Fear not," James said with a grin, then stepped away from the sink so he could pull out one of the large pans from the cupboard next to the stove. "I'll scoop some snow into this, and then we can melt it on the stove to get hot water for the dishes. It'll be easier than having to fight my way to the well. First, though, let me get another fire going. Good thing we didn't use up all the wood last night during dinner."

No, there were still five or six logs sitting next to the hearth. Not enough to keep them going all day, of course, but it should be sufficient to fend off the cold while he cut more.

"Okay," Rowan responded, since there wasn't much else she could say. He'd proven to be very efficient at chopping wood, while she'd never even lifted a hatchet. True, there had been a couple of times during her tenure here when she'd wondered if she should chop some wood in case the solar power gave out entirely, but it had always managed to keep chugging along.

Unlike today.

James flashed her a quick grin before heading into the sitting room. Already, she could feel the cold pressing on the building like an almost physical weight, and knew it was important to get a fire started as soon as possible.

Too bad there wasn't a fireplace in the kitchen. It wasn't going to be much fun to cook in here even with the heat the stove put out, but at least if they had one warm room in the building, they'd be able to survive.

She hoped.

Darby had trailed after James, and Rowan figured she might as well head into the salon, too, since there wasn't much she could do until they had some snow melted and warm water to do the breakfast dishes. Also, it would be much more comfortable in there with the fire going.

And it already was—James stood up just as she entered the room and brushed his hands against his pants, while behind him hungry flames licked at the wood he'd placed in the grate. "That should do for now," he said. "But I need to get that snow to melt."

"Maybe I should go with you," she offered. "I mean, if we fill up two pans, we'll have that much more water to work with."

But he only shook his head. "No, let me go. I'm going to get all snowy anyway when I go out to chop wood. There's no reason for both of us to get our feet wet."

She supposed he had a point there, although she didn't like the idea of staying inside and doing pretty much nothing while he went out into the storm and did all the work. However, something in his face told her he didn't want her arguing with him, so even though she followed a few paces behind, she maintained her silence as he headed back to the kitchen, fetched his coat from the hook next to the door, and retrieved the pan he'd left on the counter a moment earlier.

Then he was outside, letting in a brief gust of freezing air before Rowan hastily closed the door behind him. Darby, who'd padded into the kitchen along with them, sent her an inquiring look.

"He's just getting some snow to melt, Darbs," she said, and the dog's tail thumped gently against the floor.

Kind of sad that James had gone to all that work to get the Castle's plumbing hooked up to the solar, only to have it come to nothing after the storm moved in.

"Storms don't last forever," she said out loud. In the past, when she'd spoken to herself like this, she'd sounded tentative, as if she wasn't sure she could trust the sound of her own voice after spending so much time alone. Now, though, she thought she could detect a new confidence in her tone, something that hadn't been there a few days earlier.

Could having James around have made that much of a difference?

Apparently so. Or maybe it was simply that, whatever might happen over the next few hours or even days, she knew she wouldn't have to face it by herself.

He knocked on the door then, and she hastily opened it and stepped out of the way so he could hurry over to the stove and set the heavy pan on top. Wet, slushy footprints marked his passage, and he gave her a rueful look as he seemed to catch the way her gaze tracked immediately to them.

"Sorry about that."

"You have nothing to be sorry about," she told him. "You're the one running around out in the snow."

His shoulders hitched, and he said, "And I'm going to go back out and take care of the wood. Might as well get it all over with at once, and then we can cocoon for the rest of the day."

A flash of a smile, one that did something she wasn't expecting to her knees, and then he was back outside, letting in a swirl of snowflakes and a blast of cold air before she shut the door behind him.

Well, one way to get warm would be to mop up those footprints.

Rowan fetched a string mop from the pantry, then got to work on cleaning up the floor. True, she'd have to do this all over again when James came back, but at least the task kept her busy until the snow in the pot melted enough to use it for the breakfast dishes.

Which it did after a couple of minutes, allowing her to wash up and set the bowls on the countertop rack to dry. The kitchen had a dishwasher, but she'd never dared to use it even at the height of summer when the Castle's solar batteries were full. Even if they'd still had a little power now, she wouldn't have wasted it on something so frivolous.

The floor and the dishes were done, and James still hadn't returned. For a moment, Rowan wondered if she should put on her jacket and go in search of him, then told herself that wasn't necessary. Yes, he was out in the snowstorm, but he wasn't all that far away. And he'd told her he wanted to chop enough wood to keep them going through the rest of the day and tonight. Even if he was the best wood chopper in the world, that was going to take a little while.

She leaned the mop against the wall near the stove—she knew she'd need it again soon—and headed into the sitting room. Her exertions had kept her warm enough, but it still felt much better to be in here where the fire danced happily in the hearth. It was kind of amazing how much heat it cast into the room, since her experiences with the small fireplace in her family home had taught her fires in general were more for atmosphere than to actually warm up a space.

But the Castle had been built back when central heat didn't even exist, and she guessed the fireplaces here must have been engineered within an inch of their lives. Although she wouldn't allow herself to sit while James was still out chopping wood in the middle of a snowstorm, she did lean against the wall as she waited.

Darby, on the other hand, had no such scruples about relaxing while the humans in his life labored away. As soon as they entered the room, he went to the edge of the stone hearth, curled up on the rug, and immediately went to sleep.

*Must be nice,* Rowan thought, but she couldn't help smiling. What else was a dog supposed to do on a snowy day? He didn't seem to have a problem with going out into a near-blizzard to do his business, but she'd also noticed that he'd come right back and hadn't spent any time nosing around the property the way he did when the weather was more cooperative.

Sometime later—she couldn't tell for sure, since there wasn't a clock in here—the kitchen door banged open again, and she hurried out of the sitting room to see James setting a pile of logs on the floor on the other side of the door.

"Lots more where that came from," he told her. He sounded slightly out of breath, not so strange considering what he'd been doing for the past twenty minutes, or however long it had been. "I'm going to put it all in here so it has a chance to dry out."

"Good idea," she said. Maybe once upon a time, the Castle had had lots of racks or baskets or whatever they'd used to store their logs, but all those items were long gone, along with whatever furniture had existed here back when the place had still been a hotel. It had changed hands several times over the years, most recently belonging to the Catholic Church before a billionaire philanthropist bought the facility back in the 1990s, and all those items were long gone. "Do you need help?"

"No," James replied cheerfully. "Like I said, no point in both of us getting all wet."

After delivering those words, he headed back outside to fetch another batch of logs. All in all, he went in and out six times, while the stack of lumber took up all of one wall and threatened to spill into the hallway.

Not that it mattered—Rowan would cheerfully step over any number of pieces of pine if it meant they'd stay warm through the rest of the day and the night that followed.

"Okay," James announced as he headed over to the pot of now-lukewarm melted snow so he could wash off his hands, now reddened with cold. "That's done."

"You didn't wear gloves?" she asked, even as she wanted to kick herself for not noticing sooner.

"I had some," he said, still sounding completely unconcerned. "But they're leather and the hatchet kept slipping, so I took them off and shoved them in my pockets. It's fine."

Rowan wasn't sure whether it actually was fine but tried to reassure herself by thinking that if he'd gotten frostbitten at all, he wouldn't have so much mobility in his fingers. "If you're sure—"

"I am," he said. "And now that's taken care of, let's get some more logs on the fire. It could probably use some."

Maybe. Or at least, the fire had seemed as if it was crackling away just fine when she'd left the sitting room, but she hadn't been in there to check on it during the last ten minutes or so. Anyway, it was a good reason to leave the increasingly chilly kitchen and head back to a much friendlier place.

"Sure," she replied. "Darby's waiting for us."

"I can tell he always finds the best spot in the house," James returned with a grin.

How could someone be that cheerful after

spending all that time in the cold and the snow? Rowan had to assume he was one of those lucky people with a naturally sunny disposition...or maybe he was just happy that he wouldn't have to go back outside any time soon.

In which case, she could relate.

The two of them returned to the sitting room, where the fire was in fact showing some signs of flagging. Not a problem, though, since James added a few more logs and shifted things around a bit with the trowel he was using as a makeshift poker—the original fireplace equipment had long since disappeared—and soon enough, the flames were dancing once again in the hearth.

"Well, looks like we're set," he said after he propped the trowel up against the fireplace surround. "Now we just have to figure out what to do with ourselves." A glint in his dark eyes and he added, "Got a pack of playing cards?"

# Chapter 9

Not only did Rowan have playing cards on hand, but she was also able to produce a rather bewildering variety of board games from a storage closet down the hall.

"People didn't seem to use this stuff very much," she told Jamal after setting her haul on a side table. "They were mostly into playing games on their computers and their phones. But every once in a while, someone would pull out Scrabble or Yahtzee, so the staff decided to keep all of it."

"Good for us," he replied. "Since computer games aren't really an option at the moment."

She only shook her copper-hued head in response to that comment, although he could see the smile that played around her mouth.

Good. He found he wanted her to smile at him.

They started with Yahtzee first, a game whose rules he found easy enough to follow, since they weren't all that different from an ancient dice game his people had been playing for thousands of years. Monopoly, on the other hand, was an entirely different proposition.

"I can't believe you've never played this," Rowan remarked. They'd brought another of the tables from the dining hall into the sitting room and were playing there, as the coffee table wasn't large enough to accommodate the games and whatever food they were snacking on at the moment.

Now that lunch had come and gone—they'd had hot tea and the final bits of the roasted rabbit she'd made the day before last, since it was older than the turkey—they were making their way through a box of Ritz crackers. Jamal had never consumed such a thing before, but he had to admit there was something satisfying about the buttery taste of the crisp little wafers, especially since he was eating them in a warm, comfortable room while snow fell outside and a fire flickered in the hearth.

Or perhaps it was merely that he sat here with Rowan Aames, who had proven to be a quite satisfactory companion to be snowbound with.

"I did when I was a child," Jamal said, then realized that "James" probably would have said "kid." Well, he could only hope Rowan wouldn't notice the small slip-up. To cover his mistake, he added quickly, "But it was a long time ago."

"Not that long," Rowan said, looking amused. "I mean, you can't be too much older than me, and I just turned twenty-seven last month."

He found himself wishing he could have been here to celebrate that birthday with her. Excellent wine, roasted venison or elk...oh, he could have summoned all sorts of wonderful things for them to eat.

If, of course, he had been willing to reveal to her that he was much more than what he appeared.

Now, though, he had to do what he could to keep up the appearance that he was just as human as she.

"Twenty-nine," he replied.

"Well, then," she said, as if that was the only response their exchange required.

However, she unbent enough to explain the rules of the game to him, which seemed unduly complicated. Or perhaps it was only that his people had little use for the financial systems that had been part of the reason why humans had seemed so hell-bent on destroying their planet.

At any rate, Rowan beat him handily, which was fine. He'd never been the sort whose self-worth was tied up in whether he won a particular game or competition. No, that was much more his younger brother Omar's failing.

As they put the Monopoly board and its accompanying game pieces and faux money away, she said, "What next? Scrabble?"

He had no doubt he'd be able to beat her quite easily in that game, simply because he'd been using the English language for centuries longer than she'd been alive. Perhaps doing so would have tied up matters between the two of them, but this wasn't about keeping score.

No, this was more about him and Rowan continuing to interact, rather than each of them picking up a book and retreating to their separate corners of the couch to read. Jamal found he wanted to keep talking to her, to learn more of who she was and how she had found the strength to survive here alone for so many years. This was the first time he'd had any true interactions with a human, and she was so vibrantly, wonderfully herself that he couldn't help but be fascinated.

"Poker?" he suggested, and now she grinned outright, her warm brown eyes seeming to pick up some of the fiery hues from the hearth just a few feet away from where he sat.

"I don't know how to play," she said. Her cheeks appeared faintly pink, but that could have been due to her proximity to the fire. "I mean, I know how to play blackjack because my brother Henry showed me once, but we never got around to five-card stud or any of the fancier stuff."

"No time like the present," Jamal replied. He wasn't deterred by this development; in fact, teaching her even some of the simpler forms of the game would take a while, and would also help to pass the afternoon hours until it was time to venture into the chilly kitchen and concoct some kind of dinner from their turkey leftovers.

She still didn't look entirely convinced, but she didn't protest as he picked up the deck of cards she'd brought out with the other games and shuffled them expertly. It had been some time since he'd played poker, true, and yet he thought he remembered the fundamentals of five-card stud well enough. His brothers had thought him foolish for engaging in such a human pastime, just as they hadn't entirely understood his reasons for consuming books and films and other pieces of mortal culture, but he'd always found those endeavors fascinating, for they were so utterly unlike the djinn experience of the world. Even so, his familiarity with humankind hadn't extended to believing their society was worth saving.

That was their own fault, though. A few hours of amusement here and there did not justify the continuation of their species when so much more was at stake.

At the moment, though, he didn't wish to think about any of that. No, he only wanted to focus on the woman who sat across the table from him, her red hair practically molten in the reflected firelight. She was looking especially beautiful in that particular moment, skin warmed by the fire, her gaze intense as she watched him shuffle the deck and then begin to deal the cards, her face as pure and lovely as a painting by a Renaissance master.

Then her mouth quirked slightly, breaking the impression of being the living embodiment of a Botticelli portrait. "You're really good at that," she said, head tilting toward the cards as he deftly laid them out. "You sure you don't have a past as a dealer in Las Vegas or something?"

The mere vision of him sitting at a poker table in Nevada and dealing cards to mortals made him want to chuckle. In fact, he went ahead and let himself make an amused sound, simply because that sort of past seemed equally implausible for the man he was pretending to be.

"No," he replied. "Some friends and I got interested in poker a while back—we watched a lot of competitions on TV and taught ourselves how to play. And I always wanted to be that guy who could shuffle cards like he was performing a magic trick or something."

"Well, it looks like you succeeded." Rowan's gaze moved toward the cards he'd laid in front of her. "So...what do we do now?"

"Usually, we would have put in an ante before I

even started dealing our cards," he told her. "But it seems kind of silly to play for money when it's not worth anything anymore. So, let's just leave the betting part out for now."

"We could play for crackers," she suggested with a grin, and he shook his head.

"I think we already ate half the box," Jamal replied, which was only the truth. They'd been unopened, but he was still somewhat surprised by how crisp and fresh they'd been. Well, food manufacturers back in the before times had pumped many of their offerings full of chemicals. Luckily, those sorts of ingredients would have no ill effects on a djinn. "We can worry about betting later."

"All right," Rowan said. She didn't look disappointed, which meant she probably had suggested playing for crackers as a joke.

"Do you know about pairs of cards and straights and flushes?" he asked next, and to his relief, she nodded.

"I remember that much. It's all the other stuff that sort of escapes my brain."

Perhaps because she'd had no need to hang on to such admittedly esoteric knowledge now that the world had changed so much. It would have been much more important for her to focus on the necessities of staying alive rather than the intricacies of card games.

And even when she'd gotten beyond the day-to-day struggles of survival, she'd still spent her time making a record of the world before, of not just her own life but the lives of the people she'd known, the books she'd read, the lyrics to songs that very well might never be sung again.

An odd sadness stirred in him, one he did his best to push away. Humans had done this to themselves and had no one else to blame. The djinn had only been the means of delivering their doom...not the cause.

"We both have one card face up and one down," he said. Time to focus on the here and now, and not what had happened four years ago. "It's knowing what's in the face-down card that will help you decide what to bet."

"But we're not betting," she pointed out, and he couldn't help smiling.

"True," he said, "but you still want to try to psych me out, to make me think your hand is better than mine even if it isn't."

"Got it," she replied, then lifted a corner of her face-down card so she could get a peek at what it concealed. Her expression didn't even flicker, telling him that even if she didn't know all the rules of the game, she definitely had the "poker face" part of it down pat.

His own cards were the Queen of Hearts and the King of Hearts. In five-card stud, the chances of getting a straight flush were astronomical, so he didn't even bother to hope that the next one he dealt himself would be either a jack or ten of hearts.

Good thing he hadn't been counting on it, because he dealt himself a five of clubs and an eight of diamonds to Rowan. She already had the eight of spades showing, meaning she had a pair to his nothing.

But of course, she could have no idea that he was sitting on cards that were basically worthless, and he knew he had to do his best to ensure she couldn't see that unfortunate fact reflected in his expression.

In the next round, he got a five of hearts, so at least he had a pair to match hers. It still wouldn't beat her, but better to have even a little something than a set of utterly mismatched cards.

"If we're not betting, it's kind of hard to tell whether you have anything worthwhile," she remarked as he dealt the next set of cards.

"True," he allowed. "But we can both see that we each have a pair, if nothing else. Also, this is where bluffing comes in. There are plenty of times when a player can be holding not much of anything, but if his bets make the other players think he's got something, then there's still a chance they might fold."

"I'm not folding," she said. Her brows were drawn together, and she looked far more intense than a simple game of no-stakes poker should have necessitated.

Once again, Jamal wanted to smile, but he kept his expression impassive. She might have been so focused because she didn't want to look up from the table to see the snow falling more heavily than ever just outside the window. They had plenty of firewood, and even if it seemed as if it might start to run out, he could use his djinn powers to make sure what they had lasted through the night, but he could see why she might be so worried. He had to admit there was something somewhat disconcerting about the way the snow kept coming down with no sign of stopping.

It wasn't that this part of the world didn't get its fair share of snow.

It was that it had never seemed to do so much at one time before this.

However, the weather had been shifting ever since most of humanity and its works had died, and Jamal supposed it wasn't so strange that storms might be stronger and wetter now that global warming was no longer a factor.

Whatever happened with this storm, though, he knew he would be able to keep himself and Rowan safe, and that was the most important thing.

"Of course you're not folding," he responded, and dealt the final card.

She received another eight, and he had to fight to keep himself from frowning. What were the odds that she would get three of a kind? Perhaps he hadn't shuffled the deck thoroughly enough.

But it was too late to worry about that now, although he couldn't quite prevent his lips from thinning as he laid the last card of his own hand in front of him.

The two of diamonds. Of course.

"Reveal your cards," he said, and, now that she didn't need to hide her reaction to the cards anymore, she grinned widely and flipped over the one that had been hidden the entire time.

The eight of clubs.

He blinked. "Four of a kind? It's too bad we aren't playing in the real Las Vegas."

Her mouth pursed, but he guessed she was more amused than offended by the sideways jab at her hometown. "This Las Vegas is real, too," she said. "Although I'll admit that way more people have heard of the one in Nevada." Her expression sobered, and Jamal noted the way she swallowed before she added, "Or at least, they'd heard of it once upon a time."

The sadness in her voice and expression was so palpable, it practically hung in the air between them like a living thing.

He didn't want her to be sad. He wanted to see her smile the way she had a few moments earlier, wanted to see her beautiful amber-brown eyes light up with amusement.

After picking up their cards, he shuffled them back into the deck and said, "Rematch?"

---

Rowan had to admit she hadn't thought it would be so much fun to sit there and play cards with James. Despite her brothers teaching her to play blackjack, their family had never been the card game type or much for any kind of board games, either. No, they'd liked to go out and hike and play softball and participate in much more physical activities.

No one would be playing softball around here while a snowstorm was raging, so it seemed cards were the next best option. Not just poker, either, but silly kid stuff like Go Fish and War, games she hadn't played since she was a little girl and sleeping over at her best friend Kaylee's house.

Eventually, though, Rowan could see the day getting darker and darker outside the windows. By that point, the snowdrifts had to be almost two feet high, and she could only be glad that James had worked so hard to make sure they had enough fire-wood to get them through the night. They'd have to sleep in here—she still wasn't sure how that was going to work—but at least they wouldn't have to worry about freezing.

A worry had been nagging in the back of her mind that maybe the temperature would keep dropping and dropping, and they'd end up burning books or maybe her stacks of carefully written memories just to keep themselves warm, like what had happened in that movie where some kind of insane polar vortex had plunged the upper half of the United States into a new Ice Age, but that hadn't happened. No, it was cold, and probably going to be colder still during the overnight hours, and yet she could tell they hadn't dropped anywhere close to zero, even with the way the snow kept falling.

"We should think about dinner," she said. "Something we can do on the stovetop."

"Do you have any pasta?" James asked. He'd just come back to the table after adding a few more logs to the fire, and the sitting room felt so cozy that Rowan kind of hated the thought of leaving it to go to the unheated kitchen.

She'd definitely have to bundle up to cook dinner.

"Lots, actually," she replied. It had been one of the things she'd brought back in bulk from her foraging expeditions in Las Vegas, only to realize it was going to be a real pain to deal with when she didn't have running water to fill the pot and only an induction burner to heat it. The end result was that she still had boxes of spaghetti and linguini and fettuccini sitting in there, along with bags of rotini and farfalle. "But shouldn't we be eating the turkey instead?"

"I was thinking both," James said, looking undeterred. "We can shred some turkey and toss it with olive oil in the pasta. And maybe some olives or even sun-dried tomatoes if you have anything like that in the pantry."

That sounded good. No, she didn't have sun-dried tomatoes on hand, but there were olives and even parmesan cheese in a can—she'd grabbed whatever she could that seemed as if it would have a long shelf life, although she hadn't yet tapped into the parmesan, worrying that it wouldn't last nearly as long once it was opened.

But now she'd be sharing it with James, and it would definitely make their pasta toss taste a lot better.

"It's a plan," she said. "Let's go rustle up some grub."

He grinned at her, and the two of them headed to the kitchen—after stopping to pull on their jackets.

The contrast between the unheated kitchen and the warm sitting room was so vast that for a second, Rowan wondered if some deadly polar vortex really had descended on them.

But no, this was just what it felt like inside when you didn't have a heat source and the temperatures were barely brushing twenty degrees outside. All the same, she was very glad when they turned on the stove and started heating the water. No, it might not make a huge difference in their overall comfort level, but any little trickle of warmth was better than nothing.

At least she didn't have to worry about letting the cold escape when she opened the fridge to get out the turkey, not when the air in the kitchen was probably around the same temperature. James shredded the turkey while she gathered the rest of the components from the pantry, but after that, there wasn't much to do except wait for the water to come to a boil.

His lips weren't exactly blue, but she could tell he wasn't enjoying himself, even with a puffer jacket shielding him from the worst of the cold.

"I'm missing July right about now," he commented, and Rowan gave an understanding nod.

"No kidding. I think I'd kill for a ninety-degree day, even though I used to hate the heat."

"You're a winter person?"

Her nose wrinkled. "I like the in-between times. Fall and spring, even though this part of New Mexico can be crazy-windy in the spring. But at least the temperatures aren't as extreme."

Yes, a warm spring day in late May, after any threat of snow or frost was past, but before the summer heat descended and made things less than tolerable. Just perfect eighty-degree temperatures and blue skies...sitting on the patio at the Plaza Hotel and having a cocktail and watching the people in the park across the street.

The kind of lazy, lovely day she hadn't experienced in far too long.

Rowan didn't even realize tears had begun to trickle down her cheeks before James was over there, reaching out to pull her close. And all right, it was stupid to be crying over something as silly as a May day...it wasn't as though spring wouldn't eventually arrive, even though it might not feel like it right now...but she knew it was so much more that had caused her to break down.

It felt good for him to be holding her, as though he'd brought his own warmth with him, an echo of the time of year she missed so desperately. Maybe she should try to pull away, and yet she knew she wouldn't. He'd come here just in time to save her from having to endure this storm on her own.

No, it was the simple fact of not being alone for the first time in more than four years. She'd only known James for two days, but there was no way she could deny the way she reacted to him—or rather, the way she would have allowed herself to react if the situation had been normal.

It wasn't normal, though. Nothing would ever be normal again.

His lips touched the top of her head, and something inside her seemed to melt, seemed to make her cling to him that much harder.

"I'm sorry," he said.

Now she did pull away, just so she could gaze up into his face. He didn't look at all embarrassed by her show of emotion, and instead only reached down so he could use his thumb to brush away the tears on her cheek, cold in the unheated space.

"What do you have to be sorry about?" she asked. "I'm the one who just lost it."

His mouth twitched a little...a mouth she knew she couldn't let herself look at for too long. "I guess I was just feeling bad that I couldn't snap my fingers and make it summer again."

Now it was her turn to offer a lopsided smile. "I doubt even a djinn can do that."

Something flickered in his dark eyes. "No," he said. "Not even a djinn."

And then he lowered his head, that oh-so-distracting mouth coming closer and closer....

It was a very gentle kiss, almost tentative, as though he didn't quite know how she was going to react and wanted to be able to pull away quickly, just in case.

She didn't want him to pull away. No, despite how cold it was in here, her entire body seemed to burn with the kind of heat she hadn't felt in a long time. Pressing close to him, she deepened the kiss, letting him know this was all right, this was exactly what she wanted, even if she couldn't have expected them to end up in this place so soon.

That kiss didn't last as long as she'd hoped, though, because a hissing sound brought them both back to the here and now, to the reality that the pot of water had finally reached its boiling point and was now bubbling over onto the burner. James hurried to the stove and turned down the heat, then shifted back toward her and smiled, if a little awkwardly.

"Guess we weren't paying attention," he said.

"Guess not," she replied. The rush of heat his kiss had awakened in her hadn't completely dissipated, but she was in enough possession of her faculties to grab the package of rotini and shake it into the water, which now had dropped down to a much gentler boil.

And if her fingers were trembling a bit as she set the empty bag down on the countertop, well, she'd just have to hope James hadn't noticed.

His gaze was still on her, gentle, maybe a little worried. "Are we okay?"

She looked up at him, at the gorgeously chiseled lines of his jaw under its scruff of beard, at the mouth with its slightly fuller lower lip...a mouth that had just been touching hers a few minutes earlier. Once again, she was struck by how handsome he was, how he had the face of a male model or an actor, someone whose pure, male beauty should have been appreciated by thousands of admirers.

How she'd never in a million years thought that someone so gorgeous would be interested in anyone like her.

But he was...and she couldn't help thinking it wasn't just because they'd been marooned here together. He must have seen something in her, some spark she thought had been extinguished over the past couple of years.

"Yes," she said, her voice steady, "we're okay."

# Chapter 10

HOW COULD HE HAVE ALLOWED HIMSELF to kiss her?

Oh, she was beautiful, he wouldn't dispute that.

Beautiful and strong and intelligent, and far more engaging than he'd ever thought a human woman could be. He'd always believed they must be dull and plodding, weighed down by a sense of their mortality and afflicted by all the pains and illnesses that preyed upon mortal bodies. He certainly hadn't expected a creature of fire and iron will like Rowan Aames...and now he was beginning to understand why Aamir had succumbed, when before this moment his actions had appeared incomprehensible.

Jamal had no doubt that his older brother would laugh if he were to learn of the way he had stumbled, had fallen prey to a mortal woman's wiles.

No. That was not correct. Rowan had done nothing to trap him. She had only been herself.

And that, it seemed, was more than enough.

They'd both been subdued as they finished preparing their dinner. It was so frosty in the kitchen and the hallway connecting to the sitting room that Jamal knew their food would be cold before they ever sat down, so he directed a little of his djinn energy into it, just enough to keep it warm, if not piping hot. And Rowan seemed shaken enough from the intimacies they'd just shared that she didn't seem to notice anything amiss.

No, instead she'd gotten another bottle of wine to have with their meal, and appeared a little steadier once they were both sitting down and had their food in front of them. She didn't offer any kind of toast, however, but only sipped some of the chianti just as soon as he'd poured it for her.

Which was fine. The important thing to him was that she appeared to be doing what she could to get past their current awkwardness.

"The wood seems to be holding up," she remarked before scooping up a forkful of rotini and turkey.

"Yes," he agreed. Of course it was; his djinn powers were helping the fire along as well. It was not his element, but such a simple task didn't require him to possess that kind of gift. "We'll be fine until morning."

"I hope it stops snowing."

He hoped it would, too. Or...perhaps not. As long as the snow continued to fall, they had a reason to be caught in this place together. Once the weather cleared up, Rowan would expect him to get on the road again. She hadn't mentioned his offer to take her with him, and quite possibly she didn't know what she should do next. They'd shared a kiss, an acknowledgment of the attraction between them, but they had done nothing more than that.

Yet.

Jamal couldn't quite ignore the heat that flickered in him as he looked at her. The kiss had been satisfying in its own right, and yet he knew his body wanted more than that, more than only the sensation of her lips pressed against his.

No, he wanted all of her.

Whether she would be open to such things, he couldn't say for sure. Now her expression, if not precisely guarded, was still neutral, as though she was doing her best to avoid giving anything of her emotions away, even if they were no longer playing poker.

"Well, it has to stop sometime," he said, doing his best to keep his tone light. "It's unusual that it's lasted this long. I'm guessing we'll wake up to sunshine tomorrow."

A flicker came and went in her eyes, probably at the way he'd said "we." But there was no point in dancing around the issue—even if they didn't sleep together in the usual human sense of the phrase, they would still have to share this space tonight.

Otherwise, she would surely freeze.

A faint smile played around her lovely lips. "Want to bet on that?"

"Sure," he said easily. "If it's sunny, then you have to make coffee."

"That's not much of a bet," she returned, now with an amused light in her amber-hued eyes.

"I didn't want to make it too high stakes, just in case I was wrong."

She chuckled then, and a bit more of the palpable tension in the room seemed to ease a little. "Okay, it's a bet."

They both fell silent as they returned to their food, but it was a companionable silence, one that somehow felt right. From time to time, Rowan would feed Darby a bit of turkey, or Jamal would also pause to give the dog a tidbit here and there, and again, this seemed good to him, the way the three of them were sharing a meal.

"What does Darby do when you're writing?" he asked at last, and Rowan tilted her head, possibly a little surprised by the question.

However, she seemed to decide there was nothing that out of the ordinary about it—after all, the stacks of papers and notebooks in the dining hall down the corridor gave mute testimony to how much time she'd expended on the endeavor—so she gave a small lift of her shoulders and said, "It depends. Sometimes I'll just let him out and leave the kitchen door open while I'm working, and other times he'll curl up nearby and wait it out. It mostly depends on what the weather's like and whether he feels like roaming around or would rather stick close to home."

"You're never worried that he might not come back?"

She set down her fork and reached for her glass of chianti. "No. The moment I found him, I could tell he was going to be my dog. I guess I was lucky in that."

Yes, she was—more than she knew, for the djinn had ensured that all the animals who'd lost their families would always have plenty of food and all the shelter they needed, even as they were left free to roam as they willed. As far as he'd been able to tell, they were just fine with this arrangement and had seen no need to look for new masters among the humans who had survived the Heat and the reavers who followed.

Not Darby, though. For some reason, the dog had understood that Rowan needed someone at her side to provide some kind of solace during all those years of isolation.

"Good dog," he said, and Darby came over to claim another morsel of turkey, tail wagging happily.

"Yes, he's a good dog," she said. Her gaze moved from the cattle dog, who'd settled himself on the rug between their two chairs, obviously not wanting to miss a chance at a single bite of turkey, back up to Jamal. "Do people have a lot of pets in Los Alamos?"

He had absolutely no idea. Yes, he and his brothers had surveyed the residents of the mountain town when they left its fastnesses to go into the river valley where Española was located, but they'd never gotten close enough to know what their individual lives were like. And as far as he could tell, people didn't bring dogs along with them when they worked in the fields or went through the abandoned town to look for any items that might be of use in their new lives in Los Alamos.

However, he had to believe that, while most former pets had been content to go it alone in the years following the Dying, the town that was now the only outpost of purely human civilization was its own unique case. Surely the people who lived there had adopted the animals left behind and made them part of their families.

"Yes," he said, hating that he had to lie to her like this, even as he acknowledged that telling her the truth would be far, far worse. "There were all those pets left behind, you know? So people adopted them."

"Did you?"

An innocent enough question, he supposed, but one that put him on even shakier ground; if he confessed to having a pet, she would want to know how she could have left it behind. "I had a dog," he said carefully. "But she was old when I took her in. She passed last spring."

The sympathy on Rowan's face only made the mountain of lies he'd just told her that much worse, as if someone had compelled him to walk across broken glass. "I'm so sorry," she said.

"It's all right," he responded, and hoped the carefully neutral tone he'd adopted would tell her that he really didn't want to talk about it. "She had a good life. But that's part of the reason why I volunteered to go out and do some exploring—it wasn't as though I had anyone to look after except me."

Rowan must have gotten the hint, because she didn't say anything, only gave a sympathetic nod before picking up her fork once again. After a moment, she ventured, "And there...there wasn't anyone else?"

Jamal knew she wasn't talking about his fictional dog anymore.

Well, at least he wouldn't have to lie about that particular part of his life.

"No," he said. "There wasn't anyone."

Maybe the faintest of nods. She ate a mouthful of turkey and pasta, her eyes still full of questions.

However, she didn't ask any of them, only ventured that maybe they could play cards again after dinner. That seemed a safe enough pastime to him, especially since he knew it was still early in the evening, and to go to sleep now would only result in them waking up far sooner than they should.

Or perhaps she was merely putting off the inevitable time when they would have to put away the cards, would have to shift the table to one side so there would be enough space for them to lie down on the rug in front of the fireplace. Although Jamal had to admit to himself that he was looking forward to that moment, he couldn't say for sure whether Rowan felt the same way.

Whatever happened, he wanted to make sure she took the lead. Perhaps that way, he wouldn't feel so guilty about what was developing between them.

---

They'd had to bundle up to move the dishes into the kitchen, although they'd decided to leave them on the counter for now. Darby had gotten his last licks in—literally—by cleaning each of their plates, so whatever little residue was left could be handled the next day, when, Rowan fervently hoped, the sun would be out and the solar panels on the roof and set up to one side of the Castle would finally get the full charge they needed.

But after that was done, James had said, "We might as well bring our bedding down now, since we've already got our coats on."

This was true, and made sense. At the same time, she kind of hated the thought of moving all those blankets and pillows down to the sitting room, because then the scenario of them sharing that space tonight would become all too real.

Then again, it would have been silly to take off their coats and play cards, and then have to put them back on again, so she only said, "Makes sense."

The two of them headed up the stairs, although Darby clearly had no desire to leave the warm sitting room behind and elected to stay in his favorite spot in front of the hearth. A little of the heat from the room had drifted up the stairs, so the first part of their climb wasn't too uncomfortable. By the time they reached the second-floor hallway, though, Rowan could see little puffs of mist coming out with each breath, illuminated by the hand-cranked flashlight they'd brought with them.

Gathering James's belongings didn't take very long. They took a brief pause to brush their teeth, although neither of them was in the mood to splash ice-cold water on their faces after such a pleasant meal. It was a bit more work to bundle up all her quilts and blankets and her sleeping clothes, but eventually they were able to descend the stairs and deposit everything on the sitting room floor, where Darby seemed delighted to have something new to make a nest in.

"No, Darby," she admonished him as he began to burrow himself into James's sleeping bag.

"It's fine," James said. "You know he's going to end up there once we're asleep anyway."

He had a point. The dog always did like to snuggle next to the nearest human, even when the weather was hot, and she guessed he'd be ecstatic to have two people's warmth to share tonight.

"All right," she replied, then directed a stern eye toward the dog. "No claws, Darby."

The dog let out a whuffle that she supposed was his way of acknowledging the admonition, and she couldn't help smiling a little. There was something about having a dog around that always brought her back down to earth.

But then it was time to head back to the table, where James had already picked up the deck of cards and begun to shuffle them. Rowan couldn't help admiring the way his long, strong fingers manipulated the deck...and couldn't quite stop herself from wondering what it would be like to have those hands running over her body.

*Stop it,* she scolded herself. *Just because he kissed you earlier doesn't mean anything has to happen tonight.*

Yeah, right.

However, she managed to pull out a chair and sit down, and look over at him with what she hoped was a safely neutral expression. Whether she pulled it off or not was another story; the couple of glasses of wine she'd drunk earlier normally wouldn't have made her even tipsy once upon a time, but it had been years since she'd allowed herself any more than half a glass with a meal, and now she felt a little swimmy.

"I'm not sure I'm in the mood for poker," he told her. "How about a quiet game of Go Fish?"

"Sounds good to me," she replied. Yes, it had turned out that five-card stud wasn't so complicated, although she had a feeling it would be much more difficult when actual betting was involved. However, Go Fish seemed a lot more suited to her current mental state.

He handed over the cards. "You can deal this time."

Rowan took them and awkwardly shuffled

them a few more times, even though she knew James had pretty thoroughly mixed them up just a moment before. However, it seemed better to do this, if only to reinforce her role as the dealer this go-'round.

As she laid their cards on the table, he said, "You're amazing, you know."

Heat flooded her cheeks, but she did her best to sound unruffled as she replied, "Oh, I'm not so sure about that."

"Well, you should be," James said. He clasped his hands on the tabletop and gazed directly at her, obviously not worried about whether he was making the situation more awkward by the minute. "To have survived here like this all alone for so long? I don't know too many people who could've managed something like that."

She managed a lopsided smile, then picked up her set of seven cards. "Oh, I think most people are capable of a lot more than they think they are. Besides, if I was so amazing, I probably would have figured out a way to hook up the plumbing system to the solar a long time ago."

This argument didn't seem to dissuade him. Like her, he retrieved his cards so he could survey the hand he'd been dealt, but his expression didn't shift. "I don't think that has anything to do with it. You didn't have any background in that kind of stuff. The only reason I was able to do it was because I've been working on so much solar and wind power in Los Alamos."

Okay, he probably had a point there. Still, she didn't want to linger on the subject of her apparent awesomeness, not with the sexual tension between them crackling like the logs that snapped and popped in the fire a few feet away.

"Got any sevens?" she asked, and he smiled.

"Go fish."

The game progressed normally enough after that, with James managing to beat her after a lot of back and forth and taking one another's cards. She suggested a rematch, and that time she came out on top, concluding their game with a jaw-cracking yawn.

"I'm beat," she announced, and laid her cards down on the tabletop. Although she'd hoped to keep playing until they were both too tired to think of doing anything except sleep, it seemed clear enough that James had a lot more stamina than she did and wasn't anywhere close to calling it quits.

For a moment, she thought he might protest, but then he also put down his cards. "Probably a good idea. It's been a long day."

She supposed it had. Or at least, it felt as if about a hundred years separated the Rowan and James of yesterday from the Rowan and James of today. Funny how one kiss could suddenly change everything.

"And Darby's definitely ready for bed," she added, tilting her head toward the dog, who'd burrowed himself into the sleeping bag and looked as if he didn't plan to go anywhere any time soon.

A quick flash of a smile before James said, "Yeah, I'll have to be careful about dislodging him."

For some reason, that brief exchange seemed to lessen the tension between the two of them. Rowan smiled back, then murmured something about getting her jammies on.

Maybe all those layers of clothes would provide something of a barrier...or maybe not.

James didn't protest, or try to come closer and suggest that maybe there were a few things they needed to get out of the way before she climbed into her sweatshirt and leggings and socks. In fact, he even obliged her by turning away and going over to the fire to stoke it up one last time so she could yank off her jeans and sweater and long-sleeved T-shirt and into the warm, comfortable items she'd been using to sleep in ever since the weather turned cold.

That made it much easier to slide into the pile of bedding they'd brought down, and to have the blankets and quilts pulled up to her chin before James came over, sat down on his sleeping bag, and slipped out of his jeans. Underneath, he wore thermal underwear, and it seemed he thought that and a long-sleeved T-shirt would be enough to keep him comfortable.

Thank God that he hadn't decided to sleep in his underwear and nothing else. True, even with the fire going, it wasn't really warm enough in here for that, but she'd had a boyfriend who'd insisted on wearing boxer briefs and nothing else at night no matter how cold it was, and for all she knew, James was the same way.

Apparently not, though.

He slid into the sleeping bag, taking care not to be too abrupt with Darby, although Rowan could tell he wasn't going to allow the dog to hog the entire thing. They'd already snuffed out the candles they'd been using to illuminate the space, so the room was dim, lit by the ever-changing flames in the hearth and nothing else.

She lay there for a moment, wondering what would happen if he tried to kiss her good night. It seemed that wasn't his plan, or maybe he was just doing his best to stay warm as well, because he only said, "Good night, Rowan."

"Good night, James."

And that, it seemed, was that.

Closing her eyes was the best course of action, and yet the second she did, all she could think about was how hard the floor felt beneath her, and how, despite the warmth drifting out from the hearth, it seemed as if the cold of the basement was somehow moving up through the floorboards and the thin Persian rug, seeping right through all the quilts she had placed both beneath her and on top of her.

To her embarrassment, her teeth began to chatter. At once, James shifted in his sleeping bag. "Are you okay, Rowan?"

"F-fine," she managed, and she thought she heard him chuckle.

"This probably wasn't the best arrangement," he said, then pushed himself up to a sitting position to survey her in her bundle of quilts and blankets. "What we really should do is unzip the sleeping bag and spread it out over the rug, then pile all the quilts and blankets on top of us. That way, we'll have more insulation beneath us, and we can share our body warmth."

He spoke so matter-of-factly, as if it wasn't a big deal for the two of them to be cuddling together. Maybe it wasn't. Maybe he'd also realized it was way too cold tonight to be doing anything except using each other to stay warm.

"You think that'll work?" she asked, knowing she sounded dubious at best.

"Only one way to find out."

Another push, and now he was standing, much to Darby's chagrin. The dog shook and moved a little closer to the fire, obviously realizing it was best for him to stay out of the way until he'd figured out what the humans were up to. James picked up the sleeping bag and unzipped it so it was one big blocky rectangle, then sent a glance in Rowan's direction, telling her it was time for her to hold up her end of the bargain.

Fine. She got up as well and gathered the blankets and quilts, then waited off to one side as he spread the unzipped sleeping bag across the rug. Once he was done, she dropped the pile of bedding on top of the bag, then smoothed it out as best she could so it looked like an actual stack instead of just a big wad of fabric.

"Perfect," James said, then knelt and flipped the covers back. "Give it a try."

She lowered herself to the floor, then pulled the blankets and quilts over her. Yes, that was better—the Arctic-rated sleeping bag did a much better job of keeping the cold from coming up through the floor, and the covers seemed to help to hold the heat in rather than letting it escape on all sides.

"Better," she allowed.

A chuckle, and then he slid under the covers next to her. Almost at once, she could sense the way his body heat combined with hers, making the setup almost comfortable.

Almost.

"Much better," he said. A pause, and then she felt him move closer.

Part of her wanted to freeze in place and hoped

she could fool him into believing she'd already fallen asleep. However, a much larger part of her brain wanted nothing more than to have him reach out to her and pull her close.

Which was what he did...after a pause during which he'd obviously tried his best to gauge what her reaction would be. But then his arms went around her, and she found herself snuggling closer, so very glad of the heat of his body and the strength of his embrace.

When he held her like that, she felt safe for the first time in years.

Their mouths met, tasting of toothpaste and mint, and a different kind of warmth flared all through her. It seemed impossible that someone as smart and capable and gorgeous as James Aguilar wanted her, but in this moment, while the snow fell outside and the fire flickered in the hearth...and Darby seemed to have interpreted correctly that they didn't want him plopping down between them...Rowan put all that away.

Sometimes it was better not to think.

The kiss deepened, and then James's mouth was hot against her neck, kissing her in the spot that had always somehow driven her wild, had made her melt into the moment. His hands went up under the sweatshirt she wore, fingers moving against her bare breasts, and she gasped aloud, sure his touch was almost enough to make her climax right then and there.

Not quite, however. That might have been a flash of his teeth in the firelit dark as he pushed the sweatshirt up so he could run his tongue over her nipple, and she moaned this time, knowing it wasn't going to take much, not after so much time had passed since the last time she'd been with anyone.

That was why, when his hand slipped inside her leggings and touched the throbbing bud between her legs, the orgasm flared in her only a moment later, giving her a release she hadn't even realized she'd needed until this moment. Yes, she'd taken care of herself as best she could during all those years of isolation, but what she'd done alone couldn't come close to what having a man touch her would do.

Not just any man, though.

James.

He held on to her as she shuddered her way through the climax, then kissed her again, mouths locked together while they hurriedly pulled at leggings and sweatshirts and T-shirts, anything that prevented them from being together like this, flesh to flesh, skin hot with a warmth that had nothing to do with the fire burning a few feet away. She took him in her hand, felt how big and heavy and ready he was, and he moaned as she touched him, running her fingers against his shaft.

Not for too long, though, because he shifted, and now he was pressing against her, so ready. As was she, still wet from the orgasm that had blazed through her a few moments earlier.

No words, only their eyes locked on one another for a single endless moment. And then he was inside her and she gasped, wrapping her legs around him so she could pull him in even deeper, feeling him fill her empty spaces, knowing that this would never have felt as good with anyone else.

Time passed, but she had no sensation of it, her world narrowed down to only the feeling of him inside her, the realization that she was close again, that another climax was about to hit with the force of a tidal wave.

She moaned aloud first, and then she could feel him release, feel his heat fill her. A flicker of worry —they definitely hadn't used any protection—but then she let it go, let that moment of doubt fly away like a wayward balloon caught in a strong breeze.

How could anything go wrong when she had James here with her?

They clung together for a long moment, but then at last he pulled away, his breath ragged in the darkness. Not too far, though, because he placed another kiss on her mouth, this one infinitely gentle.

"You're incredible," he whispered.

"So are you," she said, and he gave another one of those warm, friendly chuckles, the ones that somehow reminded her of the hot chocolate she used to love so much, with a sprinkle of cayenne to give it some extra kick.

His arms went around her, and she snuggled close, using his shoulder as a pillow.

Yes, now she was truly warm.

# Chapter 11

He'd kept the fire going through the night, even though the carefully tended logs should have died down at some point. If Rowan asked, he would tell her he'd slipped out from under the covers to add more wood, but he thought she was lost enough in sleep that she wouldn't have noticed if he'd gotten up.

The important thing was to make sure she was safe and warm.

Should he take himself to task for what had passed between them the night before? He supposed some people would think he had been careless at best and an utter hypocrite at worst, but he saw no point in self-recrimination.

Not when he knew he was not the same man who had arrived here two days earlier, or at least, he was not the man he'd thought he was. If anyone had asked, he would have said he cared nothing for love, was more than content to go through his long life on his own.

Now he knew that being alone was the last thing he wanted.

He got up from their makeshift bed and pulled on his thermal underwear, although he didn't bother with the T-shirt. Darby shook himself and stood as well, and Rowan stirred.

"What time is it?" she asked, her voice still blurred with sleep.

"I have no idea," Jamal replied, which was only the truth. There were no clocks in this room—and even if there had been, he doubted they would have shown the correct hour. For a djinn, telling the exact time was a foolish concept, thanks to his people's long lives, but he knew humans in general craved that knowledge. "But let me look outside."

He went over to the window and pushed aside the heavy curtains; unlike the rest of the Castle, this room's furnishings echoed some of its bygone days as a hotel, and so the drapes hadn't been replaced with the much more institutional blinds that covered the windows in the student bedrooms upstairs.

A true winter wonderland met his eyes—snow several feet deep as far as he could see, with a bright sun making the landscape that much more dazzling. There didn't seem to be a single cloud in the sky, which meant they should have power soon.

"It's probably midmorning, judging by the angle of the sun," he said.

Those encouraging words made Rowan sit up and send him a startled glance. Her hair was mussed from sleep, but she looked all the more adorable because of that. "Did you say 'sun'?"

"I did," he replied. "Come and see."

Unlike him, she'd pulled her sweatshirt back on after they'd finished their lovemaking the night before. Her long legs, however, were still bare, lithe and lovely, as she walked over to the window to get a look for herself.

Jamal recalled feeling those legs wrapped around him the night before, driving him even deeper into her, and a rush of need went through him.

*Later,* he told himself. While Rowan was acting naturally enough with him now, he didn't want to do anything that might make her feel as if he was pressing her for something she might not desire. For all he knew, she'd come to him last night driven by an animal need for closeness and warmth, and nothing more.

But no, she paused at his side, then went on her tiptoes to press a kiss against his cheek, even though her own cheeks flushed faintly as she did so. "I'm so glad we could wake up to a sunny morning," she told him.

"So am I," he replied. "Told you the storm wouldn't last forever."

Her nose wrinkled, although her warm brown eyes laughed up into his. "True, you did," she said. "I guess at the time, it just felt like it would never end." She looked away from him then, face alight with the promise of a new day. "This is great, though. We should have plenty of power to get everything running soon, but it's probably a good idea to let things charge for about an hour or so just to make sure we have enough. The system is set up to shut down before the batteries are totally depleted, so I don't think we damaged anything. I'd just like to baby it a bit."

"We can do that," Jamal said. "In fact, why don't you stay in here and keep warm while I make us some coffee? That'll be a good way to get the day going."

"It's going to be really cold in the kitchen," she pointed out, but he only shrugged.

"I'll wear my coat. But no point in both of us freezing, right?"

Something in her expression made it look as if she wanted to argue, but she seemed to decide to let it go. "All right. Can you take Darby with you, though? I'm pretty sure he needs to go out."

The dog was already standing by, tail wagging,

so Jamal knew Rowan was only pointing out an obvious truth. "Sure," he said. "Just hang tight here—I put a few more logs on the fire right before you woke up, so it should stay warm for a while."

She glanced over at the fire, which was still dancing happily away. "Thanks for that. But I think I'll get back under the covers while I wait."

"Good idea."

He bent and gave her a quick kiss, and was gratified to see the way her eyes lit up from the casual caress. As far as he could tell, she wasn't feeling awkward at all about their morning after, as though she'd realized there was nothing wrong about what they had done and she might as well do her best to accept this natural progression of their relationship.

Or at least, it would have seemed natural to anyone who didn't know who...or, more to the point, what...he truly was.

Not for the first time, guilt nagged at him, but he pushed it away as he shrugged on his jacket and headed out of the sitting room and down the corridor to the kitchen. Perhaps he had come here on false pretenses, but he doubted anyone could say he had forced her last night. The only thing he had done was initiate things, knowing he might have to back off quickly if it turned out she was not as interested in him as he'd thought.

But she'd returned his kisses with equal heat,

and he had known she'd wanted him just as much as he wanted her. True, she might not have been quite as amorous if she'd known he was a djinn, and yet....

He wouldn't allow his thoughts to go any farther than that. In fact, right then, he rather wished his brain would shut up and leave him alone so he might enjoy the afterglow of a night spent sleeping with a beautiful woman. After their first encounter, they'd both fallen almost immediately into a deep sleep, so there hadn't been a repeat of that first passionate joining, but he saw no reason to believe that they wouldn't also share a bed tonight, even with the power back on.

They would just have to decide which bed to use.

As Rowan had warned him, the kitchen was bitterly cold, so much that he could see his breath as faint mist in the icy air. However, because he'd come here alone, it was easy to use his djinn powers to heat the water and prepare the coffee, although he made sure to use the same amount of time as the task would have required if it had been performed by a human, and to dirty the same pans and other utensils. Darby helped, simply because the dog appeared to also be cheered by the sunny morning, and had spent a good span of time nosing around the snowy yard and reacquainting himself with all the smells there.

Still, it felt good to return to the sitting room, where the fire continued to burn in the hearth and the temperature was much more comfortable. Rowan had taken advantage of his absence to get dressed in the clothes she had been wearing the day before, and he experienced a pang of regret.

It would have been pleasant to see her bare legs for just a while longer, even as he was forced to admit that it wasn't quite warm enough for that in here.

"Thanks," she said as she took the mug of coffee from him. "And Darby's been taken care of?"

"Yes," Jamal replied. Clearly, she wanted to be all business this morning, so he would go along for now. Even so, he was interested to see if she would be quite as brisk tonight when it came time to go to bed. "He went outside and found all kinds of new smells, and then I fed him breakfast."

"Very efficient," she said with a smile. It faded a little as she added, "We should probably figure out our breakfast at some point, but I'd kind of like to wait until we can use the power again."

"It shouldn't be too long," he told her. "The sun's really bright this morning, and it doesn't look like there are any clouds at all." He paused there, then asked, "How long do you think it will take for all this to melt? I'm not very familiar with this part of the world."

Rowan blew on her coffee before replying. When she spoke, she sounded hesitant. "And I'm not familiar with storms like this. What we got from just this one is almost what we'd get during an entire season. Mostly, it depends on whether there's more snow on the way, or whether this was just a freak early-season snowfall and we'll be back to our usual mid-fifties and low sixties soon. If things go back to normal, then it should only take a couple of days for things to melt in the sunny spots. It's going to be a muddy mess, though."

That he could well imagine. He had no idea how well-groomed the grounds here had been back when the college was running and full of students, but now large portions of the area surrounding the Castle were bare dirt, just waiting to turn into the clay-heavy mud that seemed to predominate in northern New Mexico.

"Well, we don't need to go anywhere right away," he said, and something in Rowan's expression seemed to shift, to become almost shuttered.

"But you'll want to go eventually," she returned.

Was she expecting him to stay here with her? On the surface, that prospect didn't seem very practical, even if he had been the human he was pretending to be. It would make much more sense for her to go to Los Alamos, even if he couldn't accompany her there.

For some reason, he didn't like that idea very much. He'd gone to bed with her the night before without much regard for what might happen next, and yet he now realized this wouldn't be as easy as having a casual tumble and going on his way. Even if they could not have a future together, he still wanted to make sure she was someplace safe, someplace where she would be surrounded by people who could ensure she prospered. It seemed the least he could do, even if it was not what some part of him—a part he did not wish to acknowledge—truly desired.

"It's the logical thing to do," he replied, even as he pushed away an unbidden image of a winter idyll where the two of them spent the next few months here together, making love, planning meals and playing cards and reading to one another. As pretty a picture as that might have been, he knew it could never come to pass. The elders had made it very clear that a djinn could not cohabitate with a mortal unless the djinn made their human lover their Chosen.

And while Jamal would not condemn his brother Aamir for doing that very thing, he also didn't believe he cared for Rowan enough to sacrifice his freedom in such a way. She was beautiful and clever and would make an excellent partner for a mortal man one day, but his feelings for her didn't go beyond a certain admiration...and desire.

Oh, yes, he definitely desired her, even more now that he knew how sweet she tasted.

"But we don't have to make any big decisions this morning," he added before she had a chance to reply to his words. "It's just something to think about."

"All right," she said, although something in her tone still didn't sound entirely convinced. "I'll think about it."

---

Strange how they could be so normal with each other, as if nothing in particular had happened between them. But Rowan reflected that was the way these things usually went—you went on a date that got hotter and heavier than you'd imagined, and then you woke up at his apartment and had coffee and went out to breakfast, and acted as though everything hadn't suddenly shifted overnight.

Except she knew no one had made her react the way James had the night before...and she kind of doubted anyone else ever would.

Which meant, she supposed, that she should thank the Castle for the way it had sheltered her over the past four years, and head off with James Aguilar to make a new life in Los Alamos.

Most people would argue it was stupid to stay

here alone, even if it turned out that she and James didn't have a love for the ages after all.

To be honest, she didn't know what to think, except that the mere sight of him made her breath catch, and she felt easier and more herself with him than she had with anyone she'd ever known. Despite that, she had to believe it was way too soon to consider herself in love with him.

No one fell in love that fast, right?

In lust, sure. Last night's lovemaking had been incredibly satisfying, but she still craved more. She guessed the reason why James hadn't initiated anything this morning was that he didn't want to wake her. Whether it had been the cushy sleeping bag beneath her or the release those earthshaking orgasms had provided, Rowan wasn't sure, but she knew she'd slept like the proverbial rock.

As it was, they had a completely normal breakfast of toast and more coffee, and midway through, the lights on the microwave and the oven flared back to life, letting them know the solar power had kicked in.

Which meant she could have a hot shower. The sex had been great, but she really wanted to get cleaned up. In the past, she'd shared morning-after showers with her boyfriends and wouldn't have been averse to the prospect today...except that the showers on the dorm floors were strictly utilitarian, with barely enough room for one person in their narrow stalls, let alone two.

Well, maybe someday. Of course, that meant she had to allow for the possibility of her and James having an actual future, of them leaving here and going to Los Alamos, where there might or might not be showers roomy enough for two people.

She'd already been entertaining the idea of leaving with him, and yet she still didn't know quite what she should do. Somehow, it felt like something of a betrayal to leave behind the place that had sheltered her for the past couple of years, even if logic suggested it was the smartest thing to do.

"Do you want to shower first?" she asked him, and he shook his head, even as the corners of his mouth turned up slightly.

"No, you go ahead," he replied. "I'll work on getting the kitchen cleaned up."

"Thanks," she said, reflecting it was kind of a miracle that he'd offered to handle the chore. When she was a kid, her brothers would rather have mowed the lawn than do the dishes—and often did, since her parents expected everyone to pull their weight even while not doing much to dispel embedded beliefs about the division of labor based on sex, cooking lessons notwithstanding.

Well, they'd been great parents, if not the most progressive people on the planet.

Thinking about her family made a familiar wave of sadness move through her, and she did her best to push it away. She thought she'd come to terms with the loss during her years of isolation, but every once in a while it managed to surface again, like the wreck of a ship reemerging as the tide went out.

"I'll save you some hot water," she added, doing her best to keep her tone light.

James's dark eyes crinkled at the corners. "I appreciate it."

Rowan left the kitchen, noting how Darby chose to stay behind with their new companion. She couldn't say that the dog had transferred all his affections to James, but she could tell he was just fine with the current arrangement of having more than one human to keep him company.

Another point for packing it all in and getting the hell out of Dodge while they still could. With the storm gone, they should have some time before another batch of snow came along, and it just made sense to use the clear weather to travel to Los Alamos. More than ever, she longed for the days when you could look at your phone or check online to see what the weather was going to do for the next few days, but now all she could rely on were her instincts. This recent storm had been unseasonably early for something so fierce, which made her think the chances of another one following on its heels were pretty low.

At least, she hoped they were.

But it felt great to get clean again, and although it was time to wash her hair, she still managed to get out of the shower within fifteen minutes. The space heater had done a decent job of warming the bathroom, and she could tell temperatures were going to rise a lot today, maybe as much as thirty degrees warmer than they'd been just the day before. That was how it worked in this part of the world at the change of seasons, though—you never knew exactly what it was going to do, and that was why you always needed to have a variety of clothes on hand to deal with the shifting conditions.

Today, she guessed she wouldn't have to bundle up too much, so she put on a lighter-weight sweater than she normally would, along with a fresh pair of jeans. Over the past few years, she'd collected a lot of clothes from the local Walmart and various other shops around town, just so she wouldn't have to do laundry more than once every two weeks, so she had a lot to choose from. Boots, though, because even if temperatures hit sixty today the way she thought they might, it was still going to be a slushy mess outside.

She met James coming up the stairs, Darby at his heels, and did her best to stifle a smile. "It's all yours."

“And the kitchen’s done,” he responded. “I’ll meet you back downstairs after I’m finished up here.”

“Sounds like a plan,” she said. She could tell they were both trying to act casual, even though a flare of warmth went through her as his dark eyes met hers and she knew this supposed normality was a surface construct at best. “I’ll be in the sitting room.”

He nodded, then went into the room he’d been using, where she assumed any changes of clothing he had would still be stored somewhere in his rucksack.

No point in hanging around when he was just about to disappear into the shower, so she continued down the stairs and into the sitting room, where their bedding still occupied a large space on the floor.

Would they sleep here again tonight? No reason, she supposed—with the solar panels charging the batteries and plenty of power to keep the space heaters going, it just made more sense to go back to their rooms...or at least, one of their rooms. It would be a squeeze for both of them to occupy one of those narrow dormitory beds, but on the other hand, the close proximity should be enough to keep them both plenty warm.

A smile playing around her lips, she gathered up the blankets and quilts and folded them carefully, then zipped James's sleeping bag back together and rolled it tightly before placing it next to the rest of the bedding. That task done, she put another couple of logs on the fire, even though at this point, doing so wasn't really necessary, thanks to the space heater he'd left running in here before he went back upstairs.

But the bright flames looked cheerful, especially when contrasted with the snowy landscape revealed outside after she opened the curtains. The entire world was blanketed in white, although she noticed the way the icicles hanging from the eaves had already begun to melt under the sun as it rose ever higher in the sky, and how the snow that lay on top of the walkway that led to the Castle's front entrance had begun to look a little patchy. At this rate, they might have a clear path to the parking lot before the day was over.

Not that they would be going anywhere today. The snow would need to melt a lot in more places and not just on the paved surfaces before they could safely get moving. Still, looking at the signs of snowmelt cheered her up, reminding her that one storm didn't mean they'd be encased in ice for the next four months.

With the sitting room tidied up, Rowan found herself going back out into the corridor and down to the dining hall. It was much colder in there, although the room's numerous windows let in a flood of bright sunlight, and she could tell it had also warmed significantly from the way it had felt only the day before.

The stacks of papers and three-ring binders remained where they'd always been, and as she gazed at them, she found herself frowning. It was one thing to possibly say goodbye to the Castle, and something else altogether to leave behind everything she'd labored over for the past three years. Was she willing to walk away from all this? What if her writings were all the memory that existed of the world that had once been?

"*Oh earth, unhappy planet born to die*

*Might I your scribe and confessor be,*" she murmured, and from somewhere behind her, James said,

"Did you write that?"

Surprised, she turned around. He stood a pace or two away, his hair damp, telling her he must have washed it as well.

"Sorry," he said before she could respond. "I didn't mean to startle you."

"It's okay," she said at once. "But no, I didn't write that quote. It's from a poem I first saw in a book I read a long time ago."

He came over to stand next to her. That close, she could practically feel his body heat, welcome in the chilly air.

"What was the book about?"

"The end of the world," Rowan replied. The irony of the situation wasn't lost on her, and she added, "Except in that case it was brought about by stupid people with nuclear bombs and not djinn. Still, it always kind of haunted me. I looked up the poem online and saw it was by a woman named Edna St. Vincent Millay, so I read the rest of it, even bought a copy of the book it was in."

"Do you still have it?" James asked, his expression genuinely curious.

"No," she said. "I kind of went on a purge of the stuff I collected in middle school when I was about to graduate high school, so the book of poems got donated. But I found it in the library here." She stopped there and gave a rueful shake of her head. "Maybe that's what partly gave me the idea to write down everything I could remember. I didn't know if there was anyone else left to do it, so I figured I might as well be our world's 'scribe and confessor.'"

"It was a good idea," he said, and his hand stole into hers, his fingers warm and strong against her chilled ones. "And just because you might have to leave all your writing behind now, that doesn't mean we can't come back and get it in the future. I'll bet it would all fit in the back of an SUV."

He sounded matter-of-fact and cheerful at the same time, as if they'd already made the decision to go.

"What if I don't want to leave?" she asked, and his grasp on her hand tightened a little.

"It doesn't really make sense to stay here, does it?"

No, it didn't. The logical side of her mind knew that, but....

He now took her other hand and turned her so she faced him. Staring up into his almost too-handsome features, she didn't see anything in his expression except concern for her. Some men might have been impatient over what on the surface seemed like a silly stance to take, but James didn't appear to be one of them.

"I get it," he said. "Or at least, I think I do. But you'd be a lot safer in Los Alamos."

"I thought you said the djinn weren't hunting humans anymore."

His mouth tightened a little. "They aren't," he replied. "But djinn aren't the only danger in the world. There are wild animals and weather events like the one we just made it through. And besides that, this building is old. Yes, you mentioned it was refurbished and modernized in the nineties, but that's been thirty years ago now. Sooner or later, it's going to need work again, lots of work. There could be problems with the roof or the windows or the foundation. Do you really want to be stuck out here while the place crumbles around you?"

Rowan wished she could argue with him on

those points...and yet she knew James was right. Already she'd noticed a few leaks in the rooms on the upper floor, but because she hadn't been living up there, she'd done her best to brush aside her concerns about the damage those leaks might cause. The thought had crossed her mind that maybe she should try to get up on the roof and see how the water was getting in, although she'd realized that doing so would have been way too dangerous.

Besides, she didn't know the first thing about fixing a roof.

"No," she said, and although she didn't exactly sigh, she couldn't quite hold back the breath that escaped her lips.

He pulled her close so he could wrap his arms around her and hold her tight. It felt so good to have him there, to realize that yes, the sex had been amazing, but just being in the warm circle of his embrace was almost as wonderful. The hug told her he was genuinely worried about her...and maybe would miss her more than he wanted to admit if she didn't give in and decided to stay here.

And to what point, really? The Castle had given her shelter for several years, but it wasn't home, wasn't the place where she'd grown up and where she had any truly happy memories. She'd barely worked here for two months before the Heat swept across the world, and she'd only stayed because she was too frightened to go anywhere else.

"Okay," she whispered. "I'll go."

# Chapter 12

Although Jamal's first reaction upon hearing Rowan had relented and was willing to leave the Castle was relief, he realized a moment later that he'd created a massive problem for himself. Yes, he could pretend to be James Aguilar, an ordinary human, for most of the journey to Los Alamos, but at some point, he would have to admit the truth and let her know he wasn't quite the mortal she thought him to be.

He had every reason to believe the ensuing scene would be quite ugly, and yet he still thought he had done the right thing. All those words he'd said to her a moment earlier were nothing more than the truth; she'd been lucky so far, but if the building continued to deteriorate, eventually it would become unsafe. Better for her to be far away in Los Alamos, where he had to believe its human inhabitants were doing their best to make sure their infrastructure remained intact.

Now he placed a finger under her chin, tipping her face up toward his. "It won't be right away," he told her, his tone gentle. "We've got to let a lot more of this snow melt before it's safe to get on the road."

"True," she said. "But I guess I should try to get some more of this organized before I go. Everything that isn't in a binder should be hole-punched and put in one, just because it'll be easier to move if and when we're able to come back and get it."

This seemed like a reasonable enough plan, and would also give them something to do while they were waiting for the snow to melt. And while he couldn't control the weather, he could convince the ground beneath the snow drifts to warm slightly, just enough to make everything go away a little faster than it normally might. Some might have questioned his haste, but he could not help thinking about how the elders had caught Aamir dwelling with Isla, and how they had been forced apart until Aamir realized he wanted to take the human woman as his Chosen. Jamal had no wish to be reprimanded by the elders like a child who had disobeyed, so it seemed better to leave the Castle before they could even discover he and Rowan were here.

"That's a great idea," he said. "Let's get to work."

---

Because Rowan had already gathered as many three-ring binders as she could find on campus—supplemented by more that she'd looted from the Walmart in town—most of what they needed was already on hand. True, she'd only been using one hole-punch device because she hadn't needed any more than that, but James found a second one in what used to be the college president's office, and they were off and running.

Now that she'd decided to leave, she found herself curiously at peace. Really, it was the only smart thing to do. They'd organize this mess and gather their belongings, and then decide how long they should linger before getting on the road to Los Alamos.

"How long do you think it will take us?" she asked as they punched holes in stacks of paper covered in writing and Darby lay on the floor nearby, looking somewhat dejected because they weren't doing anything that involved food. At least she'd been taught cursive and had always had what she thought was pretty handwriting, so the pages were somewhat aesthetically pleasing. As for the dog, well, they'd break for lunch soon enough and could feed him some morsels of leftover turkey.

"To walk to Los Alamos?" James said, and she nodded. "It's about a hundred miles, so maybe three or four days, depending on the weather and the roads. I haven't been along that stretch of I-25 because I came into Las Vegas from the north, so it's hard to say."

That description of their proposed journey didn't sound quite as daunting as she'd feared. Three days on the road, and then they'd be among people. She still didn't know for sure what was going to happen between the two of them, but every passing moment in James's company made her hope a little more that this thing they shared was real and that once they were in Los Alamos, they might actually be able to succeed at being a couple.

A few days ago, such a prospect would have been nothing more than an idle fantasy. Now, though, she thought it might actually come to pass.

"And there really aren't any djinn?"

He chuckled. "Oh, there are djinn. It's just that it seems like they've stopped attacking people. I've been all over the northern part of the state and never had a problem. That's part of the reason why we've been slowly expanding out of Los Alamos. For a long time, we only went into Española to work the fields and gather what we could from the town, but now we've got a few people living there."

That revelation surprised her, although she supposed one place was as safe as another if it was protected by one of Miles Odekirk's devices. Thinking of the boxes that had been humanity's salvation, she said, "Weren't you still taking a risk by traveling without one of the devices? You'd think they would have given one of them to you, just to be safe."

James had just punched a set of holes in the page that had Rowan's best recollection of her mother's strawberry shortcake recipe. After he set it aside, he said, "Well, it was kind of important to show that it was safe to travel without one. And I think I've proved that."

"True," she allowed. If there had been any djinn out there, waiting to pounce, you'd think one would have gotten James the second he stepped outside the protected zone...or maybe not. Maybe the djinn had wanted to lure him into a false sense of security so they could get him when his guard was down.

That hadn't happened, though, and Rowan knew there was plenty of empty land out there where he would have been miles and miles away from any possible help. No, it sure sounded as if he was right and the djinn had backed off, for whatever reason. And that meant the two of them should have an uneventful walk from Las Vegas to Los Alamos. They might be pretty footsore by the time they reached their destination, but they wouldn't have to face anything except the usual hazards of the road.

James set aside the three-hole punch he'd been using and pushed back his chair. "I think it's time to take a break. Why don't we go outside and see what the weather is doing?"

Yes, that sounded like a good idea. They'd been at this for nearly two hours and had made a bigger dent in the pile than she'd first thought. Funny how much faster things went when you had two people working together.

She also pushed back her chair, then rose. Darby climbed to his feet, tail wagging, obviously hopeful that they were about to take a lunch break.

Well, first a peek outside, and then some food.

The three of them made their way down the corridor and out the front entrance, where she was surprised to see actual bare patches in the snow, while the walkways were nearly clear.

"It's sure melting fast," she remarked, and James squinted up at the sky.

"The sun's helping a lot."

True. She'd scrounged a lawn thermometer from the Walmart and set it near the path so she'd be able to get a read on the temperature as she was coming and going, and was surprised to see it was already in the upper fifties. It looked as though her guess that temps would reach sixty before they began to descend in the late afternoon had been right.

"At this rate, we'll be able to get out of here tomorrow," James said. His dark eyes scanned the sky and the horizon, obviously looking for any signs of trouble brewing.

There weren't any, though. Not a cloud in the sky, as far as Rowan could tell. In this part of the world, that didn't always mean a lot, but only a very light breeze touched the pines on the hillsides above the campus and rustled in the bare branches of the cottonwoods down near the springs, and that was a good sign.

Bad weather always came with the wind.

"Yes," she said, taking care to keep her tone light. Some part of her was still conflicted about leaving this sanctuary behind, but she knew that was her fear talking and she should ignore it. If nothing else, this amazingly mild weather should be her signal that it was time to go. She and James and Darby would walk out of here in the sunshine, and after that?

Well, she supposed she'd find out soon enough.

---

They got through a surprising amount of Rowan's unbound writings that afternoon. Not all of them, but enough that he could tell she was content with the work they had done, and wouldn't argue about leaving the following day if the weather continued to cooperate.

Jamal believed it would. Not because he had a true weather sense the way an air elemental would, but all of his people had their connections to the earth and the wind and the sky, and he guessed they had entered a period where conditions would continue to be mild for at least a few more days, possibly as much as a week. That would be more than enough time to get to Los Alamos...or at least, the border of the zone the devices protected, where he would have to part ways from Rowan.

An inner voice whispered to him that this haste was foolish, and it would make much more sense to linger here for a few more days so he could maximize his time with her. But as much as he'd come to enjoy her company...and as much as he looked forward to tonight, when they would be able to share a real bed...he also knew that doing so was unwise. Better to leave as soon as possible and take advantage of the break in the weather.

To that end, he helped her decide what to take with her—she had a surprising amount of clothing for someone who'd been living here in isolation for the past four years—and also promised her that they would leave everything in the kitchen and the bathroom neat and tidy when they departed the following morning.

"I know it's kind of silly," she said that night over dinner. They'd used the turkey leftovers and some root vegetables from the cellar to make a surprisingly hearty soup, and drank another of the bottles of wine she also kept down there to remain cool no matter what the season of the year. "After all, I doubt anyone's going to come this way after we're gone. But after everything this place has done for me, I just feel like it deserves to be left in decent shape."

"I understand," Jamal said, and he thought he truly did. Some might have said this was only a building, but besides Darby, it had been the only thing of consequence in her life for far too long. "And we'll make sure it's clean and everything's closed up tight. Who knows? Maybe someday there'll be enough people to expand in this direction. There had to be a reason why Las Vegas sprang up here in the first place."

"I learned in school that it was a land grant by the Mexican government, way back in the 1830s," Rowan replied. "But I think the land was valuable because of Gallina Creek. Water's pretty scarce in New Mexico. Then later, the railroad came through and the place boomed."

"And the water is still here," Jamal said. "So I

can see why people might want to come back eventually."

"Here's hoping." Rowan lifted her glass of merlot, and he gently clinked his against it.

"Here's hoping," he echoed, and wondered exactly what he should be hoping for.

*For this not to end,* he realized, but changing course now made no sense. No, he and Rowan had already agreed they would leave tomorrow, and trying to alter their plans would only raise far too many uncomfortable questions.

The conversation shifted there to what they might expect on the long road to Los Alamos. Jamal explained that the fastest way to get there would be to follow the highway, since because they were on foot, they'd be able to weave around the abandoned vehicles without too much trouble.

"Maybe we should try to find a motorcycle," Rowan suggested, but Jamal only shook his head.

"Anything that's been sitting for that long probably wouldn't run," he said, which was true. Djinn had no need to worry about such things, but he'd heard gas could go stale and batteries die after sitting unused for months or years, and certainly enough time had passed for both types of malfunction to be a real issue.

Her expression fell, but then she nodded as she picked up her spoon. "You're right," she replied. "It's been so long since I've used anything except an e-bike that I kind of forgot about that stuff. Walking can get tedious, but at least it's not complicated."

No, it was not. Even the djinn form of locomotion for those who weren't air elementals wasn't terribly difficult—they blinked themselves from the place where they stood to the next spot they could see, and would move that way over and over again until they reached any destination they hadn't previously visited. It was a form of travel that was surprisingly efficient, eating up miles and miles in a short amount of time.

Unfortunately, since Rowan had no idea he was anything other than human, it wasn't one they could avail themselves of now.

"It'll go faster than you think," he said. "Especially with the snow disappearing so quickly. By noon tomorrow, the way should be mostly clear—especially on the highway, since it should melt even more quickly there."

She nodded, although he got the feeling her thoughts had moved elsewhere. And if the flicker of her gaze upward was any indication, she was thinking about what was to follow this, their last dinner at the Castle.

However, she didn't say anything about that, only made a noncommittal sound before sipping some of her soup.

Well, he would leave it alone. There was not so much of this dinner left, after all.

In fact, they finished their soup and their wine not too long after that and gathered their bowls and glasses so they could wash everything and put it in the dish drain on the counter. When they were done, though, Rowan turned toward him.

"My room has the most comfortable bed," she said. "I know, because I tried all of them before I chose that one to sleep in."

"Just like Goldilocks," he joked, and her warm brown eyes lit with amusement.

"I guess so," she replied. Then her gaze met his. "It'll be a little cramped, but…."

Already heat moved through him, even though they stood a few feet away from one another. Without answering, he reached out and twined his fingers with hers so he could pull her close, could kiss her lovely mouth and taste the traces of merlot on her lips.

She responded by parting those lips, letting him taste her more, even as he felt himself harden against those stiff, uncomfortable "jeans" that humans insisted on wearing. Once again, he found himself wishing she knew the truth about him, just so he could blink the two of them upstairs and directly into her room, and not have to waste any time walking there.

But this was not the time…or rather, he would

not allow it to be...so he had to content himself with taking her by the hand and hurrying up the steps and into her room, where his fingers found the hem of the teal sweater she wore and pulled it up and over her head. Despite the relative warmth of the day, it was chillier in here than he'd expected, and he murmured a brief, "Sorry," so he could lean over and toggle the switch on the space heater near the nightstand.

Warm air immediately began churning into the room, and Rowan seemed to take that as a signal that turnabout was fair play, since she grabbed his long-sleeved T-shirt and pulled it off as well. Her hands as they moved down his shoulders to his chest were not cold at all, telling him she was just as eager for this encounter as he was.

They fell onto the narrow bed, fingers flying as they pulled off socks and jeans and underwear, pausing only so they could draw the covers over them to protect themselves from the still chilly air in the room. Jamal detected just the smallest sigh from the foot of the bed, probably a resigned Darby settling himself on the floor until his people were finished with their current activities.

*You may be waiting a while, Darby,* Jamal thought with an inner grin.

After that, though, there was nothing more than Rowan, nothing more than the sweet taste of her flesh, the surprising strength of her hands as she stroked him before taking him into her mouth.

Ah, God. Jamal leaned back against the pillows and reveled in the sensation of her pleasuring him, of the delicious strokes of her tongue against his shaft. He would not allow himself to climax, though—no, he wanted to do that while buried in her, so once he knew he was getting close to the danger point, he pulled away from her and shifted so his mouth moved down her wonderfully flat belly, down to her mound, so he might suckle on her.

She gasped, her hands burying themselves in his hair as he tasted her, licked her, until he could tell from the way her breathing sped up and her moans grew intense that she was about to come. And yes, there were more of her delicious juices, which he lapped up before shifting so he could enter her.

Ah, that was what he wanted most, to feel himself deep inside her, to have her lithe legs wrapped around him as she drove him deeper. His mouth found hers, and they kissed, finding their rhythm, moving faster and faster until the orgasm hit, so intense that the world seemed to spin around him, even while she gasped aloud as well as she reached her own climax.

And then to hold on to her while her breathing quieted, to press his lips against her tumbled hair and know it was the color of pure copper, so rare among his people. To realize that he wanted nothing more than this...only to lie here with Rowan in his arms, to know they were safe and warm and the only two people in the world.

Well, at least for a little while.

## Chapter 13

Sometime after she and James had made love, Darby jumped onto the bed and smooshed himself up against their feet, and Rowan, still flushed with the aftermath of the encounter, only chuckled and reached down to pat the dog on the head before she snuggled against James once again. As she'd thought, it was awfully cramped in here, two people and a dog crammed together in this twin bed, but she didn't mind. It felt cozy and warm, and she thought this was fitting for their last night here at the Castle, to all be together in bed, making their own odd little family.

*Family,* she thought, mouth lifting in a small smile, but that was her last rational thought, as sleep claimed her just a moment afterward.

Bright sunlight filtered into the room when she

awoke hours later to find James watching her with sleepy dark eyes.

"Morning," she said, and he reached over to push a strand of hair away from her face.

"Morning," he replied. His gaze moved to the clock sitting on the bedside table, which she'd done her best to keep as accurate as possible, even though it had been mostly guesswork for quite some time.

Seven-thirty.

For her—at least since the world had ended—that was sleeping in. Most of the time, she woke with the dawn, knowing she had many things to do in order to keep herself alive. In a way, though, she was glad. They hadn't set a timetable for their departure this morning, sharing an unspoken agreement that they'd leave when they left, and wouldn't worry if they got a late start.

After all, it wasn't as if anyone in Los Alamos was expecting them.

"Well, at least we're rested for our walk," she said, then sat up, although she kept the quilts and blankets pressed against her bare breasts. Not out of modesty...it wasn't as if James hadn't already gotten an eyeful the two times they'd made love so far...but because it was still cool in here despite the space heater gamely working away down on the floor by the nightstand.

"That's true," he agreed. "Coffee?"

"Perfect."

They got out from under the covers, both of them hurrying to grab the clothing they'd discarded the night before. The sweatshirt and leggings she usually wore to sleep in weren't too far away, just in the dresser on the other side of the room, but her sweater and jeans were closer.

Darby shook and jumped down from the bed, happy that his people were up and moving, which meant they'd be able to let him outside. And after they'd gone downstairs into the kitchen and Rowan had opened the door so he could go out, she saw that even more of the snow had melted than she'd thought. Yes, large patches remained under the trees and in any other shady spots, but all the walkways were clear, and although she could only see a corner of it from where she stood, it looked as if the nearest parking lot was also free of snow.

And the sun was already up and shining brightly in a cloudless sky that mirrored the one from yesterday.

"Looks like another perfect day," she said as she closed the door and turned back toward James, who'd already been busy filling the kettle so he could place it on the stove.

"That's what I was hoping for. We should be able to get on the road pretty soon after we eat and shower."

Good thing she'd washed her hair the day before, since she wouldn't have to worry about waiting to let it dry before she went out into the cool morning air. At the same time, she found herself thinking it might have been good to have one or two details to delay their departure. Now that the day had come, she found herself more nervous than she'd expected to be.

*Well, what did you think was going to happen?* she asked herself as she went to get a pair of mugs down from the cupboard. *It's been four years since you went anywhere other than Las Vegas. The world out there is a scary place.*

Maybe not quite as frightening as it had been at the beginning, but still, she realized she was taking James's word that they wouldn't encounter any djinn on the road to Los Alamos, would only have to contend with whatever wildlife they might encounter.

Which might not be all that much, since she had to believe that coyotes and bears had better things to do than roam around a deserted highway when they had all of northern New Mexico to wander looking for food or prey.

James poured some ground coffee into the machine—she got the feeling he didn't want to waste time grinding beans this morning—and said, "It's going to be fine."

About all she could do was send him a rueful smile. "Was I that obvious?"

He set down the bag containing the coffee and came over to her so he could wrap her in a warm, welcome hug. "A little," he replied. "And I get it. But once we're away from here, you'll see there's nothing to worry about. Also, it's not like we're going to rough it. We'll swing by the Walmart and get you a sleeping bag, too, but my plan is to stay at whatever houses or hotels or other places present themselves along the way. It's not like I expect you to sleep under the stars or anything."

Rowan's arms tightened around him. It felt so good to be here like this, with the reassuring strength of his embrace and the rich, friendly scent of coffee filling the air. Right then, she wished nothing would change, even as she realized they'd be able to share this same kind of closeness in Los Alamos. Their surroundings would be a little different, but this...whatever it was that had grown between them...it would still be there.

"Good to know," she said. "When I was a kid, my family went camping a lot, but I'm kind of out of practice these days."

"We'll only sleep outside if you really want to," James told her, although the light tone in his voice made it clear he was teasing her a little.

"If it was June or July, I might take you up on that," she replied, making sure to keep her words equally casual. "At this time of year, I think I'll skip it."

His dark eyes crinkled in amusement. "Wise choice."

Darby scratched on the back door then, so she went over to open it and let him in. He immediately tracked mud all over the kitchen floor, and she let out a sigh and fetched the mop so she could clean up the mess.

"I guess that's the downside of a fast melt," James remarked. The coffee was done brewing, so he picked up the carafe and filled a mug for her.

"You can say that again," Rowan said. She rinsed the mop in the sink and got to work cleaning up the rest of the mud, figuring that gave her enough time to allow her coffee to cool a bit. "But I'd rather be fighting mud than snow."

He nodded, then brought his mug of coffee to his mouth so he could take a cautious sip. Rowan noticed how he didn't tell her it was silly to expend her energy on cleaning up Darby's mess when they were going to be leaving in a couple of hours. No, James could clearly tell she was determined to leave the Castle in as good shape as possible, even if it might take a little extra time and energy.

However, when he said they should throw out anything from the refrigerator that they wouldn't be taking with them, she didn't argue. The canned stuff in the pantry was one thing; it would last for years, if not forever. But there was no point in leaving behind anything that was sure to spoil.

That was why, after they made some bundles of provisions for the road, they took everything else out to the compost heap and the trash cans she kept behind the building.

"I'll leave the lids off, though," she said as they dumped the last of the stuff from the fridge. "That way, the raccoons can get at it."

James's eyebrows tilted at an amused angle. "I'm pretty sure they'd be able to get that trash even with the lids on."

All right, he had a point there. Still, leaving the trash freely available felt like a little parting gift for the raccoons, even though the cute little critters had driven her nuts more than once as she did her best to keep them from getting into the garbage and making an utter mess out there.

That task made her feel a little lighter, as if removing the food from the refrigerator was the final step in releasing her from this place. Yes, they still had to pack, but that wouldn't take very long. All her writings had been put in folders and stacked in the dining hall, so they would be easy to pick up in case she—or anyone else—ever came this way again. There really wasn't much left to do.

In fact, after eating the last of the bread with some jam, all they had to do was go upstairs and brush their teeth one final time, then fetch their things. Rowan had found a large backpack in one of the student rooms a while back and had used it to transport items from her foraging expeditions in Las Vegas, so that was what she deployed now to carry the belongings she would take with her to Los Alamos.

And one last thing.

She opened the single drawer in her bedside table and pulled out the framed photo it contained. The picture had been taken at her brother Henry's wedding, so she and her parents and her brothers were all dressed up, Charlie and Henry looking stiff and formal in their charcoal gray suits, her father in a lighter gray suit and her mother in a pretty blue-gray dress that worked well with her red hair. Rowan had been a bridesmaid, so her gown was a deeper shade of blue, and she wore much more makeup than she ever had in her day-to-day life. In fact, with the makeup and her coppery hair worked into long, loose curls, that image of herself almost seemed like a stranger, or maybe like someone she'd known a long time ago but whose name she couldn't even remember.

"That's a nice picture," James said from behind her shoulder, and she startled, then realized of course he would want to see what she was looking at, since he'd been only a few feet away packing his own things. "From a wedding?"

"My oldest brother Henry's," she replied. "It was in May...right before."

No need to say anything other than that. James would know just as well as any other human still alive today that everything would be forever divided between now and before, that nothing had ever been the same after that terrible week in late September.

No response, only a soft kiss against her hair, once again telling her how lucky she was that it had been James whom she'd found washing up in the spring only a few days earlier. He could have been a cold man, or a mean and angry man, but he was none of those things.

No, he was perfect.

She shoved the photo into her backpack and zipped it up. It was something she'd gone to claim on one of her trips to Las Vegas, and even then, a little more than a year after the Dying, she'd seen the changes in her family home, the way the paint on the siding was already beginning to fade and chip, how the lawn her father had once dutifully mowed every other day was now a mass of weeds. At the time, she'd had the wild idea that she should try to tidy up, should remove the weeds and do what she could to preserve the place, even as she realized that was a crazy idea. She might as well have lit a signal fire to let the djinn know exactly where she was.

If there had even been any djinn around at that point. James had made it sound as though things had been safe for around the past two years or so, but she hadn't seen any evidence of the vicious elementals after that first month following the Dying. Most likely, they hadn't seen any reason to hang around in a place that was so obviously deserted.

"I'm glad you have it," James said softly. "Ready?"

She nodded. Sure, there were probably a few minor tasks she could have handled before they left, but she knew trying to tackle them would have been a delaying tactic and nothing more.

A breath, and then she said, "I'm ready."

---

Something about seeing the photo of Rowan's family awoke an odd, niggling ache deep inside him. Of course, Jamal knew she must have lost them in the Dying, just like all the other mortals who still lived and walked on this earth had lost their families, but still, that glimpse of their faces had made them seem real, something more than a number or part of a huge, undifferentiated mass. All of them dressed up and smiling, putting on their best faces for the camera. Rowan had obviously inherited her red locks from her mother, a pretty woman who looked as though she'd been in her late forties or early fifties at the time the photo was taken, while her father and her brothers all had the same mid-brown hair.

However, since he could tell Rowan didn't want to talk about them, he'd let it alone after placing a kiss against her sweet-smelling hair. This was not the time for confidences, after all, not when he knew they would be parting forever at the end of this journey.

He found he didn't like that idea very much, even though he was the one who'd pressed her to leave the Castle and go to Los Alamos to be among her own kind. However, there was nothing else he could do. While it might have been amusing to entertain himself with notions of whisking her away to his home in Jackson Hole and spending the winter with her there, he knew the elders would never allow him to do such a thing.

Especially now, when they'd already caught Aamir trying to break the rules in exactly the same way. He had no reason to believe the elders had been watching him more closely than they might have watched any other djinn...but at the same time, he could see how they might want to do that very thing, just to make sure the entire al-Qadir family had learned their lesson.

No, he and Rowan took their backpacks downstairs and fetched the food—both theirs and

Darby's—from the kitchen, then headed out. Just like the day before, the sun shone warmly overhead, and if it weren't for the telltale patches of snow that still lingered beneath the trees or in other shady spots, he might have thought the storm of several days ago had been a dream and nothing more.

It was real, though. It was real, because he knew without that storm, he and Rowan might never have found their way into each other's arms.

They walked along the road and into town, where she guided him to the local Walmart so they could find a sleeping bag for her. This detour also allowed them to grab a box of energy bars, just in case the food they'd brought with them wasn't sufficient to last the entire distance.

"I'm surprised you didn't take all of these already," he said after they'd stuffed the energy bars in his rucksack and secured the newly acquired sleeping bag to the backpack she was carrying.

Her shoulders lifted—only a little, because she wasn't as mobile now with that overstuffed pack to carry. "I took some," she replied. "But I never knew if someone else might come this way, and I didn't see the point in picking the place clean when I was doing okay with the rabbits and the trout and the stuff from the garden. And now I'm glad I didn't eat all of it, because otherwise we wouldn't have had anything to bring with us."

Once again, he thought of how resourceful she'd been, and yet at the same time still worried about others even while she was trying to manage her own survival. He somehow doubted many other humans would have acted the same way.

Or perhaps they would. If the past few days had taught him anything, it was that he understood very little about mortals despite all the books he had read and the films he had watched. The reality was so much more than he had expected...Rowan was so much more, with her passion, her kindness, her utter grit, for lack of a better word.

He would always be grateful to her for teaching him a lesson he might never have otherwise learned.

They set out from the Walmart, this time making their way to the highway Rowan called "I-25," presumably because it had been an interstate in the time before, connecting New Mexico and Colorado. Unlike the roads around Santa Fe and Taos, which had been cleared years before by the djinn known as the One Thousand, the highway here was still littered with cars. Not as many as there had been in Albuquerque or Denver, of course, because this part of the world had always been sparsely populated, but still, there were enough that trying to negotiate their path on even a motorcycle might have been dangerous.

Rather, dangerous to Rowan. Jamal knew that an accident would pose very little trouble for him, as any injuries he suffered would have healed themselves almost as quickly as they occurred.

"Where do you plan to stay tonight?" she asked after they passed the last exit at the south end of Las Vegas. Something in her expression was resigned, as if she knew now there would be no turning back from here.

"Probably Pecos," he replied. "Or maybe Glorieta. I doubt we'll be able to get much farther than that since it's still a good twenty miles at least from there to Santa Fe. This'll be the longest stretch of the trip, but there just isn't much between Pecos and Las Vegas."

Rowan only nodded; Jamal guessed she must have made this trip plenty of times by car, since he could tell that tiny Las Vegas had been seriously lacking in amenities, and she probably knew as well as he did what sort of towns and settlements lay along this stretch of highway.

However, thinking of Santa Fe made him frown inwardly—he knew that the One Thousand and their Chosen occupied the state's former capital, and there was no way they could take the most direct route through town to get to Los Alamos. No, he would have to concoct some sort of story about the streets at the heart of the town being clogged with vehicles and unsafe, forcing them to take what had once been the truck relief route on the outskirts of the city. That area was still technically a part of the Santa Fe settlement, and yet the scouting he and his brothers had done seemed to indicate that very few djinn had taken homes there. It should be safe enough.

He hoped.

Out here, more snow still remained in the empty fields to either side of the highway, since he had done nothing to help along the melting process the way he had with the grounds immediately surrounding the Castle. However, the sun was bright and fierce, and that, combined with the dark surface of the road, made it so the way in front of them was barely even damp any longer.

Partway through the day, they stopped at the side of the highway to drink from the water bottles they'd filled and have a snack, and allow Darby to run off into a clump of bushes to do his business. He and Rowan would also have to do something about that at some point, but since she hadn't made any comments along those lines so far, he guessed their own bathroom breaks could wait a while longer.

Once they were walking again, she said, "There used to be a gas station a few miles ahead. I'm trying to hang on until then."

"Thanks for the intel," Jamal replied. "I was starting to worry, especially since there aren't even any trees to hide behind out here."

No, there weren't. Off in the distance, he'd

occasionally spotted ranches with a few bare trees clustered around them, but the land closer to the highway was noticeably empty. It would have been difficult to have any kind of privacy.

But Rowan's memory had been correct, and they only had to walk three more miles or so to get to the gas station she'd mentioned. It was a rundown-looking place, probably not all that well-maintained even before the Dying, but the past four years of being left untouched guaranteed at least there was no remaining biological matter to worry about, and they were quickly done and back out on the road.

"Do you think we're making good enough time?" Rowan asked, craning her head up to take a look at the angle of the sun.

Jamal feared they weren't—they hadn't left the Castle until nearly ten, losing several valuable morning hours—but he didn't see the point in worrying her now until it became apparent they wouldn't reach Pecos before nightfall. "We're covering some ground."

Because she was wearing sunglasses and a baseball cap, he couldn't see much of her expression. However, it was impossible to miss the sideways flick of her glance toward him. "That's not an answer."

"It's hard to say," he replied. "I don't know this part of I-25 very well."

At least that hadn't been a lie.

"Well," she went on, apparently undaunted, "if you don't think we can make it, we can stop for the night in San Jose. It's a tiny town, but it's close enough to the highway that we won't have to go miles out of our way."

As she spoke, they approached a sign indicating that San Jose was ten miles away, with Pecos twenty-two. Since it was now well into the afternoon, he knew there was no way in the world they'd be able to walk twenty-plus miles in the three or four hours of daylight left to them, not when they were both carrying heavy packs.

"All right," he said. "San Jose it is."

---

There wasn't an off-ramp for San Jose, but Rowan and James and Darby were able to cross over to the northbound side of I-25 so they could scramble down the embankment and make their way into town by that route.

Well, "town" was kind of an exaggeration. Mostly, San Jose was a wide spot in the road, with not much more than a couple of double-wides, a few houses, and a large corrugated structure Rowan guessed had once been used to store hay or alfalfa. Nothing there looked exactly inviting, but they headed for the biggest of the houses since it looked to be in the best repair, two stories and made out of the same ruddy-hued stone that had been used to construct the Castle.

The front door wasn't locked, which didn't surprise Rowan too much. She'd noticed that lots of people had left their houses unlocked during the Heat, although she had no idea whether that was because they were so delirious from the fever that they didn't know what they were doing, or simply because they'd never been the type to worry about that kind of stuff because they figured their neighborhood was safe.

This house had quite a collection of sturdy, rustic furniture painted in bright colors, probably from Mexico. Rowan knew those sorts of pieces tended to be expensive, just because her mother had one painted cabinet in a similar style that she'd been inordinately proud of. It was surprising to find that kind of furniture here, and she wondered if maybe this house had been some kind of vacation getaway for someone with money.

Whatever the reason for the decor, the house felt solid and safe, if a little dank and chilly. There hadn't been any way they could bring a space heater along, obviously, but James scouted around the property and found some wood that wasn't too damp, and after peering up into the flue, he declared the fireplace safe and lit them a fire.

That made things much better, and they huddled together in front of the hearth and ate a spare meal of turkey leftovers and a granola bar broken in half. While it would have been better for them to cover more ground today, Rowan found herself content enough. She was here with James and Darby, and they'd found shelter for the night. With the sleeping bags, they could camp in front of the fireplace and be relatively comfortable until it was time for them to get moving tomorrow morning.

After they zipped their sleeping bags together and climbed inside, she said, "I guess it's a good thing we grabbed those energy bars. If our trip goes an extra day, we're going to need them."

James reached over and pulled her close, although she could tell he was only trying to give her some warmth and comfort, and not initiate anything. As much as she wanted him, she could understand that. This house might have stood empty for more than four years, but it still wasn't theirs. Having sex on the floor of the living room would have seemed rude.

"We might be okay," he said. "If we get an early enough start tomorrow, we can make up some time."

His tone was so cheerful that she knew he wasn't annoyed with her for taking so long leaving the Castle this morning. That hadn't been her intention, though—it was just how things had worked out.

"Well, I don't see myself sleeping until nine, that's for sure," she joked. "I mean, what time is it now?"

"I have no idea," James replied. "Past sundown, but that's all I've got."

Yes, the world had grown dark while they ate in front of the fire. Probably, the hour was barely past seven, but what difference did it make? There was something to be said for going to sleep when you were tired and getting up when you were ready to start the day. Clocks really didn't factor into that kind of lifestyle.

That was why she didn't have a problem with laying her head against his shoulder and gently drifting off to sleep...or waking the next morning when the world outside was little more than a gray blur. She and James both got out of the sleeping bag, since they'd slept fully clothed except for their boots, and she let Darby out in the yard while James went exploring. A moment later, he reappeared, a wide grin on his lips and a full bucket swinging from one hand.

"They had a well," he explained as he set the bucket down on the hearth. "I had to switch it over to manual, but I found the bucket right by it, so it was easy to get some water."

"Seriously, is there anything you can't do?"

Rowan asked. She'd been dreading having to dole out only a small amount of water to splash on her face and wash her hands and brush her teeth, so having an entire bucket to work with seemed like heaven. No, she wouldn't be able to shower, of course, but she'd already resigned herself to that not-so-pleasant reality.

His grin didn't fade. "Oh, probably a few things."

She made a face at him, but that didn't prevent her from refilling her water bottle with well water and putting some more water in Darby's travel bowl as well. James refilled his bottle, too, and then they both rinsed off their faces and hands before grabbing a quick breakfast of another granola bar and a few bites of turkey for some energy to last them through the morning.

Because they'd gotten up so early, the sun was barely peeking over the ridges to the east as they made their way down San Jose's one and only street, and back onto the highway. The sky was clear, promising another day of easy walking, but Rowan was still glad of the puffer coat she wore. Even though daytime temperatures would probably rise into the low sixties again, it felt as if it was hovering around freezing now and might take hours to get anywhere near comfortable.

That was all right, though—they set a brisk pace, as if both of them wanted to eat up as much ground as possible today. Not much talking, but that was all right, too. She thought it was just fine to have James next to her and Darby ranging ahead, tail wagging as if he thought he'd been taken on the best adventure ever.

When they reached Pecos at a little past noon, James sent an inquiring glance in her direction.

"We've got six hours of daylight," she said. "Even if we can't make it all the way to Santa Fe, we'll at least be able to reach Eldorado."

"Another town?"

"Sort of," Rowan replied, trying to figure out the best way to explain the place. "It's kind of a suburb of Santa Fe, even though it's around ten miles outside the city center. But there are houses there, and even a grocery store if you go about a mile off the highway."

"Sounds good," James said. "I guess I've seen the sign for the turn-off, but like I said yesterday, I don't know this part of the world all that well."

Neither did she, but her family had driven this stretch of I-25 enough times that she mostly knew where things were, even if she wasn't super-familiar with all the various points of interest. It just made sense to have a backup plan in mind in case they couldn't quite reach their intended destination after all.

"Well, Eldorado it is," she replied, adding, "just in case."

He nodded, and they continued down the highway. As they moved along, she realized this stretch of the road was a lot hillier than she'd remembered and thought it was a good thing that they'd decided on Eldorado as an interim stopping place. Going up and down all these various grades was taking a lot more time than she'd anticipated.

However, they managed to chug up that last hill just before reaching the turn-off, although Rowan found herself breathing heavily by the time they were done, and very, very glad that they were about to descend toward their chosen off-ramp.

As they reached the crest, though, her eyes narrowed.

Was someone standing in the middle of the interstate, blocking their way?

No, she realized, her heart seeming to stop in her chest.

Not just someone.

A djinn.

He wore dark robes that fluttered in the breeze, and she couldn't see his face clearly because his tall form was silhouetted against the setting sun. But there was no mistaking the cool menace in his voice when he spoke, even if the words didn't make any sense.

"Hello, brother," the strange djinn said. "I thought I might find you coming this way."

# Chapter 14

How could Omar have located them here? True, the three al-Qadir brothers had a closer connection to one another than most djinn did with their siblings, simply because only a few years separated them rather than decades or even centuries. But still, if Omar had known where he was all this time, why had he waited so long to strike?

*Because he wanted you to think all was well,* a cool voice somewhere deep within told Jamal. *He wanted to catch you when you were at your most vulnerable, when you were weary and footsore and believed you were close to this evening's destination.*

For of course he would not have tried something like this anywhere closer to the Santa Fe djinns' territory. As far as Jamal knew, no one had settled in Eldorado, for they still had plenty of options for housing much closer to the city center.

Next to him, Rowan was white-faced, even with the warm light of the lowering sun bathing all of them. And yes, she should be afraid...although perhaps not for the reasons she thought.

"You will let us pass," he said, making sure to keep his voice calm and steady. "This has nothing to do with you, Omar."

At those words, Rowan stared up at him in shock, even as Darby hung back, clearly understanding this was people business and that he needed to stay out of it. "You *know* this djinn?"

"Of course he does," Omar cut in before Jamal could reply. "For he is my older brother." And as her mouth dropped open, he added, wearing a smug smile, "Ah, I see dear Jamal has not been entirely truthful with you, has he? But I already suspected as much, considering he wears the guise of a human."

"You—" Rowan began, but Jamal shook his head. He would not command her to keep silent, but he hoped she would understand that this was not the time for arguments. Later, perhaps...once they had survived this encounter.

"I am taking this woman to Los Alamos," Jamal said, still doing his best to maintain his composure. Inside, he was perhaps not quite as calm, and yet he knew the best thing he could do was try to defuse the situation rather than be provoked into an outright confrontation.

But since his hotheaded brother was involved, he knew his chances of succeeding at such an endeavor were not very good.

"Indeed?" Omar returned with a sneer. In looks, he was very like his two brothers, with night-dark hair and eyes, although his features were just a bit more finely chiseled, his straight nose an echo of their mother's. "I was unaware you had decided to start a taxi service for humans. It seems some of our brother Aamir's madness has now spread to you as well."

Was it madness? Jamal did not think so, although he had to admit some of the other reavers —his younger brother included—might have something to say on that subject. All he knew was that it had become paramount to him to make sure Rowan reached Los Alamos safely...even if somewhere deep inside, he wished they would never have to part.

Rowan's hands were on her hips, and even though she was still almost preternaturally pale, her flame-colored hair even brighter in the orange shimmer of the setting sun, she didn't look afraid.

No, she looked angry.

"What does any of this have to do with you?" she demanded of Omar. "James...I mean, Jamal... told me that djinn weren't even hunting humans anymore. So what difference does it make if he takes me to Los Alamos?"

Looking at her, Jamal could not help but admire her bravery, especially after experiencing the shock of learning he was not what he pretended to be. However, he also knew his younger brother would not appreciate her show of courage.

No, not at all.

Omar's lips thinned. "It makes a difference to me, for he and our older brother swore an oath to continue with the eradication of the human race, even after the other djinn put aside their swords and moved on to a more peaceful life. Aamir has already betrayed us, and I will not allow Jamal to do the same."

As he spoke those last words, the ground beneath them rumbled, and cracks began to appear in the asphalt. Next to him, Rowan stared around in shock, for she most likely had never experienced a true earthquake. New Mexico was not a seismically active state, and although it might have suffered a tremor here and there, it would have been nothing like this. Poor Darby was already huddled on the ground, tail tucked between his legs, as if he knew there was nothing he could do except hope his people would somehow protect him.

"Get down," he commanded, and even though Rowan's eyes blazed and he knew he would have many questions to answer after all this was done... assuming they survived...she did as he said, dropping to a crouch so she would not be knocked off her feet in the event of another quake.

For himself, he straightened and cast aside the human disguise he'd been wearing so he might face his wayward brother, djinn against djinn. Even so, he knew he had to try once more to show Omar that it did not have to be this way.

"This woman has caused no harm," he said. "She has lived quietly, in isolation, since the Dying. She is not the reason why we set upon our course all those years ago."

Omar's nostrils flared in disgust. "She is human, and that is reason enough. Too many mortals already dwell in Los Alamos, and I see no need for there to be any more."

Once again, the earth shook, and the faint cracks that had already appeared began to widen. Now they were gaps of a few inches each, manageable enough, and yet Jamal knew this was only the beginning.

Since it was clear that his brother would not be moved, he did not bother to waste further breath on arguments. No, he met him with the same weapon, earth elemental versus earth elemental.

The ground didn't merely shake, but instead rolled, sending chunks of asphalt flying in Omar's direction. He ducked, features contorted with fury, while somewhere behind him, Rowan let out a startled little shriek. Out of the corner of his eye, he could see she remained crouched on all fours, desperately trying to ride the tumultuous earth the way a cowboy might try to hang on to a bucking bronco.

"All this, for one stupid human?" Omar said. "You have lost your way, brother, and it seems it is my duty to help you find it again."

Another rumble of the highway beneath their feet, only this time, the seismic wave seemed to crack at the end, sending Rowan flying into the air. Jamal ran to catch her, snagging her by one wrist and pulling her into his arms before she could fall to the heaving roadway.

Terrified brown eyes met his. "Are you all right?" he murmured, and she nodded.

"What—what are you going to do?"

"Whatever I have to," he said, then set her back down.

His will pushed deep into the earth, setting off a geyser of dirt that erupted from the asphalt surface and struck Omar full-on. He stumbled backward, eyes hard and glittering as obsidian.

"You will regret that," he snapped, and again the ground shook beneath Jamal's feet.

But he had been expecting that, and sent an answering tremor in his brother's direction, causing the stressed asphalt to crack even further, opening up a fissure that Omar just barely managed to jump across.

Face contorted, he extended a hand, and the highway convulsed again, the surface beginning to show a spiderweb of cracks. Jamal had no idea how much torture the material could take, but he doubted it could go on like this forever.

He didn't quite lose his balance, but he had to put out his hands to steady himself. After he had done so, he realized that Omar had meant the tremor as a distraction and nothing more, because he made a great leap so he landed where Rowan was standing, and reached out to seize her by the arm so he might pull her toward him.

*No.* Whatever his brother intended to do then —disappear with her so he might torture her in private, or simply throttle her in front of Jamal's eyes—he knew he could not allow it to happen.

And there was only one thing...one terrible, desperate thing...he could do to stop his brother.

The question was, did he have the courage?

Since the alternative was to witness the woman he cared for being murdered before his eyes, Jamal knew there could be only one answer to that question.

Straightening, he glared at Omar and called out, "Rowan Aames is my Chosen, and my protection is given to her!"

At once, Omar let go of Rowan's arm as if it had suddenly become a hissing viper.

"Are you mad?" he demanded. If he had been a fire elemental, flames of rage surely must have danced around him. As it was, the ground below their feet rumbled once again, but not with enough force to cause any of them to lose their balance.

No, the tremor was merely Omar's way of venting his fury.

"I am not mad," Jamal replied, feeling oddly calm now that the fateful moment had passed. "But I also cannot allow Rowan to suffer any harm. She is my Chosen now, and you should know all too well the fate of those who have dared to lift a hand against a djinn's partner."

His brother's hands knotted into fists. However, Jamal somehow understood that Omar would cause Rowan no further harm. The risks were far too great, and the younger djinn, impetuous and angry as he might be, had no desire to have the elders banish him to the outer circles for the crime of harming a Chosen.

Instead, his mouth curled into a contemptuous smile. "Enjoy your victory, brother. I am certain you will soon learn it was a hollow one."

And then he disappeared, leaving Jamal and Rowan standing alone on that stretch of buckled and ruined highway, with Darby still crouched against the broken pavement as if he did not quite know what he should do next.

Rowan turned toward Jamal, spots of angry color showing in her pale cheeks.

"Just what the *hell* is a Chosen?"

---

Rowan didn't know what her brain had a harder time accepting—that the awful djinn named Omar had actually disappeared, or that the man standing in front of her was the terrible elemental's brother.

James—*Jamal,* she reminded herself—looked subtly different now, maybe a little older and harder, and even more preternaturally handsome than he'd been when he'd appeared to her as James Aguilar. How he'd made his regular human clothes disappear and be replaced by the dark, vaguely Middle Eastern–looking robes he wore now, she wasn't sure.

Djinn magic, she supposed.

He watched her, dark eyes wary. However, his voice was gentle enough when he spoke.

"Chosen...that is a very long story, and one I would prefer not to relate here."

Well, she supposed she could see how a cracked and ruined highway out in the middle of nowhere with night falling might not be the best place for an in-depth convo. Voice shaking a little, she said, "Then where?"

Jamal came closer to her. "We will go to my home to talk. After that...."

The words trailed off, and before she could react, he'd come close to her and put his arms around her waist. She began to pull away, knowing she didn't want this kind of contact with him, now that she knew he was a djinn, but his grasp on her only tightened, even as he reached out to Darby. The dog shook and got slowly to his feet, and came over so Jamal could lift him with his free hand.

"This is how your people must travel with mine," he said. "It will only take a moment, but don't let go, no matter what."

Not exactly the most reassuring words in the world. He'd hardly finished speaking, however, before the dusky highway around them disappeared and they stood in the living room of a strange house, one done very much in the lodge style, with rustic paneling on the walls and an absolutely breathtaking view of what she thought might be the Grand Tetons, purple with dusk, outside the floor-to-ceiling windows.

"This is your house?" she asked after Jamal had let go of her and Darby, who dropped to the Navajo rug and looked around in confusion before apparently deciding the best thing to do was lie down a few feet away and hope that no one would notice him. "What, no Arabian palace?"

Despite the edge in her voice, Jamal smiled slightly, looking much more like the man she had first met. "All of us were given human homes to live in," he replied. "Some chose to knock them down and create something more in line with the palaces we occupied in the otherworld, while others were happy to leave their human dwellings as they were. For myself, I was not here enough to care either way."

"Because you were busy killing humans," Rowan said, her tone flat. In a way, she was surprised at herself for reacting so calmly to the situation. Shouldn't she be absolutely freaking out, worried that he was about to send her into oblivion the way he had so many others?

Maybe she was just overloaded. Or maybe she'd realized if he'd really wanted her dead, he could have stood by and let his brother do the deed.

"Once, yes," Jamal said. He inclined his head toward the large dark green leather sectional that dominated the room. "I think it would be better if you sat down."

Now that she thought about it, her legs did feel shaky, like someone had replaced her knee joints with rubber instead of bone. She managed to go over to the "L" of the sectional and sat, then stared up at Jamal expectantly.

"All right," she said. "I'm sitting down. Now are you going to tell me about all this Chosen crap?"

Something about the set of his jaw seemed to tense, but instead of replying right away, he sat down as well, making sure a decent distance remained between them.

"I would not say it is 'crap,'" he said. "But I can see you are upset, so we will not worry about that for now."

"Of course I'm upset," she snapped. "You lied to me. You made me think you were a regular human. And then we...."

She let the words trail off, mostly because she couldn't even begin to think of what to say. How was it possible that they'd been intimate when it seemed as though the djinns' only goal in life was to stomp on humans the way they might a bunch of cockroaches that had invaded their kitchen?

"Yes, we did," Jamal said, again in that curiously gentle tone. "It is something that has happened between humans and djinn on occasion over the centuries. Those liaisons were casual, and most of the time, the mortals involved had no idea that their partners were anything but other humans. Chosen, though...that is something different."

"Different how?" Rowan demanded.

To her utter shock, a glass of red wine appeared

on the inlaid juniper coffee table next to her, a match to the glass that had just materialized in Jamal's hand. "You might want to have a drink."

As much as she wanted to argue with him, she knew he was right about that. Without bothering to answer, she lifted the wine glass, then shot him a suspicious look.

"Is there anything weird in this?"

"'Weird'?" he repeated, looking puzzled. Then comprehension dawned in his night-hued eyes, and he shook his head. "It is not drugged, if that is what you meant. It is only a Rhone blend that I thought you might enjoy."

Still wary, Rowan lifted the glass to her nose and took an experimental sniff. It smelled good, but she wasn't sure if that proved anything. Surely a djinn would make sure that any little "extras" wouldn't give themselves away by smelling bad.

But then she realized Jamal wouldn't have to resort to drugging her wine to take advantage of her. He was a djinn—he could do pretty much anything he wanted.

Oh, what the hell.

She sipped from her glass. It was good, better than any of the Walmart rescues she'd kept socked away in the Castle's basement. But then, she supposed a djinn could also summon whatever vintage he wanted, even if it was a 1959 Chateau Lafite Rothschild or whatever the hell it was she'd heard referenced in movies as an expensive vintage.

Seeming to take the way she'd gone ahead and drunk the wine as a signal to proceed, Jamal said, "There were some among the djinn who did not agree with the eradication of the human race. We called them the One Thousand. Each of them took a human as their partner. Those humans are Chosen."

So...did that mean she was now Jamal's partner? Just a day earlier, she would have been happy to know he wanted to make things at least semi-official between them. Now, though...now she couldn't help wondering exactly what she'd been signed up for, utterly against her will.

"Go on," she said, and sipped some more of her wine.

From the way his brows pulled together, she got the impression he'd been expecting more of a reaction than those two short words. However, Rowan was doing her best to hold it together, to not let panic set in. Yes, he'd saved her from his brother...but for what?

"The Chosen are still human," Jamal went on after a pause. "But they also have something of their djinn partners' strengths as well. They never grow old, will never be ill or suffer an injury that won't heal almost instantly."

For a beat or two, Rowan only sat there, her

brain trying to catch up with the astonishing revelation he'd just made. Wait....

"Does that mean I'm immortal?" she demanded.

Now it was her turn to wait while he drank some wine. "We assume so. Or rather, those who were Chosen have only been that for four years, so it's a bit soon to comment on their immortality. But they have not aged during those years."

So...did that mean she would be twenty-seven forever? Once upon a time, she might have said that was a pretty good age to be stuck at, old enough to have gotten some life experience under her belt, but still definitely young enough to have all her health and vigor...and yes, her looks. Not that she'd ever expected to win any beauty contests, but enough people had called her pretty that she supposed she was.

"But you didn't take a Chosen," she said, her brain still doing its best to pick away at this sudden turn of events and try to make sense of everything. "You were off killing humans."

"My brothers and I were reavers," Jamal replied. If he was at all embarrassed to admit to being a mass murderer, he didn't show any sign of it. "We had taken it upon ourselves to eradicate those who had brought this world close to ruin. But never women, never children."

Was she supposed to be glad that she'd never

been at risk of dying at his hands? Cold comfort when she hadn't heard him deny all those other deaths.

"But why make me Chosen?" she asked. "I mean, your loyalties clearly don't lie with humans, right?"

"They do not," he said calmly. "But it is forbidden for djinn to harm those who are Chosen. I knew my brother was either going to kill you on the spot or take you away someplace else where he could carry out his revenge. The only way to save you was to make you my Chosen then and there. Once you were Chosen, Omar knew he would be risking banishment to the outer circles if he harmed you. That was why he left you alone and vanished."

She supposed that was something. But....

"If none of you supposedly killed women and children, then why did you think your brother was going to kill me?"

A long pause followed that question, during which Jamal sipped again from his glass of wine. At last, he said, "Because he was too angry to see reason. All he saw was that another of his brothers had betrayed him."

Although Jamal hadn't provided any details, it wasn't too hard to figure out that their older brother...Aamir?...had apparently fallen in love with a mortal and made her his Chosen. Rowan supposed that for someone like Omar, who didn't seem like the most level-headed person in the world, doing so would have seemed like the ultimate betrayal.

So seeing Jamal with another human woman must have made Omar go right around the bend.

Not the sort of brother-in-law she'd once envisioned having. Then again, during the past couple of years, she'd done her best to resign herself to the sad reality that she would never have a partner in life, let alone any in-laws.

Now, though, she didn't know what in the world was supposed to happen next. The terrible brawl between the two djinn brothers was over, but the ground still felt awfully shaky beneath her feet.

Rowan knew one thing, though.

"You didn't ask me," she said clearly, and Jamal blinked, puzzlement clear in the dark eyes she'd once thought she was getting to know.

"I didn't ask you what?"

"You didn't ask me if I wanted to be your Chosen," she replied, and at once he frowned.

"It was not the sort of situation where there was time to ask your opinion," he returned.

That reply felt like an obstinate refusal to see exactly how he'd screwed up. Before she could say anything, though, he continued.

"None of the One Thousand asked their partners to be their Chosen. It was not deemed necessary, since the alternative was to face certain death."

Rowan set down her glass of wine. The few sips she'd had should have helped to mellow her a little, but right then, she only found herself burning with righteous anger.

"So, rape is justified as long as you're saving the life of the victim."

He flinched at the ugly word, but he kept his gaze fixed on her face as he replied, "No one was forced. Or at least, that is not the impression I have of the situation. Those who were Chosen were grateful to their partners for giving them a life they could never have expected."

*And hadn't asked for,* Rowan thought, but she could tell Jamal would never see eye to eye with her on this topic. Even though he was not one of the One Thousand, he was still a djinn, and as far as she could tell, they seemed to believe their actions were always justified.

"Did I force you?" he asked, and her eyes narrowed.

"No," she replied, then added before he could respond, "but you sure as hell lied to me. Do you really think I would have slept with you if I'd known you were a djinn?"

He also set down his wine glass. However, even though she could see the angry glitter in his eyes, he sounded measured enough as he said, "Most likely not. But that is neither here nor there. What we need to do now is discuss our next steps."

Was he really that clueless? No matter how good it had been with him when she'd thought he was James, that didn't change the ugly fact that he'd foisted Chosen status on her without asking whether this was even something she wanted.

"I'll tell you what the next step is," she said. "You're going to take me to Los Alamos—or at least as close as you can get—and then we're both going to forget that any of this ever happened."

His jaw clenched again. "I'm afraid that's not possible."

She pushed herself up from the sectional, and he stood as well. He'd always had almost a foot on her, but for some reason, he seemed even taller now in those forbidding dark robes he wore. Still, she refused to let herself be intimidated.

"Why not?"

"Because," he said, a rasp of annoyance entering his voice for the first time, "you are my Chosen, and that means we must live in the community of djinn and Chosen in Santa Fe. That is what the elders have decreed—a djinn and his human partner must live in the closest such community to the location where the mortal was originally from."

Maybe once upon a time, Rowan would have been thrilled to live in Santa Fe—the town had always seemed exotic and exciting to her, with its ancient architecture and numerous high-end restaurants and shops—but now anger only flared in her again.

"So, I have no say in my life, in what I do or where I live?"

Jamal came closer. She could tell he wanted to reach out and take her hands in his, so she crossed her arms instead.

Once again, a frown tugged at his brows, but he didn't comment on her stubbornness. Instead, he told her, "It is more that you will have a different life. In time, I think you will come to realize this is the best thing that could have happened to you."

He had a mighty high opinion of himself, didn't he? Angry words rushed to her lips, but she managed to hold them back. Getting in a screaming match wasn't going to do much to argue her case.

"Right now, it seems like the worst," she said. "I don't want to spend the rest of my life with someone who lied to me about what he was." She looked down at Darby, who had remained crouched next to the sectional the whole time, looking miserable.

Dogs always hated it when their people were fighting.

Guilt flashed through her, but she knew she couldn't back down, not when it was so patently obvious who was in the wrong here.

"Then I fear we are at an impasse," Jamal replied, his voice much colder than it had been a moment earlier. "For the rules are quite clear. I cannot let you go to Los Alamos, not when you are my Chosen. You can only go to live in Santa Fe."

"Do I have to go with you?" Rowan asked, and his eyes widened slightly.

It appeared he had never considered that angle on the situation.

"What do you mean?"

"I mean," she said, enunciating each word, even though she guessed he knew exactly what she was driving at, "that it sounds like I have to go to Santa Fe, but maybe we don't have to live together. You stay here in this house, and I'll live with the other Chosen. No harm, no foul."

He didn't answer right away, only watched her with that same grim set to his mouth and that same angry flicker in his dark eyes. In a way, he looked more handsome than he'd ever been, like some brooding hero out of a gothic romance novel, and yet, she much preferred his smiles.

Or at least, the smiles he'd worn when he was pretending to be James Aguilar.

Smiles that had been a lie.

"Oh," he said slowly. "I think there may be a

great deal of harm. But if this is the way you want things to be, then I will agree to your terms.

"You will go to live in Santa Fe...alone."

# Chapter 15

Perhaps there was something he could have said, some argument he could have presented to tell Rowan that her current course of action was madness. But as much as he wracked his brains, he could come up with nothing that he thought remotely persuasive.

*She will be safe there,* he told himself. *That is the most important thing.*

True, he supposed. All the same, his soul twisted at the thought of her living in Santa Fe without him. He'd been so sure that once he'd explained himself to her, had told her why he had done what he'd done, she would understand and return to his arms. They had shared so much at the Castle and on the road, and he thought they worked very well together. Making her his Chosen had been a spur-of-the-moment decision, one he'd had no time to contemplate if he wanted to keep her alive, but he thought he would do it all over again if it meant keeping her from harm.

But she hadn't understood, had countered every argument of his with one of hers, until he realized he could not continue to fight her on this.

All he could do was hope that one day she'd realize she'd made a mistake and would ask him to finally join her in Santa Fe.

First, though, he had to take her there…and there was only one place they could possibly go.

*Aamir,* he thought, reaching out with his thoughts the way their people could, *it is Jamal. I require your help.*

*Jamal?* his brother replied, even his mental voice sounding startled. *What is the matter?*

*I saved a woman from Omar,* he replied. *But she is not ready to truly be my Chosen. I thought she could come and stay with you first while your people there find a suitable home for her.*

A silence followed that request, one that felt even more startled than Aamir's first words. But then he said, *I see much has been happening of late. I certainly never thought you would take a Chosen of your own.*

*I only did so to protect her from Omar,* Jamal said, even though he knew in his heart of hearts that the matter was somewhat more complicated than that. *For now, it is better for her to be there in Santa Fe.*

*And we will take her in,* Aamir said at once. *Have no fear of that. This is my home—I will let Isla know we are expecting a visitor.*

A brief flash in Jamal's mind of a large white house that sprawled along a ridge line to the east of Santa Fe, with a wide terrace that probably offered spectacular sunset views. It would be too late to see the sunset tonight—night had fallen while he and Rowan argued here in his house in Jackson Hole—but perhaps she would be able to view it tomorrow.

Without him.

But now he knew where his brother and the woman Isla resided, so it would be easy enough to travel there in the manner of his people. Well, as easy as it could be when the woman he carried thus was so unwilling to be held in his arms.

The mental exchange had taken place in the blink of an eye. He fixed a smile on his face as he told Rowan, "I will take you to Santa Fe now."

---

Jamal dropped her and Darby off on the terrace of a spectacular house that overlooked Santa Fe. The night remained clear and a full moon had risen, providing extra illumination in addition to the fancy wrought-iron fixtures that glowed on the white walls of the building behind them.

"This is my brother's home," he said. "He and his Chosen will be out shortly to greet you." He paused, and then Rowan heard his voice clearly in her mind.

*You need only call out to me this way, and I will come to you when you are ready.*

She drew in a breath and almost wished he still held her, just because the shock of hearing him in her thoughts this way was enough to send her reeling.

*How...what?*

*It is how we djinn can communicate with our Chosen,* he told her. *No matter how far away I am, I will hear you.*

He reached out to touch her hair, a tender caress she hadn't been expecting, considering the way they'd spoken to each other only a short while earlier, and then disappeared.

Darby let out a short bark, obviously not happy about seeing one of his people vanish like that. Rowan bent down to give his ears a reassuring scratch and immediately straightened when she noticed one of the French doors that fronted the terrace beginning to open.

A tall man—a djinn—emerged, accompanied by a strikingly pretty woman who appeared to be a few years younger than Rowan. The light from the outdoor lamps was bright enough that she could tell the djinn looked very much like Jamal, with the same inky hair and eyes, the same chiseled features, although a little harsher than Jamal's, a little less friendly.

But no, that wasn't a very kind descriptor, because he smiled upon seeing her, and held out a hand. "I am Aamir, Jamal's older brother, and this is Isla Dunbar, my Chosen."

"Hi," Rowan replied, wondering if they found this moment as awkward as it felt to her. Even though she believed she was in the right about the current situation, she couldn't help thinking that it was kind of a big ask to have the brother of the man she'd just rejected take her in as a house guest.

Isla came over and bent to hold out a hand to Darby, who gave it a curious sniff. "What's his name?"

"Darby," Rowan supplied immediately, glad that the other woman had offered such a good way to break the ice. "I found him in Las Vegas. He's been my best buddy these past four years."

The dog's tail began wagging, as if he understood they were talking about him.

"He seems like a great dog," Isla said. "But let's go inside—it's cold out here."

Yes, it was, now that the sun had completely disappeared and taken its unseasonable warmth with it. Rowan noticed patches of snow here and there in sheltered spots, although it didn't look as though they'd gotten as much precipitation here in Santa Fe as she and Jamal had in Las Vegas.

She and Darby followed Aamir and Isla into the house, whose interior was just as gorgeous as its exterior, with traditional Saltillo tile floors and expansive windows. The place had probably been built to take advantage of the nighttime city views, although now a great deal of the town appeared to be dark, with some lights clustered around the center, where she guessed most of the One Thousand lived. What had Santa Fe's population been, back before? Tens of thousands, which meant the vast majority of its houses were now unoccupied.

But not this one, where many of the lights were on and a cheerful fire flickered in the plaster hearth at the far end of the room. Rowan was glad of that—and glad of how Isla immediately whisked her away to one of the spare rooms.

"The house has five bedrooms," she said as she led Rowan down a long hallway on the opposite side of the house from where they'd entered the living room off the terrace. "Kind of overkill, but djinn always tend to pick the biggest and best places, you know?"

No, Rowan didn't know that, although she had to admit that Jamal's house in Jackson Hole had seemed pretty impressive, based on the one room she'd seen.

She didn't want to think about that house, though, not when doing so only brought back memories of the way they'd argued there. Of course, she'd been in the right, but she'd never been one for confrontations, and she kind of hated that the last time they'd been together, they'd been fighting.

Before she could dwell on that uncomfortable subject any longer, Isla led her into a large room furnished with a queen bed and simple, rustic pieces that Rowan guessed had been very expensive back in the day. Original paintings of northern New Mexico landscapes hung on the walls, and a large window looked into what she thought was a central courtyard, where a lighted fountain splashed away in the darkness.

"I thought this would be the best room for you because it has its own bathroom," Isla said, opening the door to reveal a glimpse of a space with warm handmade tile in a friendly shade of green, and a large vanity with dual copper sinks. "And there's plenty of space in the closet."

"I don't have much," Rowan replied as she swung her heavy backpack from her shoulders. Darby was already nosing around the space, familiarizing himself with all the new smells.

"Well, we can fix that," Isla said with a grin. "Plenty of good shopping here in Santa Fe—or rather, lots of stuff for the taking. It's not like we have to worry about money anymore."

Probably not, especially since it seemed as if djinn could create whatever they wanted from thin air. "Thank you for letting me stay here," Rowan said. "I know it's kind of a lot."

At once, the friendly smile Isla had been wearing faded a bit. "Well, from what Aamir told me, it sounds like his brother kind of put you in a tough position. We're fine with offering you crash space while you get things figured out, but you'll need to talk to Julia about getting your own place at some point."

"'Julia'?" Rowan echoed. It sounded as if Isla and Aamir would only be willing to put up with a house guest for so long, which meant that tomorrow, she might as well get the ball rolling in terms of finding permanent lodging here in Santa Fe.

Isla looked as if she was glad that the conversation had shifted to a more neutral topic. "Julia Innes. She's the Chosen of Zahrias al-Harith. He's the leader of the djinn here, and she used to be one of the people who ran Los Alamos. Anyway, she's kind of made it her responsibility to help any newcomers find a house."

"Newcomers?"

A small dimple showed in Isla's cheek as she smiled again. "People like me and Aamir. I mean, most of the djinn here chose their partners during the Dying, but there are a few who found their Chosen afterward. Because all the djinn whose partners lived in New Mexico needed to live in Santa Fe, they ended up here, and Julia helped them find houses."

"Like a real estate agent?" Rowan asked, and despite the circumstances that had brought her here, she couldn't help returning the other woman's smile.

"Sort of. She's got a stack of listings she gathered from the various realtors around town, and she gives them to you so you can pick the place that will work best for you." Isla's gaze strayed to the fountain outside, splashing in a courtyard that was too cold now for anyone to enjoy it in person. "This house was on the top of the stack, and Aamir and I loved it so much that we didn't see any reason to look at any other places."

Rowan could see that. The place was huge and well-appointed, and probably had some of the best views in Santa Fe. At the same time, she wondered if this Julia Innes person would expect her to choose something similar. A house like this felt awfully large for one person to be rattling around in. Maybe there was a spare condo or townhouse she could use.

"Well," Isla went on, "I'll let you get settled in. We were planning to eat in a few minutes, so just come on out when you're ready. And I'll have

Aamir conjure some bowls and food for Darby. What does he like?"

The offhand way she mentioned having her djinn partner produce supplies for the dog reminded Rowan once again how much easier life could be when you never had to worry about running short of food or whether a particular item you needed was actually available.

"He'll eat anything," she replied. "When we ran out of one kind of dog food, we just moved on to a different one. But he did like the Blue Buffalo stuff when we still had it."

"Blue Buffalo it is. See you in a couple of minutes."

Isla headed out then, presumably to meet up with Aamir in the living room or maybe the kitchen. Since she hadn't seen any signs of food preparation, Rowan guessed that dinner would appear much the same way those glasses of wine Jamal conjured had...by appearing out of thin air.

Maybe one day she'd get used to that.

---

Jamal stood in the center of his living room and resisted the urge to hurl the wine glass he held at the nearest wall. However, since that would have been a waste of good wine, he instead lifted it to his lips and took a large swallow, followed by another.

It didn't exactly help, but at least it wasn't splattered all over his living room.

Did Rowan not realize that he had also made a huge sacrifice in making her his Chosen? He'd had no wish to be encumbered thus, not after spending his entire adult life making sure any romantic encounters he had were brief and uncomplicated... but he also couldn't bear to have her die at Omar's hands. And yet she was the angry one, saying that he hadn't involved her in the decision and that she could never trust him because of the way he'd lied to her about who he truly was.

He had to allow she was on firmer ground there. It had been wrong to hide his identity from her, and yet he knew they would never have become friends if she'd known he was a djinn.

Then he wanted to laugh at himself. Yes, they'd been friends at first...and then had become so much more.

Why could she not see past her anger and realize they worked well together, even if their connection had been born out of false pretenses?

It seemed she had a temper to match her hair. Thinking of that, Jamal wondered if perhaps this was all for the best. She could have her life in Santa Fe, and he would have his existence here in Jackson Hole, with no worries about having to deal with her unpredictable rages.

However, he knew that view of the situation

wasn't quite fair. She hadn't shown much of a temper when they were working together at the Castle. True, she hadn't been afraid to challenge him if he made a suggestion she didn't agree with, but for the most part, she'd been a most accommodating companion.

And now he knew he was looking for reasons why it was better for them to be apart when deep down he knew the opposite was true.

"Driven to drink, I see," came Omar's unwelcome voice from behind him, and Jamal turned to see his brother standing near one of the windows, an unpleasant smirk pulling at his lips.

"I did not invite you here," Jamal said distinctly, then drank from his glass of wine again to show what he thought of his unbidden guest's comment.

A shrug. "No, but I thought it best to check on you and make sure you hadn't committed some other foolhardy act in service to that human you were trying to protect."

Jamal felt his eyes narrow, but he knew better than to lose his temper. That was the very outcome Omar no doubt wanted from this confrontation, and he certainly wouldn't give him the satisfaction.

"'That human,' as you say, is now staying with Aamir and his Chosen in Santa Fe," Jamal replied, taking care to maintain an even tone. The subject of their oldest brother's defection was still a sore one with Omar, and Jamal knew hearing his name would only irritate his intrusive sibling that much more.

"Oh, are they taking in strays now?" Omar shot back. "Then I suppose I can see why they would allow that woman in their house, along with that mutt she had with her."

For some reason, the disparaging description of Darby only made Jamal more inclined to throw his brother bodily out of the house. However, while he could easily fix any damage an altercation between the two of them might cause, he found he was not much in the mood for such work.

"They are offering her hospitality until she finds a home for us," Jamal said. He was loath to admit to his brother that his Chosen relationship with Rowan was a sham and that she had no intention of being his partner in eternity. Better to make it sound as if she was doing the work of getting settled in Santa Fe while he closed up his house here in Jackson Hole. True, there was not much work involved in such a procedure, since all he had to do was blink his belongings to his forever home in the former state capitol, but he had no intention of telling Omar any of that.

"How...domestic," Omar sneered. "Is she going to procure a house next to Aamir's, so that all of you can have block parties and picnics and whatever other foolish pastimes humans engage in to pretend they aren't all going into the dark in the end?"

An image of him wrapping his hands around Omar's neck and giving him a good throttling passed through Jamal's mind, but he did his best to shove it away. He'd suspected for centuries that half of what his younger brother said was intended to provoke a reaction and nothing more, and he certainly wouldn't give him the satisfaction of seeing how much his troublesome sibling had angered him.

"As to that," he said, knowing there was an edge to his tone that he couldn't quite hide, "I do not know, for I have allowed Rowan to make the decision. I trust she will come up with a situation that will suit both of us very well."

Even though he'd only said those words to push back on his brother, Jamal realized they were the truth. Whatever was happening in Santa Fe, he knew Rowan would make a good choice when it came to her home...to their home, he hoped. It might take days, or weeks, or even months, but he had to believe at some point she'd realize they needed to reconcile.

Did she really want to spend the rest of what would be a very long life surrounded by people happy in their relationships while she remained alone?

With all his soul, he hoped not, for he knew he could not bear such a thing.

For now, though, he needed to do what he could to rid himself of Omar, who'd only uttered a contemptuous chuckle at Jamal's previous words.

"Have much joy of her," Omar said. His black eyes glittered with malice as he added, "For now it seems I have no brothers."

He vanished then, presumably going back to his home in Placitas, a hilly settlement a few miles north of Albuquerque. Jamal stood where he was for a long moment, body tense, wondering if his brother might return to plague him once again, even though it seemed as if he had delivered his parting shot and had nothing more to say.

But the minutes ticked by, and it became clear that he was gone for good.

Jamal pulled in a breath, then magically refilled his glass.

It was going to be a long night.

# Chapter 16

"You really don't have a condo or a townhouse or anything like that?" Rowan asked Julia Innes. A few minutes earlier, Isla had driven her to the La Fonda hotel at the heart of town, explaining that they used it as a sort of meeting place and center of whatever business they might need to conduct, and that was where Julia wanted to meet with her. Isla had handed Rowan a walkie-talkie, telling her to reach out when she was done with her business. That made sense, she supposed; even with djinn energy running everything, they obviously hadn't seen the need to try to revive the cellular networks when anyone they'd need to talk to was right here in Santa Fe.

Julia looked down at the stack of papers in front of her with something close to dismay. She was tall and blonde and beautiful, and a little older than some of the other Chosen Rowan had seen while Isla was driving her through town, as though her djinn—Zahrias?—had gotten together with her after the initial choosing had taken place.

"Obviously, there are empty units like that here," she said. "But I never collected any sales data on them because I knew everyone settling in Santa Fe would want a bigger place. I suppose you can just wander until you find a condo complex and then look inside to see if there's one that'll suit you. None of them have been cleaned out, though."

Which seemed to be Julia's oblique way of telling her that she was very likely to find one of those sad little piles of gray dust, the only thing left behind after a victim of the Heat succumbed to the deadly fever. Although Rowan had swept up plenty of those in the aftermath of the plague, that had been years ago now, and she wasn't sure she wanted to repeat the experience.

Also, even though she'd wanted to be modest and self-sacrificing, she knew deep down that she'd always wished for a big, fancy house, the kind of place where she'd have room for all her favorite things, even while acknowledging to herself that was probably never going to happen.

"Well, give me what you've got," she said. "There have to be houses that are less than four thousand square feet, right?"

A corner of Julia's mouth lifted in a half-smile. "A few," she replied. "Here you go."

And she handed over the stack of papers, along with a folded map of Santa Fe. It had probably been printed for tourists to use, but Rowan had to admit it would be useful now that she couldn't use a phone to guide her. In fact, she'd left her phone behind in Las Vegas, as she hadn't touched the thing in years and hadn't seen the point in dragging it along when space in her backpack was so limited.

"Thanks," Rowan said. She'd visited Santa Fe enough times that she knew the general layout of downtown, but obviously, there hadn't been much point in roaming through the residential neighborhoods when she and her family had only been here to play tourist. The map would come in handy for exploring the listings Julia had given her...and to guide her back here to the La Fonda when she was done.

"I hope you find something that works for you," Julia went on. "I see that Isla gave you a walkie-talkie, so you can contact me if you need anything else. I'm on Channel 33."

Was that their way of having something like a phone number? Everyone got their own channel?

But no, they'd have to share some, just because there weren't a thousand-plus channels available on a walkie-talkie. Still, it seemed as though the setup was working for them so far.

She thanked Julia and headed outside. Isla had offered to take Rowan to the small lot off Cordova where they kept a few vehicles for people in the community to use, but she'd only said she preferred to walk. Maybe she'd regret that decision if she ended up having to wander hither and yon to find the house she wanted, and yet it still felt better to go on foot. After all, it wasn't as if she hadn't had plenty of practice walking these past four years. She'd taken the e-bike when she was going all the way into Las Vegas from the campus, but those were the only times when she hadn't relied on her own two feet.

Still, she paused outside the hotel to glance at the map and at the addresses on the papers Julia had given her, doing her best to arrange them so the closest houses were first, followed by the ones that were a little more far-flung, like Isla and Aamir's. At dinner the night before, Aamir had explained that his former home in Telluride had been located in the mountains, and that was the reason why he and Isla had selected a house that was up in the hills and a little ways away from everyone else. Rowan could see why such a location might have appealed to them, but she thought she'd rather have something lower down, maybe with a large, flat yard so she could garden.

If nothing else, tending plants would help keep her occupied.

A listing just like that was near the top of the stack of papers, a large hacienda-style house off Canyon Road. It was a walk of about a half mile from where she stood, but it shouldn't take her too long to get there, especially since they'd been blessed with yet another bright, sunny day.

Almost all the leaves had fallen from the trees here, but it was still a lovely walk, thanks to the interesting architecture that surrounded her. It seemed as if there was something new to see on every side, not to mention the djinn and their Chosen who occasionally passed by and smiled at her, the elementals in bright, silken robes that were a definite contrast to the much more sober garb Jamal and his brother had worn, the mortals in regular human clothes, even though most of it looked fairly high-end, like stuff they would have gotten from the fancy boutiques here in the city.

The image of Jamal's face flashed into her mind then, tight with worry, his dark eyes pleading with her to understand why he had done what he had done. Rowan did her best to push the vision away, mostly because she'd already vowed to herself that she wasn't going to allow herself to think about him until she was settled here and had a chance to breathe. Yes, she'd agreed to find a house, but she was going to get one that appealed to her, not something she'd settled on because she thought Jamal would like it as well.

She didn't want him affecting her decisions.

It was something of an uphill climb to get where she was going, but eventually, she reached the property in question. Even though this part of town was upslope from the area around the Plaza where the La Fonda was located, as she'd hoped, the plot itself seemed flat enough, dominated by a big white stucco house surrounded by a matching wall and the cutest blue-painted wooden gate.

Rowan let herself through that gate and walked along the pea-gravel path that wound its way to the front door. The yard had been xeriscaped with more gravel and gorgeous huge sandstone rocks and all sorts of native plants, and even at this time of year, when almost everything had gone dormant to wait its way through the long winter, something about the grounds felt serene, almost Zen-like in their simplicity.

And was that a greenhouse she spied around the corner?

It was actually two greenhouses set side by side, with what used to be a vegetable garden just beyond, all of the beds now plowed under and awaiting the return of spring. Past the vegetable garden was a decent-sized patch of grass, yellowed with frost but still something that would work for Darby. She'd never been very good at estimating plot sizes—it wasn't as if she'd planned to go house hunting any time soon after getting her first real job, which had provided its own housing anyway—but she guessed this place had to be at least an acre, maybe more, something she thought had been rare in the heart of Santa Fe where land was so expensive.

Why hadn't anyone else snapped up this gem? Did the inside not match the outside?

When she went in, though, she saw that theory wasn't correct in the slightest. All right, the place didn't seem to have been updated to match the California casual, light wood and modern finishes sort of style that seemed to be featured on all those home improvement shows her mother used to watch, but still, Rowan didn't think they would have worked here, would have fought the home's architecture, with the arches that defined the entrance from one space to another, and the big kiva-style fireplace in one corner, with hand-painted tiles from Mexico decorating its raised hearth.

The house was much larger than she'd been looking for...five bedrooms and four bathrooms...but she fell in love with the kitchen, which had big stainless-steel appliances and an island so large, she probably could have slept on it if she'd been so inclined. And the interior had that same sense of serenity she'd sensed in the yard.

*Darby,* she thought, *will love this place.*

The dog had stayed behind at Aamir and Isla's house, with the djinn promising to watch over him and possibly even play fetch. Rowan had gotten the impression he was fascinated by the dog, and in fact, Isla had told her on the drive into town that they'd been talking about getting a pet, and leaving Aamir to dog-sit while Rowan went house-hunting was probably the perfect way to convince him that a dog was exactly what they needed.

Did she want to keep looking, or did she think this house was the one? It didn't seem as if anyone else lived in this neighborhood, although she had to admit she hadn't exactly gone poking around to see if any djinn and their Chosen had settled here. From what Isla had said at dinner last night, everyone in Santa Fe had taken up various hobbies and were often occupied at home, although they met in the town square from time to time to gather for dances and concerts or a variety of holiday celebrations.

And Rowan had to think that if any of the other houses in this neighborhood were occupied, then she should have seen at least someone out and about. It was too nice a day—especially for early November, and especially after the snowstorm that had just passed through—for people to stay inside.

She thought being isolated here might be a

good thing. At least that way, she wouldn't have to deal with answering questions about why she was in Santa Fe at all when her djinn was nowhere in evidence. Or maybe people wouldn't have to ask because the story would have already circulated around town. She had a feeling a group as small and tight-knit as this one seemed to be didn't have a lot of secrets from one another.

After spending so many years on her own, Rowan didn't know how she was supposed to feel about that prospect.

*You don't have to feel anything at all,* she told herself. *It probably would have been the same in Los Alamos.*

True. But if Jamal had really been who he was pretending to be, at least she wouldn't have had to face the stigma of being the only Chosen who didn't have a djinn around.

And if wishes were horses, as her father used to say, all beggars would ride.

"Okay," she said aloud, hoping the sound of her voice would help to steady her. "I think I'm home."

---

Should he reach out to Aamir and see how Rowan was faring? Or should he let it alone for now and hope she would come to her own conclusions about her decision to leave him behind?

Jamal had been stewing over that conundrum for most of the morning, going back and forth, not sure whether contacting his brother would look like an act of desperation, or whether maintaining his current silence would make it seem as if he didn't care what his Chosen was doing. The problem was, neither option seemed all that appealing to him.

No, what he really wanted was to talk to Rowan, and he knew that wasn't going to happen unless she relented and decided to reach out to him. Considering the taut set of her jaw the night before when he'd dropped her off at Aamir's Santa Fe home, he doubted that day was going to arrive any time soon.

But even if he couldn't be where she was now, he could at least visit the place where they'd spent time together.

Already the Castle seemed forlorn to him, although Jamal guessed that impression was mostly his imagination trying to paint a picture of something that wasn't even there. The sun shone brightly today, and nothing material had changed about either the building or the landscape that surrounded it, except now almost all of the snow had melted, leaving barely any sign of the storm that had trapped them inside only a few short days ago.

He went inside and noted the chilly temperatures almost absently, as they didn't affect him and he no longer had to pretend to be a human who suffered from the cold. All was as they had left it, Darby's muddy paw prints mopped from the kitchen floor, the bed made, the hearth cold but neatly swept out.

What else had he been expecting to find? They'd locked the doors and made sure everything was secured, so it wasn't as if he was going to encounter a pack of raccoons who'd decided to make the former hotel their permanent home now that the human who'd lived here for so many years had finally vacated it.

But some of Rowan's clothes still hung in the closet of the room that had been hers, simply because there hadn't been enough room in her backpack to take all of those items. Jamal touched one of the sweaters, feeling the soft nap of the knit under his fingertips, and fancied he could detect the sweet smell of the shampoo she used still clinging to the garment.

He wouldn't bend to sniff at it, though, mostly because he thought such behavior would be far too undignified. Yes, it seemed as if her presence suffused every corner of this place, but she was gone and he refused to act like some lovesick puppy.

Especially since he'd never been in love with her in the first place. He enjoyed her company, and she was a most satisfying partner in bed, but he would go no further than that when it came to analyzing his feelings about Rowan Aames.

Even if he thought, somewhere in a place he didn't want to admit to himself, that a man who wasn't in love wouldn't waste his time wandering the halls of a building where the woman he cared about had once lived.

Frowning, he descended the stairs on foot rather than simply blinking himself to his destination. As he went, he couldn't help thinking of the way Darby used to bound down these steps, excited beyond belief that his people were going to let him outside or feed him a morsel or two as they prepared dinner.

Did Darby miss him? Or was he too excited about settling into his new home in Santa Fe to worry about what had happened to the man who'd shared his and his mistress's lives for a few short days?

Jamal found he didn't much want to think about that, either.

He opened the double doors to the dining hall and went inside. Bright sunlight streamed through the warm panes of stained glass, green and amber, that framed the windows, but he did not find himself especially cheered. How could he, when more evidence of Rowan's presence here surrounded him on almost all sides?

The notebooks remained where they'd left them, of course, and Jamal wondered if she'd told anyone about her writing, about the library of memories she'd left behind. It would be an easy enough thing for a djinn—perhaps Aamir—to blink them to Santa Fe, but that couldn't happen if they didn't know those notebooks existed.

Before he even realized what he was doing, Jamal's feet had carried him over to the nearest table, and a hand reached out to lift the notebook from the top of the pile. The first page was dated only a few weeks before he'd appeared at the Castle, and he guessed that was why it had ended up there, since it made sense that her older writings would have already been buried in a stack somewhere else.

*I used to like this time of year,* she'd written. *But now every time the leaves start to turn and the days get shorter, all I can think about is enduring another winter here. My mother would have probably told me I should be grateful for being alive, but that seems to be harder and harder the longer this goes on. The only thing keeping me going is Darby. I'd never forgive myself if I checked out on him, so every day I get up and do my chores, and every day I sit down and write something in these notes, even if I can't help feeling like the whole thing is an exercise in futility.*

Jamal glanced away from the page, assailed by the same sort of uneasy sensation he might have experienced if he'd unexpectedly caught a glimpse of a stranger undressing.

Had Rowan really been that close to taking her own life? She seemed so vibrant, so determined, that he couldn't quite fathom how she might have arrived at such a low point.

Then again, every human...every djinn, if he wanted to be honest with himself...had times when they questioned their existence and whether it was truly worth continuing. Even his own parents, troubled by the prospect of wiping out the human race, had drunk the draught of the dark sleep and died together rather than face a world where their people would carry such a heavy burden of guilt on their shoulders. Others of their kind had done the same thing throughout their history, ready to move on when life no longer had any attraction for them, and yet both Aamir and Jamal had wondered if the means and the reason for their parents' departure was partly what had fueled Omar's unwavering rage toward all of humanity. Aamir had always viewed the cleansing as a necessary evil, and Jamal had shared that view, if somewhat reluctantly.

But their youngest brother had only wanted revenge.

Heart heavy, Jamal closed the notebook. With Rowan gone, he had free rein to look through all of her writings if he wished, but he decided he would not invade her privacy any more than he already had. Perhaps at some point, she would want these things fetched for her, but for now, they would stay where they were.

He went out the main entrance and stood on the steps, letting his gaze wander across the property. Because of the storm, he had not had much chance to explore any of the other buildings, and a pale structure with an oddly pitched roof line caught his eye as it rose from within a glade of pine trees.

Since he had no real wish to return to his home in Jackson Hole any time soon, he thought he should go ahead and explore.

As he approached, he saw a sign with an arrow pointing toward the white structure.

*Dwan Light Chapel.*

Odd name. Had someone misspelled "dawn," or was Dwan someone's surname?

The going here would have been muddy—he got the feeling that Rowan generally didn't venture out here during the cold months—but his powers made the red, clay-heavy mud turn solid and dry so he might pass easily without getting his boots or the hem of his robes dirty. When he reached the doors of white pine, he found they swung inward at once, telling him that she'd seen no reason to keep them locked.

Even though he had visited many exotic locales and viewed many fine buildings throughout his long life, his breath still caught as he looked around and saw all the delicate colors of the rainbow reflected on the plain white walls. Overhead, multiple windows had been placed to create prisms in the bright sunlight, the reason for the chromatic effect.

It was utterly simple and yet utterly breathtaking at the same time. He found himself moving into the center of the space, and then over to one of the plain benches of formed concrete that were the only furniture in the chamber. It made sense, he thought, to give visitors a place to sit and contemplate the rainbows, while at the same time not creating anything that might serve as a distraction from the pure design of the space.

He sat there and breathed in, letting the quiet hush of the place fill his soul. Perhaps he and Rowan were estranged now, and yet he had to hope she would relent at some point. No, he would not flatter himself and try to frame his intrusion in her life as the one thing that had given her hope and a reason to go on living, but at the same time, his arrival still must have woken her up and allowed her to understand that sometimes fate stepped in when one least expected it.

At least, that was what he hoped. He knew he had changed, that the man he'd been when he first set out to "walk the earth" was not the same one who hadn't hesitated to make Rowan his Chosen in order to save her life.

What he was supposed to do about that, however, he had no idea.

# Chapter 17

CLAIMING THE LOVELY HOUSE OFF CANYON Road as her own turned out to be a simple enough process. Rowan contacted Julia through the walkie-talkie and told her she'd found the perfect space, and a moment later, the woman appeared with her djinn partner Zahrias to congratulate her on her choice.

"It is a fine house," the djinn leader commented. Now that Rowan had been around him a bit more, she realized he wasn't as forbidding as she'd thought when she'd first caught a glimpse of him, was only someone who carried more of a burden on his shoulders than most, since he was responsible for the well-being of the community here.

"It is," Julia agreed. "And, more importantly,

it's got solar. I was wondering what we were going to do without a djinn around to keep things running, but...."

Her words trailed off there, and she glanced away from Rowan, obviously not wanting to finish the sentence.

Of course. If she'd come here with Jamal, then he could have powered the electrical system and run the plumbing and done all the other hundred and one things Rowan had taken for granted back before...and would never take for granted again. She'd already realized the preceding evening, based on a casual comment Isla had made, that it was the djinn who kept everything going. And obviously, Jamal hadn't "fixed" anything about the system at the Castle and had only used his djinn powers to juice things while claiming that all he had to do was some simple wiring to get things back up and running.

Which begged the question as to why he'd let everything die off during the storm, rather than pretend the batteries were hanging on much longer than they had any right to. She could only guess that he'd realized she must know how long they could run without being recharged, and trying to keep them going when they obviously shouldn't have been would only have made her ask too many questions.

"Yes, that's great," Rowan said. "I suppose we could have gotten a generator or something if need be, but having solar makes the whole thing a lot cleaner."

"That it does," Zahrias responded. "But still, if the batteries get low during a period of extended bad weather, you should let us know. The power we djinn use to run your electricity and heat and everything else is negligible, and one of us will be able to come over and help get it going again without any trouble."

It did sound as if it shouldn't require much effort, which was probably why she'd never noticed Jamal showing any sign of strain to power the space heaters or even run the oven. Somehow she knew that if she went back to the Castle to inspect things more closely, she'd discover that he'd never really connected those propane tanks to the stove, but had only pretended to.

Right then, she wasn't sure if she should be angry at him for lying to her about so many things...or possibly be just a little impressed by the lengths he'd gone to in order to ensure she thought he was a human like her.

"I doubt that will happen," she said. "Darby and I won't need much."

Julia's mouth curved in a faint smile. "Maybe not, but still, I'm glad you found something close in, so someone can be here quickly if need be. In fact, Zahrias' younger brother Dani and his Chosen, Lauren, live right down the street."

So, she wouldn't be as alone here as she'd thought. Maybe that was a good thing.

She'd spent enough time on her own. It was probably time to rejoin the human race...or in this case, a community made up of humans and their djinn partners. So far, it seemed as if her fears about not being able to reintegrate into society had been unfounded, since she'd fallen back into interacting with others as though no time at all had passed since the last time she'd been surrounded by people.

"And I know Dani and Lauren's little boy, Gabriel, would just love to meet Darby," Julia went on. "How is your dog with kids?"

There was a question. Rowan had absolutely no idea, since it had been just the two of them for the past four years.

Well, until Jamal showed up.

"I don't know," she replied. "I found him... after, so there wasn't anyone else around. But he's a pretty mellow dog, so I have to believe he'd be fine being around a little boy. I guess the best thing to do would be for them to have a play date."

"Well, we can worry about that once you're settled," Zahrias put in. "We certainly do not want to overwhelm you. Gabriel can be...something of a handful."

Julia only shook her head, although another smile played around her lips. "What he's trying to say is that Gabriel is a perfectly normal three-year-old. It's not as if our daughter Amelia is an angel or anything close to it."

"We will have to agree to disagree on that one," Zahrias observed. As usual, his expression was serious enough, but an amused light in his dark eyes told Rowan he was inclined to agree with his wife on that particular subject.

Or...was Julia even his wife? Rowan had to admit she still wasn't entirely sure how all this was supposed to work. Maybe being tied together as djinn and Chosen for eternity was a formal enough arrangement that none of the people here saw any need to mess around with weddings and prenups and all that kind of stuff.

"I like kids," Rowan said, even as she hoped she wasn't telling them something only kind of approaching the truth. She'd babysat a lot when she was in high school, and several of her older cousins had already started families and brought their children along to family gatherings, but still, it had been years since she'd had to amuse a toddler.

Well, she'd just have to hope it was like riding a bicycle, and she'd be able to get back in the swing of things once she was around children again.

"Don't say that too loud," Julia told her. "Or you're sure to get drafted for babysitting duty. It's wonderful that none of us have to worry about going to jobs or doctor's appointments or anything, but people still get to the point where they'd like a break every once in a while."

Rowan only shook her head. "It's fine. I was on my own for so long that it's going to feel really good to have other people around me. Even toddlers," she added, since Julia still didn't look entirely convinced.

"But for now, we'll just work on getting you set up here," Zahrias said. "I will contact Aamir and Isla so they might bring your things to the house. If there is anything else you need, though, always feel free to reach out. Julia will make sure it is provided for you."

"Once an administrator, always an administrator," she remarked with a grin, although she didn't look too concerned about the way her husband had volunteered her to act as the settlement's unofficial concierge. "But yes, the house has been cleaned out and the pantry restocked. Otherwise, though, we left everything else in place—bedding, dishes, that kind of stuff. Still, it always seems as if there's that one thing you need and can't find."

"I'll let you know," Rowan told her.

This seemed to be all that Zahrias and Julia needed to hear, since they again welcomed her to

Santa Fe and then disappeared, presumably so they could go back to their home near downtown. However, Rowan was barely alone for a minute or two—just enough to wander back into the kitchen and confirm that yes, both the fridge and the pantry were full, and there seemed to be enough dishes and glassware and flatware to cover a sit-down dinner for at least ten people—before Aamir and Isla materialized in the living room, with Isla holding Darby in her arms. However, as soon as they appeared, she leaned down so she could let go of the dog.

"Hope you don't mind us popping in like this," Isla said as Darby ran over to Rowan and gave her a welcoming lick on the hand. "But Zahrias and Julia let us know you'd found a house and needed your stuff, so we thought we'd come over in person and make sure you were well and truly settled." She glanced around the space, gaze pausing on the hand-painted tile of the fireplace, and gave an approving nod. "I like it. It's not stuffy."

No, it wasn't. If she was going to be here forever—although Rowan supposed at some point they'd have to build her a new house, as she doubted anything in Santa Fe would be able to last for thousands of years—she might as well have a place that felt comfortable and down to earth, unpretentious. True, this "unpretentious" house had probably cost millions back before the Dying, but its dollar value didn't matter anymore.

What mattered was how she felt while in it.

"I thought Darby would like the house," Rowan replied. That seemed to be the case, because after greeting her, he'd already started roaming around the living room, sniffing at everything, doing his best to get familiar with the space. "There's a great yard, too."

Aamir also looked approving, although he only said, "Your belongings are already in the main bedroom. I assume that Julia told you to let her know if you needed anything?"

"She did," Rowan said. Even though the whole setup still felt strange and awkward to her, she couldn't help experiencing a twinge of amusement at the concern on his and Isla's faces, the way they wanted to make sure everything was perfect for her. Maybe that was their way of dealing with such an unprecedented situation. Not that she could call herself any kind of an expert, but Rowan got the feeling that this was the first time they'd had to deal with someone who'd been chosen and who wanted nothing to do with their djinn partner. "This house seems pretty well-stocked, though. I honestly can't think of anything I'd need."

"That is good to hear," Aamir said. His gaze flickered down toward his partner, and Rowan got the impression that he thought they'd done everything they needed to.

Isla, on the other hand, either chose not to get the hint, or wasn't sure whether her new "sister-in-law" was quite as set as everyone else thought she was. "But it's okay if you reach out. It's hard to think of everything, you know?"

Well, that was true. Rowan doubted that the woman she'd been four days ago would have ever thought she'd end up as a djinn's Chosen...mostly because back then, she hadn't even known what that meant.

"I know," she said gently, since she could tell Isla was only trying to help. "But right now, I think I just want to get settled in and play with Darby in the yard so he can get used to his new home."

"Then we'll leave you," Aamir replied, his tone a little firmer, and Isla seemed to get the message.

"Just call if you need anything," she said, even as her partner wrapped his arms around her waist and the two of them vanished the same way they had come.

Rowan allowed herself to release a sigh, then looked down at Darby, who'd finished circling the living room and come back to her, probably so he could get a read on what she wanted to do next.

At least Darby was familiar.

"Hey, boy," she said, bending over to ruffle his ears. "Let's go check out that backyard."

---

He'd remained in the chapel longer than he planned to, and the sun was already beginning to shift to the west when he emerged. Jamal gazed up at the sky for a long moment. No, he couldn't detect currents in the air the way some of his people could, but the way the breeze had picked up seemed to signal that these lovely, unseasonably mild days were about to come to an end.

True, adverse weather was no real problem for a djinn, and yet the idea of slogging through a storm was less than appealing. If he must continue to brood on his current situation, better to do it where he could be comfortable.

At once, he was surrounded by the familiar spaces of his living and dining rooms. Here in Wyoming, the skies had already darkened, and snow had just begun to fall. Perhaps that was what he had detected much farther south in New Mexico, where sometimes weather traveled down the spine of the Rocky Mountains, as it seemed to be doing now, rather than moving from west to east as storms blew off the Pacific and made their way across the continent.

A wave of the hand made the logs in the fireplace blaze up, but Jamal did not find himself much comforted. It would have been one thing to sit in front of it with Rowan—perhaps while cheering themselves with some mulled wine—and yet another to stand here and watch the snow fall, and know there was not a single thing he could do about it.

In that moment, spring felt very far away.

He was not alone for long, however, as his brother Aamir appeared in the living room only a moment after Jamal had awakened the fire in the hearth.

Aamir's arrival was far more welcome than Omar's had been. Jamal could not quite prevent himself from taking a step forward and saying, "You have news of Rowan?"

"I do," Aamir replied. He appeared relaxed and cheerful, and far more at ease than Jamal had seen him in years. Clearly, having Isla as his Chosen had done him a great deal of good.

Ignoring the stab of jealousy that went through him, Jamal asked, "She is well?"

"Very well," Aamir said. "She has found a house. It is quite large, and not very far from downtown. I find myself thinking that she would not have chosen such a place if she intended to live there alone for very long."

While this news sounded encouraging on the surface, Jamal would not allow himself any false hope. "Perhaps that is true," he said. "Or it may be that there were no smaller houses offered."

A corner of Aamir's mouth quirked. "I

suppose that is possible. But if she felt strongly about it, I am sure she would have found something with fewer than five bedrooms and less than three thousand square feet."

Jamal's house here in Jackson Hole was nearly double that size, and yet he was forced to admit that it felt far too large most days, as if there were still rooms and corners he had not yet explored. And he had no true idea of the size of the palace he'd left behind in the overworld, for he had constructed it according to his fancy on any given day, and there were wings where he hadn't set foot in for decades.

He had to admit that human homes tended to be much more manageable.

"That is a good size," he allowed. "Thank you for providing me with this news." He hesitated there, wondering if he should say anything further, then determined there was nothing to be gained from concealing his thoughts from his brother. "I can only wait and hope she changes her mind at some point."

Aamir's expression was grave, but then he conjured a pair of glasses filled with burgundy and handed one to Jamal. "I cannot say I know her after such a brief acquaintance, and yet I think the best thing here is time. While I understand your motivations in making her your Chosen, not only did you thrust that state upon her with no consideration, but she also had no true context for what being Chosen even meant. It was not the same with Isla and myself, for she had been in Los Alamos all that time and knew exactly what djinn and human interactions could be."

All this was nothing more than the truth. Rowan's isolation had ensured that she did not know what a Chosen was, nor that the state of affairs between humans and djinn was not precisely what it had been four years earlier.

No wonder she was in a state of shock.

"I did what I had to," Jamal said, and Aamir nodded, then sipped some of the wine he had provided.

"I know this," he replied. "And I am sorry that Omar is so driven by hate that he cannot see there are other ways to live in the world as it exists now."

Yes, he was, and Jamal knew that their younger brother, already on a crusade to rid the world of humans, was now reeling from two separate blows as he saw the only family he had left committing what he must view as the very worst form of betrayal.

Of course, Jamal and Aamir had been on a similar crusade not so very long ago. They had both changed since then, however, changed in ways they were only beginning to understand.

"But did you save Rowan merely because you did not want to see her die before your eyes, or is there something else here you are not admitting to yourself?"

The words were spoken calmly. Aamir's expression was likewise neutral, but a light of understanding in his eyes made Jamal believe his older brother comprehended far more than he wished to say openly. In a way, this interaction reminded him of the days long ago when they were all boys, not yet having reached the age of twenty, when their people would view them as adults. Aamir had always tried to act as a guide and as the voice of reason, and it had pained Jamal to see him become so extreme once the plot to destroy humankind with a deadly fever had first been hatched. More than once over the years, he had thought Aamir first began to act in such a manner in order to offer support to Omar, who had never seemed to recover from the way he believed their parents had betrayed them.

When Jamal spoke, he did his best to sound just as neutral, just as unconcerned, for he still had no great desire to admit what he held so deeply in his heart. "What is there to say?"

"A great many things," Aamir replied. "But until you are willing to say them to yourself...and to Rowan, perhaps...then there is no point demanding that you give them up to me. I will send Isla your regards."

And then he disappeared, leaving Jamal alone

again. Not sure what else he should do, he lifted the glass of wine to his lips and drank. No doubt it was an excellent vintage, but it tasted bitter as gall to him.

A bitter cup he would continue to drink for a long time...unless Rowan somehow was persuaded to change her mind.

He did not see that happening any time soon.

# Chapter 18

THE FIRST FLAKES OF SNOW BEGAN TO drift downward late that morning. Rowan was just going up the front walk after taking Darby around the neighborhood—and pausing to chat with Zahrias' brother Dani and his wife Lauren, whose hair was nearly as red as Rowan's own—when she saw the snow begin to fall.

Darby shook and looked back at Rowan, and she quickened her pace so they could get under the shelter of the covered portal at the front of the house before too many of the flakes could begin to catch in her hair. Soon enough, the two of them were inside, and she hurried over to the fireplace, which luckily she'd loaded with logs the night before, so she could dig out a lighter and get the fire going.

There, that was better. No real comparison to

riding out a storm in Montezuma Castle, where there hadn't been any central heat and not many creature comforts at all. Here at least she had the fire and a real heating system, not to mention a refrigerator stuffed full of the kinds of goodies she hadn't eaten in years—tamales and a huge pot of refried beans and a large casserole dish of cheesy enchiladas that only needed to be put in the oven to get warmed up. She didn't know for sure whether someone had made the food or whether Zahrias had simply conjured it with a snap of his fingers, and she supposed it didn't matter so much. What mattered was that she had plenty to eat, and even if she ran out of something, both Isla and Julia were only a walkie-talkie call away.

It was weird to think she had help on hand after having to do everything for herself for so many years.

And that didn't even take into account Dani and Lauren, both of whom seemed very friendly and glad to have a new neighbor on their street. Dani was a softer, gentler version of his older brother, and Lauren seemed absolutely crazy about him. Their adorable little boy, Gabriel, had been enchanted with Darby, and the dog, just as Rowan had thought, had ignored the toddler's grabby hands and cheerfully put up with being petted in a way that might not have been his favorite but knew was all the little boy could manage right then.

All in all, the morning had gone great. So why did seeing the snow coming down thicker and thicker strike such a chill in her heart?

*Because the last time you saw snow like this, you were trapped in the Castle with Jamal,* she reminded herself. *And now it's snowing again, and he's not here.*

And whose fault was that?

It was Jamal's fault, because if he'd been truthful with her, she would have had no reason to kick him to the curb.

Okay, that was probably just a little disingenuous. If he'd told her he was a djinn, she might not have had the courage to kick him out, but she sure as hell would have tried to find some way to escape.

Although the house had come with a well-stocked wine rack, Rowan knew it was way too early to start drinking. Instead, she poured some water into the kettle and set it on the stove, then rummaged in the pantry for a box of white tea she'd seen earlier while familiarizing herself with the contents of the kitchen's cupboards.

Everything here seemed so easy, from the shower she'd taken this morning to the way the stove's induction burners came right on when she turned the knob. It almost felt like being back before...even though she knew the world outside the kitchen window was very different from what it had once been, and even though she knew the

Rowan from that world would never in a million years have been able to afford a house like this.

Darby had gone straight to his bowl and slurped up water, so it was time to give him a treat for being a good boy with Gabriel and for being such a well-behaved dog on the rest of the walk. Aamir had supplied treats along with dog food, so Rowan knew they were stocked for now...and that they would be instantly resupplied whenever they started to run out of something essential.

Was life supposed to be this easy?

She had no idea, but she hoped she'd settle into this new existence at some point.

For now, though, she took her cup of tea over to the chair by the front window so she could sit down and watch the snow falling. It seemed a little thicker than the last time she'd looked, but if the temperature had dropped at all, she couldn't tell. This house had been built tight as a drum.

Not for the first time, she wondered what Jamal was doing. Was it snowing in Wyoming as well, or was this storm what the weathercasters used to call a "back door" front, due to the way it came down the Rockies and slid over the Sangre de Cristos, moving east to west? If so, it might have already come and gone at Jamal's home in Jackson Hole.

And as many times as she told herself not to think about him or what he was up to, it seemed her unruly brain just wanted to dwell on him that much more.

Well, fine. She'd just have to find something else to occupy herself.

The day before, she'd mainly focused on checking out all the kitchen supplies and acquainting herself with the big, luxurious bathroom in the main suite. Not only was there a huge shower with multiple heads and a built-in tile-covered bench, but the space also had a large standalone bathtub in front of a window that overlooked the garden. She could see herself taking a nice long soak in there; in the house where she'd grown up, she'd rarely gotten to use the tub since she had to share the second bathroom with her two brothers, and even after they moved out, she found she never had the time to indulge herself in such a way, not when she was juggling school and at least one part-time job.

And obviously, there hadn't been any soaking in designer bathtubs when she was living at the Castle. The closest she got there was bathing in the hot springs, which was only feasible for about half the year, depending on what the weather wanted to do.

But—after leaving Darby snoozing by the fire, since the dog had done all his exploring the day before and obviously just wanted to soak up some heat—she peeked into the other bedrooms one by one. It seemed clear enough that the previous owners hadn't had a big enough family to fill up all five of them, as one of the secondary rooms had been set up as an office, one as a guest space with a cute wrought-iron daybed, and yet another must have once been a library, with bookcases filling up the walls on all sides.

More than half those cases were empty, though, leading Rowan to wonder if Julia or someone else here in Santa Fe had deliberately removed the books so she could fill them with her own choices of reading material, or whether the people who once had lived here just didn't have enough books to take up all those shelves. There was enough space left over that she thought there might be room for all her notebooks.

Of course, she'd have to get someone to bring them here, but considering the djinns' apparently limitless powers, that didn't seem as if it would be too much of a problem. Having the notebooks on hand would help make this place feel more like her own home, although Rowan didn't know for sure whether she'd continue with her writing or not. It seemed as if she'd have a lot more to occupy her here in Santa Fe—hell, she was only a block away from a street that contained numerous galleries and other shops, and just exploring those would probably take her weeks. As far as she could tell, everything was open to everyone who lived in this djinn/human settlement, and if they wanted to go in and take a particular painting or piece of jewelry for themselves, it looked as if no one had a problem with that.

She walked from room to room, making mental notes, thinking it would be fun to add a vase here or a basket there so she could put her own stamp on the place. After all, Julia had told her this house was hers. She could do anything she wanted to it.

When she came back to the living room, though, her gaze moved to the dining room just beyond, the big table framed by the archway that separated the two spaces. Last night she'd eaten at the kitchen island since it had its own set of bar stools, and now she wondered if she would ever feel up to having her meals in the dining room. It felt awfully big and formal for just one person.

She had a sudden mental glimpse of them sitting at the table they'd dragged into the kitchen at the Castle, the flash of Jamal's smile as he cut a piece off the enormous turkey he'd caught earlier that afternoon and put it on her plate. Despite everything, that had been one of the best meals she'd ever had.

"Oh, stop it," she said aloud, and Darby stirred over by the fireplace, one ear perking up to see if she'd been talking to him. "It's okay, Darbs," she added quickly. The last thing she wanted was for the dog to think he was in trouble over something he hadn't even done.

Darby settled back down, snout between his two front paws, eyes closing almost immediately.

She needed to be careful. Just because she couldn't seem to stop herself from dwelling on how things had been with Jamal, that didn't mean she should drag the poor dog into her mess.

Sometime while she'd been wandering from room to room, the snow had stopped, and a few blue patches had begun to show overhead. The sight cheered her, letting her know that this particular storm was nothing like the one that had trapped her and Jamal in the Castle for days.

In fact, very little snow had accumulated, probably not even a half inch, and the street past the front yard remained clear. As she looked out the living room window, she saw a small black vehicle, halfway between a car and an extremely compact SUV, pull up in front and Isla Dunbar get out.

Rowan blinked. Why in the world would Isla be dropping by now?

*Probably to check on you,* she thought. *After all, we are kind of sisters-in-law now. She must have thought it would be a nice thing to do.*

And it wasn't as if Aamir's Chosen was dropping in at the crack of dawn or anything close to it. It would be noon in less than half an hour.

Rowan headed to the entry, a cute little

antechamber outfitted with a rustic bench and a coat tree on one side and a closet on the other. Just as Isla knocked, she went ahead and opened the door.

"I saw you pull up," she explained in response to the other woman's slightly startled look. "Come on in."

"Thanks."

As they moved into the living room, Isla unzipped the winter white puffer jacket she wore. "I hope you don't mind me barging in like this."

"It's fine," Rowan said. "I wasn't doing much of anything, anyway. Just sort of poking around. I love that the house has a library."

"Oh, that's fun," Isla replied. "It is kind of like Christmas to get these houses handed to us on a silver platter, isn't it?"

Rowan had to admit she hadn't thought of it that way, but Isla was right...except for the part where Rowan knew she'd never gotten anything as impressive as a house for Christmas.

"I was downtown anyway, going through the kitchen store off the Plaza, so I thought I'd drop by," Isla went on. "Everything looks really cozy in here."

"Yes, the fireplace is great." Rowan hesitated for a moment, then decided she might as well ask. She'd gotten the impression that her newfound sister-in-law hadn't been here all that long, but she still should have a much better idea of how things operated in Santa Fe. "So it's—it's okay to take what you want from any of the shops here?"

"Absolutely," the other woman replied at once. "It feels kind of weird at first, like you're sure the cops are going to show up and bust you for stealing, but really, everything's up for grabs. And if it turns out that you want the same painting or whatever that someone else has dibs on, it's not a big deal—the djinn will just duplicate it for you."

Kind of the adult version of being a kid in a candy store. Rowan still wasn't sure if she wanted to make any changes that big—she didn't know anything about art, and what she'd seen hanging in her new house suited her fine for now—but it was still kind of exciting to know that she could get the things she wanted without any problem. Never in her life had she experienced that kind of abundance, and she wondered if she would ever truly get used to it.

"So, where's this library?" Isla asked next.

"Right down the hall," Rowan replied. "I'll show you."

The two of them left the living room and went down the corridor where all the bedrooms were located. Since the library was the first room on the right, they didn't have to go very far.

"Looks like you've got lots of space to fill up," Isla commented.

"I do," Rowan said, although she kept her tone neutral. She still wasn't sure how to broach the subject of the notebooks she'd left behind in Las Vegas, so it seemed better to stay quiet on the subject for now. "But I can pick up more stuff from any bookstores around town, right?"

Isla nodded. "Yes. There were a couple of fun ones right downtown, and of course you can also take books from the library if you want. If you do that, though, you should write down what you took—some of the people here are trying to keep it as intact as possible, and would rather books just got checked out rather than taken permanently."

In a way, Rowan liked that idea. The items in the stores were there for the town's residents to take as needed, but the library was a resource that should stand apart.

"That's fine," she said. "I'm sure I'll find enough in the bookstores to keep me busy for a long time. Also, it's not like the shelves here are empty, either. It looks like whoever lived here was into mysteries and romantic suspense, and there's a bunch of stuff I haven't read."

"Good to know," Isla replied. She paused there, looking almost diffident. Rowan couldn't say she knew the other woman very well yet, but she hadn't seemed the shy type, had the air of someone who'd also been forced to take care of herself before Aamir came along. Then she said, "I know this isn't any of my business, but I know Aamir's brother is upset by what happened between you two. Any chance you might talk it out?"

No, it wasn't Isla's business. However, Rowan knew she was only trying to help, and it wasn't her fault that she and Aamir had kind of gotten stuck in the middle of all this by Jamal dumping her at their house in the first place.

If only she weren't still so angry with him for the lies he'd told.

"No," she said. "There's no chance."

---

Isla left not too long after that. She hadn't tried to argue with Rowan, thank God, but she still looked troubled, even as she said she and Aamir would love to have Rowan over for dinner sometime.

*So you can bug me about getting back together with Jamal?* Rowan had thought, but she'd only said that sounded like fun and she'd let them know.

Afterward, the house felt far emptier than it should have, although she refused to let that get to her. Instead, she went to the kitchen, got out the box of recipe cards she'd found in the pantry during her first inspection of the space, and then hunted around to make sure she had all the ingredients to make a big batch of snickerdoodle cookies. They had always been her comfort treat when she was a child, and she figured it was probably safer to cheer herself up with a couple of cookies than to break out a bottle of wine. If she made too many, she could always take some to Isla and Aamir, kind of as her way of saying that, although she wanted them to butt out, she also appreciated them being here for her. Knowing she had even that kind of makeshift family made her feel a little less alone.

---

That day passed, and another. The weather didn't exactly warm up, but it remained clear, allowing Rowan to get out and about and meet more of the town's residents. Everyone was friendly but also obviously doing their best to avoid any sensitive subjects, which made her think Isla must have spread the word that no one should inquire as to exactly what had happened between her and Jamal.

And Dani and Lauren invited her and Darby over so Gabriel could play with the dog, although the real reason Lauren had offered was that they wanted to feed her some of the extra-large batch of chili Lauren had made.

"It is an odd dish," Dani remarked. "But I have grown fond of it."

"Of course you have," Lauren told him. "Because I make the best damn chili in New Mexico."

Rowan couldn't help smiling at the exchange, even as she experienced a little twinge of something she couldn't quite identify as she watched their interactions. It wasn't jealousy exactly, more like... wistfulness? Need?

That sounded silly, though. It wasn't as if she wanted Dani, even though he was very handsome, and kind as well.

No, she just wanted someone to share meals with, someone who could tease her gently and who looked at her with the same kind of warmth she'd seen in Dani's eyes as he gazed at his partner.

*Well, you're not going to find it in Santa Fe,* she thought. *Not with everyone already paired off.*

And Los Alamos wasn't an option, which left her...where?

In limbo, the way she'd been for longer than she wanted to admit. Her time at the Castle had also been in an odd liminal state, not really part of the world, and she realized that, even though things were still somewhat uncomfortable now, she never wanted to go back there.

"And you're all settled in?" Lauren went on, and Rowan nodded, glad to shake off the unwelcome thoughts that had intruded just a moment earlier.

"Pretty much. It's a great house."

Rather than appear pleased by her comments, both Dani and Lauren looked troubled. Rowan could guess why, and sincerely hoped they weren't also going to pressure her to talk it out with Jamal. Why in the world should she do that when he'd already proven he couldn't be trusted to tell her the truth? For all she knew, he'd only hand her another pack of lies.

"There's someone I think you should talk to," Lauren said then, and Rowan couldn't help lifting a dubious eyebrow.

"I'm not talking to him, and that's it," she replied, and the other woman looked startled for a moment, then shook her head.

"I didn't mean Jamal al-Qadir, if that's who you were thinking of."

Rowan reached for her glass of wine, even as Dani deftly removed a morsel of cornbread from his son's hand right before he could drop it on the floor for Darby to scoop up.

"Then who?"

"Someone who's been through the same thing you have," Lauren said. "Someone who might be able to offer you some perspective."

They were going to keep harping on this, weren't they?

Well, it wasn't as if she had a whole lot of activities to keep her busy. If she'd been dumped in Santa Fe in the late spring or summer, she would at least have had her garden to work on, but now, with the days marching toward Thanksgiving and a long winter ahead of them, she had to content herself with other distractions. True, there were the greenhouses, and she was starting to put together a list of plants she might grow there, but she wasn't quite ready yet to embark on such a big project. Not when she was feeling so unsettled.

"Sure," she said. "I'll talk to this person. But I don't think it's going to change anything."

"Maybe not," Lauren said. "I suppose we'll just have to see."

# Chapter 19

Perhaps it was foolish of him to keep coming back here, but Jamal couldn't stop himself from returning to the Castle as the days went by. Only for short visits, just to make sure the building was still intact and that hordes of scavenging raccoons hadn't made off with Rowan's notebooks, but he didn't know what else to do with his empty hours. Once, perhaps, he would have contented himself with watching a film or reading a book, and yet now it seemed such pastimes were only counterfeits of the real-life experiences he desired. Each time he went there, he told himself it would be the last, and yet another day would pass, and he would blink to the empty campus outside Las Vegas and walk the hallways of the place he had once shared with her.

The one thing he would not do was open any

of the notebooks to read their contents. He was still vaguely ashamed of himself for looking inside the one, especially since what he'd found had been so personal, and most likely not anything Rowan would have wanted anyone else to see. But at least he could guarantee that her notebooks were safe.

He supposed it was possible he also kept returning here to see whether she'd asked any of the Santa Fe djinn to fetch the notebooks for her, but it seemed she had either not yet made that request, or perhaps had decided that, though her writing had kept her occupied during all her lonely days here, there was no reason for her to have it on hand now that she was among other people. Still, there might come a day when he visited the Castle and the former dining hall, and would find it as empty of Rowan's presence as the rest of the place.

What he would do then, he wasn't quite sure.

Today, though, as he stood there and surveyed the piles of notebooks, he finally allowed himself to admit the truth he had been ignoring for far too long.

He did not come here to check on the notebooks because he truly feared they might have suffered some sort of mishap, or because visiting the Castle provided even a minor diversion for him.

No, he came here because it was the place where he had fallen in love with Rowan Aames, and if he could not be with her in person, he could at least visit the room where she had left so much of herself behind, or stand in the kitchen where they'd shared that turkey dinner...or find himself in front of the fireplace in the sitting room, and remember how they had huddled for warmth under all those blankets and quilts before generating their own singular heat.

But what difference did it make if he acknowledged that truth, that he understood he had made her his Chosen, not only to save her from Omar, but because he loved her and wanted nothing more than to be at her side throughout eternity? She was still lost to him, would not speak to him. Jamal knew this for certain, because it seemed that Isla had gone to Rowan's home in Santa Fe and asked if there was any possibility they could at least sit down and talk, and Rowan had refused in no uncertain terms.

And the thing of it was, he could not even be angry with her or curse her continued obstinance. She would not be acting in this manner if it were not for the way he had hidden the truth from her, so Jamal knew the blame lay squarely on him.

He would tell her such a thing...if only she would give him the chance.

Unfortunately, that did not seem likely to happen, not if she continued to feel the same way.

Then again, only a few days had passed since he had left Rowan in Aamir and Isla's care. It was always possible she would never change her mind, and he supposed he would have to find some way to live with such a decision.

On the other hand, tempers often cooled, given time and distance, so perhaps it was far too soon for him to believe all was lost. All he could do now was wait to see what might happen.

---

Rowan didn't recognize the dark-haired woman who knocked on her door the afternoon following the meal she'd had at Lauren and Dani's home, but since Lauren had hinted at having "someone" come to talk with her, Rowan supposed this woman must be that person.

"Hi," the strange woman said. Like all of the Chosen Rowan had seen in Santa Fe, she was strikingly attractive, with hair only a shade or two away from coal black and equally dark eyes, arresting against her fair skin and elegant features. "I'm Jessica Monroe. Do you mind if I come in?"

"No, not at all," Rowan replied. She'd already resigned herself to this interview, so she figured she might as well get it over with. Besides, she had to believe that Jessica probably had a hundred other things she would have preferred to be doing this particular Friday afternoon, and that meant she would also be relieved to handle this favor to

Lauren as quickly as possible so she could go on with her day. "Come on in."

They went into the living room, and at once Darby got up from his place by the hearth and went over to Jessica, his tail wagging a mile a minute as he sniffed at the knees of her jeans and she grinned and bent down so she could scratch him behind the ears.

"He must smell my dog Dutchie," Jessica explained. "We think she's part border collie, but everything other than that is up for grabs. Who's this guy?"

"Darby," Rowan replied. It seemed pretty clear that he thought Jessica was awesome—or maybe that was just because he thought her dog smelled great. Either way, it appeared he didn't have any problems with their unexpected guest. "Can I get you something?" she asked next, figuring she should at least play the part of the polite hostess. "Some tea, or some water?"

"Tea would be great," Jessica said. "It's pretty nippy out there."

That was for sure. Although it didn't seem as if it planned to snow again any time soon, the weather had been brisk and clear, with temperatures struggling to get out of the high thirties. A cup of tea on an afternoon like that just seemed like the right thing to do.

Also, going into the kitchen and heating the

water and getting mugs gave Rowan something to do while Jessica petted Darby and made much of him…and also delayed whatever she'd come here to say.

Eventually, though, the water was heated up and bags of Darjeeling were steeping in the Fiestaware mugs Rowan had gotten out of the cupboard, so there wasn't much reason for her to stall any further. She went back into the living room and handed one of the mugs to Jessica, saying, "You can just dump your teabag into that bowl on the coffee table when you're done with it. That's what I've been doing the past couple of days."

"Sounds good." The other woman lifted her mug—bright turquoise—to her nose and inhaled some of the fragrant steam. However, she must have judged the tea inside too hot to drink, because she set it down on the coaster nearest where she'd been standing and added, "You probably want to know why the heck I just ended up on your doorstep."

"I have a feeling Lauren had something to do with it," Rowan said, allowing herself to smile a little. Something about her visitor's casual, friendly tone made her relax somewhat, since she definitely didn't have the manner of someone who'd come here to deliver a lecture. "And please, have a seat."

Jessica settled herself on the sofa, while Rowan took the armchair immediately to her left. Like

Rowan, she wore jeans and boots and a slouchy sweater, and if she had on a speck of makeup, it wasn't obvious.

No, she was just that naturally gorgeous.

"Yes, Lauren reached out to me," Jessica said. "And she told me a little about your situation. I totally understand why you're angry with your djinn."

"He's not 'my' djinn," Rowan responded at once. She knew her tone sounded stiff, but she wasn't going to worry about that. No, she just wanted to disabuse Jessica of the notion that there was any connection between her and Jamal.

One of Jessica's perfectly arched brows lifted, although she didn't reply immediately. Instead, she leaned forward to dunk her teabag in and out of its mug a few more times, then laid it in the little ceramic bowl Rowan had pointed out a minute earlier.

"Oh, but he is," she said. "You might not want to think about the situation that way, but if a djinn makes you his Chosen, that means you're always connected, for better or worse. And I get why you're angry with him—he lied about who he was, made you think he was an ordinary human. I had the same thing happen to me."

For a second or two, Rowan could only stare at Jessica in surprise. All this time, she'd thought her situation was unique. Then she found her voice and replied, "You did?"

The other woman picked up her mug and wrapped her hands around it, as if glad of its warmth after making her way up the front walk on such a chilly day. She took a sip and then said, "Yes. It was back when all of this started...or at least, that was when I first started hearing Jace's voice."

"Jace is your djinn?"

A nod. "Jasreel al-Ankara, if you want to be formal about it. Anyway, this was when I was still in Albuquerque. I heard a voice that guided me out of dangerous situations, and then it helped me find my way to Santa Fe and the house we still live in now."

For a moment, Rowan only sat there, doing her best to absorb what Jessica had just told her. She assumed by "voice" she meant she'd heard her djinn's voice in her mind, the same way Rowan had heard Jamal's. But....

"If he was only a voice, then why would you think he was human?"

The corners of Jessica's mouth lifted a little, although it looked as though she knew better than to smile outright at Rowan's confusion. "Because that was only the first part. A little while after I got to Santa Fe, Jace basically showed up on my doorstep, only he called himself Jason Little River and told me he was a member of the Taos Pueblo tribe. I was cautious at first, obviously, but he turned out to be a good guy—helped me with the house, helped me catch some goats for the property, that kind of stuff."

She paused there, and now it was Rowan's turn to put on a knowing smile. "And then I suppose one thing led to another."

"In a manner of speaking," Jessica replied, not looking at all put off by the comment. "Everything was going great, but then I overheard him talking to Zahrias in the middle of the night, and at last Jace told me the truth...about who he was, about what had really caused the Heat, and how some of his people had made it their mission to save some humans."

"Did you freak out?" Rowan asked then. When Jamal's identity had been revealed to her, she'd barely had time to comprehend what was happening, thanks to the way his evil younger brother was doing his best to wipe them both off the face of the earth. Still, once she learned the truth about who he was, she knew she'd been shaken to her core. And that was after at least knowing who the djinn were and how they'd been responsible for humanity's destruction. She had absolutely no idea how she would have reacted if she hadn't even known djinn were anything except stories you might read in a book of fairy tales.

"Yeah, kind of," Jessica replied with a grin.

Rowan could tell that, even though the experience had been traumatic, it was now far enough in the past that Jessica could smile about it. "I was so angry that I kicked him out of the bedroom and told him to stay away from me. And the next day, he tried to explain himself, but I was still so mad at him for not telling me the truth, even though he said that if he'd come to me first in his true form, there was a very good chance I wouldn't have been able to deal with it." Her smile slipped a little then, and she went on, "And he was probably right. It's not the kind of thing you can exactly wrap your brain around, you know?"

Oh, Rowan knew all too well. Or rather, while her situation was a little different, she still remembered sitting there in stunned silence as she heard Miles Odekirk's cool, dry tones coming through the radio's speaker, telling her—and any other survivors who might have been listening—exactly what they were up against, and how the world had ended because the djinn had willed it. If it had been anyone else talking, she would have thought they were crazy and were broadcasting their insane theories for everyone to hear, like that "monster shouter" guy in some of the New York scenes in the early part of *The Stand*.

But Miles Odekirk wasn't a monster shouter. He was a scientist with a highly rational mind, and something in the way he'd delivered the information about the djinn almost made it sound as if he found the entire topic distasteful, something that should have been rejected by anyone with a halfway logical brain.

And that was a big part of the reason why Rowan had believed him.

"So...you took Jace back," she said, although that piece of information seemed patently obvious, considering Jessica's presence here in Santa Fe.

"I did," Jessica replied. "Oh, I struggled with it a lot. But then I realized everything he'd done had been to protect me and keep me safe. Yes, maybe he could have handled things differently...or maybe he couldn't. The one thing I knew was that he loved me, and out of everyone in the world, he'd made me his Chosen. That had to count for something, right?"

Maybe it did. At the same time, Rowan wasn't sure whether their situations were all that similar when you got right down to it. Jasreel...Jace...had selected Jessica specifically from the survivors of the Heat, while Jamal had made Rowan his Chosen only because to do otherwise was to watch her die. Sure, she could give him some credit for that, but it still didn't mean theirs was a love for the ages or anything close to it.

Then again, if that was the truth, why did it hurt so much to be here alone?

"For you, I suppose it did," Rowan replied

slowly. "I'm just not sure whether we're dealing with the same thing in my case."

Jessica was silent for a moment. Her fingers tapped against the side of the mug she held, and it looked as though she was turning Rowan's argument over in her mind, trying to settle on the best way to respond. Then she set down the mug and shifted on the couch so she faced Rowan directly.

"On the surface, maybe not," she said. "I'm just not sure he would have made you his Chosen if he hadn't cared on some level."

And then she rose from the sofa, signaling she thought the conversation was over.

"I'll see myself out."

---

Jamal found himself going back and forth on his next course of action, not wanting to intrude on Rowan, but also loath to merely sit back and wait. This sort of vacillation was utterly unlike him, for he and his brothers had always been the sort to make up their minds quickly on a topic.

However, since every day that passed seemed to be more excruciating than the last, he decided he needed to swallow his pride and seek the advice of someone who might have a better perspective on the problem than he.

Namely, Isla Dunbar.

There was no way to hide such a visit from his brother Aamir, so Jamal did not even bother to try. Instead, he waited until a full week had passed since Rowan had gone to Santa Fe, judging that to be a decent enough span of time, and then arrived at their home in the middle of the afternoon. It was not an hour during which they should have been having a meal, and when he arrived on the doorstep and knocked, his brother was the one who answered. The startled expression he wore could have been because he hadn't expected to see Jamal in the first place, or merely surprise that a djinn would have bothered to knock.

After Aamir let him in, Jamal said, "I hoped I might speak with Isla. Is she not here?"

One of his brother's eyebrows lifted, but Aamir only replied, "Oh, she is here, but she is working in her pottery studio at the moment. If you will wait in the living room, I will go and fetch her."

Jamal thanked his brother, and Aamir headed out through the French doors that opened on that amazing terrace, presumably in search of his Chosen. Although the sun shone brightly enough, the day was cold, and he found himself hoping this studio of Isla's was well-heated, for otherwise it did not seem as if it would be very comfortable.

A moment passed, and then another. Soon afterward, both Aamir and Isla appeared, Isla in clay-smudged jeans and a sweatshirt, her thick, malt-brown hair pulled back into a messy braid.

"Hi, Jamal," she said, breezy as if this visit had been entirely expected. "Just give me a couple of minutes to get cleaned up, and I'll meet you back here."

He'd stood as she entered, the only polite thing to do, and said at once, "I am sorry to have interrupted you in your work."

"Oh, it's nothing," she said with a careless wave of her hand. "I was just finishing up anyway. Be back in a minute."

She headed down the corridor that presumably led to the bedrooms, and Aamir turned toward his brother. "I suppose I can guess why you are here today."

"I wished to have Isla's counsel."

Aamir's mouth quirked in amusement. "And not your own brother's?"

"I thought that Isla, as a human woman, might have advice to give that would be very different from what I might receive from a fellow djinn."

"True," Aamir allowed, still with that lift at the edges of his lips. "And I will certainly not mock you for this visit, not when I have been in a very similar position myself. Of course, unlike you, I was hesitant at first to take Isla as my Chosen, whereas you seem to have jumped in with both feet."

"Because I had no choice," Jamal returned,

knowing he sounded a bit too stiff. Perhaps it was true that Aamir had no desire to mock him, and yet he'd still detected a teasing note in his older brother's words.

But then Isla returned, now in a pair of clean, close-fitting jeans and a mossy green sweater almost the color of her eyes. She sent an amused glance in her partner's direction and said, "You mind giving us some space, Aamir?"

"Not at all, my love," he replied, then came over and pressed a swift kiss against her cheek before leaving in the opposite direction from whence she'd come. Jamal still did not have a precise impression of the home's layout, but he believed the secondary bedrooms they used as studies or offices were located on that side of the house.

"Some tea or coffee?" Isla asked after Aamir had gone. She took a closer look at his face and added, "Wine?"

A glass of wine would have been most welcome then, but Jamal did not wish to admit such weakness to his brother's Chosen. "Tea would be quite refreshing, thank you."

"Then take a seat, and I'll be back in a minute."

Jamal settled himself on one of the two overstuffed couches that occupied the space. As he waited, he couldn't quite keep his gaze from moving toward the windows that overlooked the terrace and the city beyond. Somewhere down there, in that maze of pueblo-style structures and bare trees, Rowan was in the house she had selected for herself. Was she reading? Playing with Darby? Perhaps she was not home at all, but out and about, doing her best to become a member of the community despite her unusual circumstances. If that was the case, then it was quite possible she would still want nothing to do with him.

He did his best to banish that thought, as well as the niggling doubt that had begun to creep in, telling him that if a week had passed and Rowan still had no desire to see him, then it was very likely that none of his stratagems would work simply because her feelings for him most certainly did not mirror his for her.

Isla returned then, a mug of handsome stoneware of earthy brown and cream with accents of turquoise in either hand. She gave one to Jamal, then sat down on the sofa that faced his, her hands wrapped around the cup.

"So, what can I help you with?"

Now that the time had come, he found himself more tongue-tied than he wanted to admit. As far as he had been able to tell, Isla appeared sympathetic to his cause, and yet he still didn't know whether he would have the courage to unburden himself to her.

But her unusual gold-flecked hazel eyes seemed

understanding, and it would have been foolish for him to come here if he could not even find the courage to speak his heart.

"Have you seen Rowan?"

Isla's head tilted slightly as she considered the question. "A couple of times," she replied. "It seems she's settling in okay. But she's also sort of... reserved. I can't tell for sure if that's just her personality or more her way of coping with the situation."

Jamal would not have thought of Rowan as particularly aloof, considering the way she'd let him stay with her and had also confided in him after they'd spent some time together. Of course, she hadn't known he was a djinn, had believed he was the first human she'd seen in a very long time. Now the situation was quite different, and he supposed he could see why she might not want to reveal her feelings to others...especially the woman who was his older brother's Chosen.

"I have given her time," he said. "I thought that was the respectful thing to do. But now I very much fear that time is not the problem here. If you have seen her, spoken with her, then perhaps you can tell me this. Do you think her anger supersedes any feelings she might have had for me? Because if that is the case, then I will do my best to leave her alone to live her life."

Isla didn't reply right away and instead sat there

with the mug in her hands, one finger tapping pensively against the glazed ceramic. Although she'd washed up, Jamal thought he spotted a smudge of pale gray clay on one of her fingernails, a detail that seemed somehow endearing to him. His heart was given to another, but he could see why his brother had abandoned all his beliefs to be with this woman.

At length she said, "Actually, I think she's that angry *because* she has feelings for you and doesn't know what to do about them. It's easier for her to shut you out than try to sit down and talk things through. And it's very possible she doesn't believe you love her at all. Do you?"

Such a direct question took him aback. Voice stiff, he said, "I should think that would be obvious."

"Well, maybe it's obvious to you," Isla replied, obviously not offended by the tone of his reply. "However, it might not be so obvious to Rowan. I won't admit to being any kind of expert—Aamir is the only serious relationship I've ever had—but if any of the movies I've watched or books I've read have told me anything, it's that women are suckers for grand gestures. So maybe you should try to think of what you can do for her."

Interesting suggestion. Jamal cast his mind back toward all the human entertainment he'd absorbed, all the films where men declared their love in some sort of unusual and romantic way. Somehow he doubted Rowan would appreciate it if he stood under her window with a large portable radio blasting out a love song, or if he climbed up to her balcony with a bunch of flowers in one hand.

If her new house even had a balcony.

"She left behind a great many notebooks when we journeyed to Santa Fe," he said after a moment. "It seems she spent much of her time alone writing down everything she could remember from the world before, and I know it was difficult for her to abandon them, even though she realized it would have been impossible to bring them along because of the way we traveled on foot."

Hearing those words, Isla's expression brightened immediately. "And I just happen to know that her new house has a whole room set up as a library. Some of the shelves are filled, but not all of them. I guess the question is, will those notebooks fit?"

"It is hard to say," Jamal said. "For of course, I have not seen this library room."

"And I doubt Rowan would be thrilled with me if I sneaked you in there to take a look." She seemed to ponder the conundrum for a moment, then said, "But there shouldn't be any problem with me going to the place where she was living in Las Vegas so I can see how many notebooks we're talking about. Why don't we do that?"

Truly, Isla's suggestion did seem like a very good solution to the problem. Since she had seen the room in question, she should have at least an approximate idea as to whether the shelving provided would be adequate or not.

"And Aamir will not mind you going there with me?"

"We'll bring him along," she replied at once. "The more, the merrier, right?"

Jamal supposed so. After all, he and Rowan had made sure to tidy the place before they left, so it was not as if his brother and Isla would see anything even remotely incriminating. And perhaps it could not hurt to have another pair of eyes on the problem, even if Aamir had not seen the library room in Rowan's house.

"I'm pretty sure he's in the study," Isla went on. "Just hang out here, and I'll be back in a sec."

She set down her mug on a coaster and went in search of her partner, while Jamal raised his own neglected mug and took a sip of the tea it contained. Sure enough, Isla returned a moment later with Aamir in tow. His expression was almost too neutral, telling Jamal that his brother, while acquiescing to the proposed expedition, wasn't quite sure it would yield the fruits the other two were hoping for.

"You will have to show me this place," Aamir said, "for of course, I have never been there before."

Easy enough; Jamal closed his eyes and visualized the warm sandstone building with its oversized turret to one side, the hillsides covered with pine trees behind it. "That is Montezuma's Castle," he said.

"An impressive place. We will meet you there."

Aamir slipped his arms around Isla's waist, and the two of them vanished. A second later, Jamal blinked himself away as well.

In the next moment, all three of them stood on the front steps of the Castle. Aamir's dark eyes scanned the landscape, keenly interested.

"You say Rowan survived here for four years, undiscovered?" he asked. "For I would say this place is rather conspicuous."

"It is," Jamal allowed, even as he opened one of the large double doors so they could go inside. "But although the structure itself is large, it is quite tucked away in this valley. I am not sure any of our people ever came this way, and if they did, they would have seen no sign of life, for Rowan was very careful to hide her presence here."

Aamir nodded. "It's most likely that the reavers working in this area scoured the town and came by here only in the beginning, then never returned. Still, your Rowan was very lucky."

While Jamal was not sure whether he could allow himself to think of her as "his" Rowan, he agreed with the rest of that sentiment. She had made it sound as if she'd spent at least a month in hiding here and had only left in search of food to supplement anything she'd found in the kitchen's pantries and whatever she'd been able to catch nearby. At that point, the reavers would have moved on, but there was always the chance someone might have come back. Obviously, though, they hadn't.

"She was," he said briefly. "Follow me—all of her notebooks are in the former dining hall."

They made their way down the corridor. Jamal noticed how Aamir kept his arm looped around Isla's waist, not for protection, but because they had come here without stopping to have her put on a jacket, and without him shielding his Chosen in such a way, she surely would have suffered from the chilly temperatures inside the unheated building.

Isla let out a murmured, "Wow," once they reached the entrance to the dining hall and she could see for herself the stacks of notebooks placed on the tables there. Still, her eyes narrowed as she appeared to take a mental count of the notebooks and compare it to what she recalled of the library she'd seen at Rowan's Santa Fe house.

"Well?" Jamal asked.

Her eyes narrowed. "It'll be a tight fit, but I think it should work. The room is pretty big—about ten by twelve, or close to it—and all the walls except for the window are covered in bookcases that go up to the ceiling. Only about half of them are full right now, which would leave the rest for Rowan's notebooks."

That was what he had been hoping to hear, and yet he couldn't help experiencing a twinge of trepidation. What if it turned out that she truly didn't want any of her writing, wanted to leave that part of her life behind? His "grand gesture" might turn out to be nothing more than a gross inconvenience. True, he could always remove the notebooks if she requested them to be taken away, but he certainly wouldn't have won any points with her.

Something in his expression must have shifted, because Aamir said, in a much gentler tone than Jamal was accustomed to hearing, "I would think it must have been very difficult for her to leave such a labor of love behind. Surely she would understand that you brought them to her because having them gone created a hole in her world."

That was what he hoped for, and yet doubt still assailed him.

Perhaps it would be better if he stood under her window with a radio, or perhaps touched the earth of her barren wintertime garden to bring it to blossom, even if doing so would go against the natural order of things.

To his surprise, Isla left the shelter of his brother's embrace so she could come over and give Jamal's arm a gentle squeeze. "You've got this.

After all, a djinn can give a woman anything in the world—the Hope diamond, a Lamborghini, a casket full of gold. But this—this is Rowan's own work, returned to her. It's the one gift you can give her that will really mean something."

"You're sure?" he asked. He wished he had her certainty, her utter belief that all this was going to turn out just fine.

"I'm sure," Isla said firmly.

# Chapter 20

Despite Isla's certainty that everything was going to be settled in the end, planning the best way to get the notebooks into Rowan's library still took some time. While sitting down with his brother and his Chosen at dinner later that night, Jamal determined that the wisest thing to do would be to come up with some reason for Rowan to be out of the house in the afternoon, perhaps tomorrow, possibly a few days hence. He thought perhaps it would be better for her to make the discovery in the daylight hours, when he could approach her at a time that would not be quite so fraught.

Isla then said she knew Rowan had become friendly with Dani al-Harith and his Chosen, Lauren, whose home was down the street from hers, and all they had to do was come up with a reason for the couple to invite her over to spend an hour or so with them. The solution presented itself more easily than they might have thought—Isla got out her walkie-talkie and contacted Lauren, who confided that, after allowing her son Gabriel to play with Darby several times, she and Dani had decided to bring home a puppy of their own.

"We can ask Rowan to bring Darby over to help socialize Sasha," Lauren said. "Dani and I had already talked about it, since Darby is such a mellow dog and we want Sasha to pick up as many good habits as possible. So I doubt Rowan will think anything is too strange about the request."

"Perfect," Isla said into her walkie-talkie. "Then just get back to me when you've got it all set up with Rowan, and we can get the ball rolling on our end."

"Will do."

Isla ended the conversation there by pressing the button on her walkie-talkie, then put it down on the table next to her place setting. Smiling, she lifted her glass of wine and said, "Well, that's taken care of."

"Not precisely," Aamir replied, although his calm expression seemed to indicate that he did not think there were going to be any problems carrying out their plan. "Rowan still has to agree to the arrangement."

"She will," Isla said, then swallowed some of

her wine. "Who's going to resist playing with a puppy?"

The brothers' eyes met across the table. Despite his worry that their plan would somehow break down along the way, Jamal couldn't help smiling a little. Perhaps there were some people in the world who might resist the lure of a fluffy new puppy, but he doubted Rowan could be counted among them, not when he knew she loved Darby and would never have brought him to live with her at the Castle if she didn't enjoy being around dogs.

"Not Rowan," he said, thinking he might as well be as positive as possible about the situation. While he'd thought humans' obsession with thinking that mere belief in a thing was enough to draw it to you was perhaps a bit naïve, he also knew there was no point in putting negative energy out into the universe.

Especially when his relationship with Rowan already had enough negative energy swirling around it.

He went on, "I'm sure Lauren has come up with the most foolproof way of drawing Rowan away from her house for an hour or two."

In fact, he'd barely finished speaking before the walkie-talkie beeped. Isla grabbed it right away.

"Are we a go?"

Once again, Jamal's mouth curved in amusement. It seemed clear enough to him that Isla was taking her part in this matchmaking scheme very seriously.

"Yep," came Lauren's cheerful tones from the walkie-talkie's speaker. "She's coming over at two tomorrow."

"Perfect. I'll let Jamal know."

"Good luck!" Lauren chirped, and then the walkie-talkie beeped again as they ended the connection.

Isla looked over at Jamal. "You get that?"

"I did," he said gravely.

Tomorrow afternoon at a little past two...for he thought it wiser to wait a few minutes for Rowan to leave, just in case she was running behind...he would go to her house and arrange the notebooks as neatly as he could in her home library.

And after she returned to the house?

Well, he supposed he would just have to see.

---

Rowan was glad the weather had remained clear and dry, if a little cold, just because she knew Darby's play date with Lauren and Dani's new puppy would be canceled if they couldn't go outside. True, she supposed the dogs could hang out in the house if necessary, but Lauren had told her Sasha wasn't housetrained yet and tended to pee when she got too excited, so it just seemed safer to have the meeting out in the backyard.

In fact, it was a good seven or eight degrees warmer today than it had been the preceding few days, making that afternoon in mid-November feel more like October than it had any right to. Although she supposed she could have kept Darby off-leash—it wasn't as if there were any other dogs around—Rowan had decided it was better to have Darby on the lead, if for no other reason than to show Sasha it was a perfectly normal state of affairs.

The dog didn't seem to mind, though, and happily sniffed here and there as he tugged at the retractable leash. Maybe he was recalling the days when his owners had walked him just like this, although Rowan honestly didn't know for sure whether he even remembered them. She'd been in his life much, much longer than they had, since he'd been barely more than a puppy himself when she found him wandering Las Vegas's deserted streets.

Dani and Lauren were waiting for them—as was Gabriel, who made a beeline for Rowan and Darby the second they appeared.

"Dabby!" he called out, and toddled over to the dog.

His parents exchanged an amused glance. Dani was holding the new puppy, an adorable little bundle of soft golden-brown fur that they thought was cocker-poodle with some terrier mixed in somewhere. It seemed that some of the djinn in Santa Fe had adopted pets early on, and were now carefully allowing them to breed—not too much, but just enough that everyone would be able to have a dog or a cat if they wanted one.

The puppy was wriggling in Dani's arms, clearly wanting to get down and meet the exciting newcomer. "Let's go outside before this little one turns me into a pee pad," he said, and Lauren grinned.

"Probably a good idea."

Like Rowan's house, the one that Dani and Lauren and Gabriel—and now Sasha—shared was a large one, with an expansive deck just beyond the living room's French doors, and a yard whose size rivaled hers as well. However, while her backyard was mostly taken up by the vegetable garden and only had a small patch of grass, theirs was nearly all lawn, with only a border of trees and shrubs for privacy.

As soon as they were on the grass, Rowan unclipped Darby's leash so he could roam free, and Dani bent so he could set Sasha down on the lawn. The puppy dashed after Darby, her feathery tail wagging furiously as her short legs did their best to catch up. Always obliging, the cattle dog turned away from the patch of grass he'd been sniffing, and the two dogs touched noses.

"It looks as if they're going to be friends," Dani remarked, and Lauren, who'd just set Gabriel down as well so he could run over to the dogs, nodded.

"All three of them, I think."

Because as soon as Gabriel had caught up with Darby and Sasha, Darby went over and licked the little boy's face. He erupted in a squeal of laughter, making Sasha paw at him, and before they knew it, he'd fallen to the grass with both dogs lapping his round little cheeks.

"I think someone's going to need a bath after this is all over," Rowan remarked, and Lauren only shook her head.

"Goes with the territory, I suppose." She paused there, and her fond gaze moved from her son to her partner, who stood nearby, also watching with a smile, but clearly ready to dive in if the roughhousing got too out of hand.

Watching them, Rowan had another of those annoying little pangs go through her. Would she ever stop comparing her life to that of the people around her? Yes, Lauren and Dani appeared to be the picture of marital...or whatever you wanted to call it...bliss, but the life they shared was very different from the one she'd chosen for herself.

And she needed to be okay with that.

Luckily, the moment passed, as they always did, and she was able to spend the next hour or so without doing anything except enjoying the way

Darby seemed to guide the play, to step in whenever Gabriel was getting a little too boisterous with the new puppy. That must have been some relic of his cattle-dog instincts, although he'd obviously never herded a cow in his life, and had been very young when the Dying happened and the world changed.

But once that hour had passed, Lauren stepped in, telling Gabriel that he shouldn't over-tire Sasha and that it was time for both of them to come inside. The little boy pouted, although Rowan could tell he knew better than to get too cranky when they had a guest over.

She took that as her signal to leave, then said goodbye and promised she'd bring Darby over for another play date soon. The dog came over to her so she could clip on his leash, and the two of them headed back to their house.

"Did you have fun, Darbs?" she asked, and the dog gave an enthusiastic wag of his tail.

However, he also seemed glad to be going home, telling her he was probably going to sleep like even more of a rock tonight. Not too surprising; she made sure he got plenty of exercise, but there was nothing like being worked over by a toddler and a puppy in tandem.

When she opened the door, he made a beeline for his water bowl. After pausing in the entry to take off her coat and hang up his leash, Rowan followed at a much more leisurely pace. It was too early to start thinking about dinner, so she thought it would be a nice idea to brew a cup of tea, grab a book from the library, and curl up in her favorite chair. The house had a fairly decent collection of DVDs, but right then she felt more like reading than watching something, wanted some time to decompress from the much higher-energy environment in Lauren and Dani's house.

While Darby slurped water, Rowan put the kettle on to boil and sorted through the tea collection in the pantry. Something herbal, she thought, since she didn't want to drink anything with caffeine this late in the afternoon.

Sweet cinnamon tea sounded perfect, so she got out a bag and fetched a mug, then waited for the water to boil. Darby, muzzle wet from drinking, came over to her, and she bent down so she could pat him on his head. His big brown eyes were just ever so slightly pleading, and she had to smile.

"Okay, boy," she said. "I suppose you've earned a treat after all that roughhousing."

She got him a biscuit from the pantry, then turned off the burner just as the water in the kettle began to make the telltale hissing and popping sounds that signaled it was about to boil. A few moments more while she waited for the tea to steep, and then it was time to sit down and relax.

First, though, she set her mug of cinnamon tea

on the coffee table, figuring it could cool while she was in the library selecting that afternoon's reading material. Darby took his treat over to his favorite spot by the fireplace and settled down on the rug to chew his way through the hard little biscuit.

Smiling—the dog always seemed to land there, even when she hadn't lit a fire—Rowan headed down the hall to the library. When she got to the doorway, though, she stopped dead, staring at the bookcases in utter confusion.

All the empty shelves were now filled with the notebooks she'd left behind in Montezuma Castle.

How the hell had they gotten there? Was she hallucinating?

No, that was ridiculous. She knew where she was...and what she was looking at.

Still, she went to the nearest bookcase and laid her hand on one of the notebooks. It felt awfully solid for a hallucination.

Who had brought them here? Aamir?

It had to be...although she had absolutely no idea how. No one here in Santa Fe even knew those notebooks existed.

As she was standing there, not sure what to do next...it felt awfully anticlimactic to pluck a mystery or a romantic suspense novel from the shelves after seeing her *oeuvre* appear out of thin air like that...someone knocked at the front door.

Isla and Aamir, coming over to see if she liked her surprise?

No other explanation made much sense.

But when she went to the door and opened it, instead it was Jamal standing there, expression studiously neutral, as though he'd had to school himself not to look too hopeful.

He wore djinn robes, but plain black ones, not the gaudy, colorful silks she'd seen on quite a few of Santa Fe's elementals.

"I hoped I could speak with you," he said.

Rowan's fingers tightened on the doorknob, even as realization struck. "Was it you?"

Dark eyes met hers. He didn't bother to ask what she'd meant by the question, and instead replied, "Yes."

Her first instinct was to tell him they had nothing to talk about. But then she thought of the notebooks lined up neatly on their shelves…and how he'd thought to do for her the one thing that actually had some meaning.

"Come in," she said, moving out of the way so he could enter the house.

She noted the way his gaze moved about the room, taking in all its various details, although his expression remained impassive. Was he doing his best not to show any reaction, lest she think he was appraising the house as his future home?

For some reason, the thought of him being

here didn't annoy her quite as much as it probably should.

However, the solemn look he wore vanished as Darby ran over to him, tail going so fast it was nearly a blur. He bent down to pet the dog, who was ignoring all of Rowan's past admonitions not to jump on people and had his front paws firmly planted against Jamal's knees so his friend wouldn't have to lean over so far to scratch his ears.

Watching the two of them, the utter joy in the dog, the bright, unpracticed smile Jamal wore, Rowan felt her irritation slip just a little. She'd thought Darby had been doing fine without the djinn around, but it seemed her dog had a different opinion on the subject, and she had a sudden pang of guilt at the way she'd deprived him of Jamal's company.

"Some tea?" she asked, realizing that her mug of cinnamon tea was rapidly cooling as it sat on the coffee table. "I just made some for myself, so the water should still be warm."

"Tea would be wonderful, thank you," Jamal replied.

"Then have a seat, and I'll be right out."

She headed into the kitchen, glad of the brief reprieve so she could try to get her thoughts sorted out. Shouldn't she be angrier with him for showing up on her doorstep like this?

Somehow, she wasn't. Maybe watching

Darby's joyous reaction to Jamal's arrival had taken her annoyance down more notches than she'd originally thought.

Pondering that conundrum, she went to the pantry and got out another bag of cinnamon tea. She hadn't asked him what he wanted, but she kind of doubted he really cared one way or another.

That clearly wasn't why he'd come here.

It seemed easier to wait until the tea had steeped for a few minutes so Jamal wouldn't have to mess around with the bag. Cowardice, possibly, but Rowan still thought it helped to hang out here in the kitchen as she tried to get her thoughts in order and did her best to ignore the sudden, irrational beating of her heart.

What was the best way to thank him for bringing the notebooks while at the same time letting him know in no uncertain terms that she had no interest in rekindling their relationship?

She couldn't come up with one, though. That could have been because she was too on edge to think clearly...or maybe some part of her had begun to understand she wasn't quite as intent on pushing him away as she once was.

*Stop being an idiot,* she told herself. *Just take him the tea and get this over with.*

Another pause to try to gather herself, to make sure she looked casual and unruffled and not as though his visit had shaken her a lot more than she wanted to admit.

Then she headed out to the living room.

Jamal sat at the end of the sofa with Darby pressed against his knee, still begging for caresses. His mouth had turned up in a half-smile, although Rowan thought it was more because he was happy to be there than because of the dog's antics.

"Here you go," she said, handing over the mug of cinnamon tea. Since her own beverage was already waiting on the coffee table, she couldn't really pretend she'd intended to sit somewhere else. Instead, she lowered herself to the cushion, glad that at least Jamal was a good two feet away from her and hadn't tried to take the spot right next to where her mug of tea sat. Darby, seeming to sense that his people needed to have an important conversation, had settled down on the rug, snout between his paws.

"Thank you," Jamal said. Once again, his gaze met hers, and this time she found it a lot harder to look away. Why did those brown eyes of his seem deeper and darker than any other eyes she'd ever seen?

She knew she could get lost in those eyes.

Once again inwardly admonishing herself to pull it together, she said, "Thank you for the notebooks. I suppose at some point I would have mentioned to someone that I wanted them here, but I hadn't gotten around to it yet."

"It is nothing," he replied, although something about the warmth in his voice told her it was a lot more than just nothing. "I did not want to think of them being left behind, and then when Isla told me you had a library in this house...."

He let the words trail off, while Rowan experienced a flicker of annoyance. Isla. It figured that her sort-of sister-in-law had helped Jamal plot all this—probably aided and abetted by his brother. At the same time, she found herself somewhat relieved that he'd been acting on intelligence provided by a third party and hadn't come snooping around the house on his own while she was out.

And then she realized Lauren and Dani must have been in on the plan as well, and had manufactured the "play date" for the dogs so she would be safely away from home while Jamal blinked the notebooks into the library.

"It looks like you've all been conspiring against me," she remarked as she picked up her mug of tea and then took a sip. Luckily, it was still warm enough to be soothing, although if she'd waited much longer, it would have started to stray into luke-cold territory.

Jamal's eyebrows lifted. "'Conspiring'?" he

repeated, then tilted his head as he seemed to consider her expression, which she guessed must have been less than amused. "No, rather, I went to Aamir and Isla for assistance once I thought of bringing the notebooks to you. She told me about the library, and I thought it sounded like the perfect place for all your writing. Surely you did not intend to leave your notebooks behind forever."

No, she hadn't, although she also hadn't thought of the best way to get them here. She supposed Aamir would have helped, and yet she knew she would have felt strange going to him for assistance when she'd made it painfully obvious that she didn't want his younger brother in her life.

But it had hurt to leave all her writing back in Las Vegas, hurt in a way she hadn't wanted to acknowledge. Some people might have thought it was foolish for her to sit there laboriously writing everything out by hand when she still had her laptop with her and could have typed out her memories and observations.

That hadn't felt right, though. Maybe she'd visualized herself as some sort of modern-day monk, hidden away in the Castle and setting down histories for people who might never read them.

All right, not a monk—her fling with Jamal had proved she was far from celibate—but still, someone who felt a driving need to write as much down as she could before it was forgotten forever.

*Might I your scribe and confessor be....*

"No, and it was a wrench to leave everything there," she said quietly. "So thank you for bringing my notebooks to Santa Fe."

Jamal drank some of his cinnamon tea, which Rowan guessed was far hotter than her own. But he was a djinn, so he didn't run any risk of burning his tongue.

For some reason, that thought didn't bother her as much as it once might have. It had been easy to reject him when he was nowhere around, had become almost an abstract figure in her mind. It felt very different to try to pretend he didn't matter to her when he sat only a few feet away, handsome features solemn, almost more beautiful in their bleakness than when he'd been smiling a few minutes earlier.

Then he set down his mug and said, "So...you accept this gift?"

"Of course I do," she replied. "I'd be kind of a jerk to tell you to send them all back when you went to the trouble of bringing my notebooks here."

She'd made that response taking his question at face value, although she had a feeling he was asking a whole lot more than simply whether she'd keep her writing here despite the tension between them.

His lips tightened for a fraction of a second, and then he said, “I waited because I thought I must. I did not want to have it seem as if I was forcing myself into your life, not when you made it clear that you had much to think about. And perhaps this is still too soon for us to have this conversation. But I have been doing my own thinking, and have realized that I should have been truthful with you from the start. Perhaps we could never have gotten past the knowledge that I was a djinn, and yet I have to hope that if I had told you the truth, you would have realized I meant you no harm. Much the opposite, in fact. From the first moment I saw you, I thought you beautiful, but then when I realized you had strength and intelligence and spirit to match your beauty, I understood there could be much more between us.”

From a human man, Rowan would have thought a speech like that was only a new and flowery way to get into her pants. But she knew now that was how djinn spoke, and she understood Jamal was baring his heart to her in a way he possibly never had to anyone else.

Her throat tightened. What on earth was she supposed to say?

Before she could reply, he spoke again.

“I understood that I was in love with you, Rowan Aames. It is something I did not want to acknowledge to myself, but after you made it clear to me that you did not wish to have me in your life, the ache of your loss was much more than I'd expected. When love is denied, it causes more anguish than anything else in the world."

His gaze had locked on her again, now pleading, although something in the dark intensity of his eyes told her he would not make any demands, would not say she must love him just because he had confessed his feelings to her. No, he only wanted to tell her where he stood, how the pain of her rejection had hurt him just as much as his lies had hurt her.

And although she'd done her best to ignore it, had settled into her new life here and made new friends and new routines, underneath everything had been an uncomfortable ache, one that seemed to tell her one thing was missing from her existence, and if she wouldn't allow herself to acknowledge it, she'd be in an even bigger world of hurt.

She'd been so very angry with Jamal because she'd fallen in love with him as well, and what was love without trust?

"Do you want me to say that I care about you, too?" she blurted out, and his eyes widened slightly, flaring with hope...and need. "Because I do, and that's why I was so goddamn angry with you. If I hadn't cared, it wouldn't have mattered so much that you'd lied."

He shifted, moving closer to her, and then he

took her fingers in his and pulled her against him. Not to kiss her, but to hold her tightly and then touch his mouth to her hair, a gesture far more tender than she would have expected from him.

"I am sorry about that," he said, his words a murmur against her ear. "If I could change things... if I had the power to go back to that moment when we first met...then I would have told you the truth. But even a djinn does not possess such powers over time and space, and so now I can only do what I can to make amends. For I love you, Rowan Aames, and my life is empty without you. Forgiveness is yours to grant, though—I will not ask it of you."

A shudder went through her. While some part of her wanted to hold on to her anger, she understood doing so would serve no one, least of all herself.

Was an eternity spent alone worth clinging to her pride and her stubbornness?

Everything hung on this moment. As if it was coming to her from a distant radio, she heard the clock on the mantel ticking, the faint, sweet tones of the wind chimes hanging from the portal as a light breeze whispered past the house.

And the soft rustle of Jamal's robes as he shifted on the leather couch, waiting for the answer that could change everything for them both.

"I forgive you," she said softly.

His dark eyes lit up, and this time he leaned in to kiss her, his mouth firm and tasting of cinnamon tea, sweet and perfect and warm.

How could she have ever thought she could live without him?

His arms went around her again, and this time they clung to one another, as if they needed as much of their bodies to touch so they could be reassured that they truly were together once again.

Jamal was the one to end the kiss, but gently, his fingers twining with hers as he gazed into her eyes. "You are certain?"

"I'm certain," she replied, then gave a rueful smile. "This whole time, I was convinced I was right and you were wrong."

"Oh, you are right about that," he said, and she found her smile broadening into a grin.

"Probably," she allowed. "But at the same time, I didn't want to acknowledge how much I missed you. Seeing you here again...hearing your voice... well, that just made me realize what a stubborn ass I was being."

He didn't try to contradict her...probably because he knew she didn't want to argue with him on that point. But his fingers tightened on hers as he said, "So...what do we do now?"

"Well," Rowan replied, doing her best to keep

her tone light, "it looks like we've reconciled. So I hope you like this house, because I really don't want to move."

"It is a very fine house, from what I've seen of it," he said. "I think we could be very comfortable here."

She hadn't thought he would try to convince her that they needed a larger, fancier house, but it was still a relief that he didn't protest. "Well, let me give you the nickel tour."

They got up from the sofa, hand in hand, and she showed him the library and the office and the guest room...and at last took him to the master suite, which he surveyed with a solemn expression on his face and a decided glint in his dark eyes.

"I think it will suit very well," he said, and Rowan lifted an eyebrow.

"Want to test it out?"

"I thought you would never ask."

And he took her in his arms, and they fell onto the bed, his kisses sweet fire, his body everything she'd been missing through this last lonely week. Afterward, they clung to one another, as if to reassure themselves that this was now their world, and they would never be apart again.

Yes, she was fine with the thought of eternity... as long as it was an eternity spent at Jamal's side.

*The End*

The Djinn Wars series continues with Omar's story in *Given*.

## Also by Christine Pope

(SERIES WITH ASTERISKS ARE COMPLETE)

### THE DJINN WARS

(Paranormal Romance)

Chosen

Taken

Fallen

Broken

Forsaken

Forbidden

Awoken

Illuminated

Stolen

Forgotten

Driven

Unspoken

Hidden

Written

Given

Mistaken (October 2024)

---

FAMILIAR SPIRITS

(Cozy Mystery/Paranormal Romance)

Spells and Spaniels

Cauldrons and Cats

Hexes and Hedgehogs

Charms and Chihuahuas

Runes and Ravens (September 2024)

---

LATTES AND LEVITATION*

(Cozy Mystery/Paranormal Romance)

Caffeine Before Curses

Muffins After Magic

Pastries and Prophecies

Eclairs and Ectoplasm

Sugar Skulls and Specters

Wedding Cakes and Wishes

---

HEDGEWITCH FOR HIRE

(Cozy Mystery/Paranormal Romance)

Grave Mistake

Social Medium

Household Demons

Perpetual Potion

Jingle Spells

Wandering Monsters

Uninvited Ghosts

Prophet Motive

Ballroom Bits

Spell Check

Brew Confessions

Charm School

---

UNEXPECTED MAGIC*

(Urban Fantasy/Paranormal Romance)

Found Objects

Finders, Keepers

Lost and Found

Finding Destiny

---

THE WITCHES OF WHEELER PARK*

(Paranormal Romance)

Storm Born

Thunder Road

Winds of Change

Mind Games

A Wheeler Park Christmas

Blood Ties

Healing Hands

Wishful Thinking

Smoke and Mirrors

---

MISS PRIMM'S ACADEMY FOR WAYWARD WITCHES*

(Fantasy/Academy Romance)

Misspelled

Dispelled

Expelled

---

PROJECT DEMON HUNTERS*

(Paranormal Romance)

Unquiet Souls

Unbound Spirits

Unholy Ground

Unseen Voices

Unmarked Graves

Unbroken Vows

---

THE DEVIL YOU KNOW*

(Paranormal Romance)

Sympathy for the Devil

Charmed, I'm Sure

A Wing and a Prayer

Wish Upon a Star

---

THE WITCHES OF CANYON ROAD*

(Paranormal Romance)

Hidden Gifts

Darker Paths

Mysterious Ways

A Canyon Road Christmas

Demon Born

An Ill Wind

Higher Ground

Haunted Hearts

---

## THE WITCHES OF CLEOPATRA HILL*

(Paranormal Romance)

Darkangel

Darknight

Darkmoon

Sympathetic Magic

Protector

Spellbound

A Cleopatra Hill Christmas

Impractical Magic

Strange Magic

The Arrangement

Defender

Bad Blood

Deep Magic

Darktide

---

## THE WATCHERS TRILOGY*

(Paranormal Romance)

Falling Dark

Dead of Night

Rising Dawn

---

THE SEDONA FILES*

(Paranormal/Science Fiction Romance)

Bad Vibrations

Desert Hearts

Angel Fire

Star Crossed

Falling Angels

Enemy Mine

---

TALES OF THE LATTER KINGDOMS*

(Fantasy Romance)

All Fall Down

Dragon Rose

Binding Spell

Ashes of Roses

One Thousand Nights

Threads of Gold

The Wolf of Harrow Hall

Moon Dance

The Song of the Thrush

---

## THE GAIAN CONSORTIUM SERIES*

(Science Fiction Romance)

Beast (free prequel novella)

Blood Will Tell

Breath of Life

The Gaia Gambit

The Mandala Maneuver

The Titan Trap

The Zhore Deception

The Refugee Ruse

---

## STANDALONE TITLES

Hearts on Fire (Paranormal Romance)

Taking Dictation (Contemporary Romance)

Golden Heart (Gaslamp Fantasy Romance)

Night Music: A Modern Reimagining of The Phantom of the Opera (Contemporary Romance)

Ghost Dance: A Sequel to Gaston Leroux's The Phantom of the Opera (Historical Mystery/Romance)

Flight Before Christmas (Fantasy Romance)

* Indicates a completed series

# About the Author

*USA Today* bestselling author Christine Pope has been writing stories ever since she commandeered her family's Smith-Corona typewriter back in grade school. Her work includes paranormal romance, fantasy romance, and science fiction/space opera romance. She makes her home in Arizona.

Don't miss out on any of Christine's new releases —sign up for her newsletter today!

*Christine Pope on the Web:*
www.christinepope.com

www.ingramcontent.com/pod-product-compliance
Lightning Source LLC
LaVergne TN
LVHW041101080826
845145LV00007B/1652

* 9 7 8 1 9 4 6 4 3 5 7 4 3 *